*For Dave,
With love &
thanks!
Best wishes
Glenn.*

Harmony's Doorway

Glenn Wakeling

Copyright © 2023 Glenn Wakeling

All rights reserved.

ISBN: 9798376373477
Imprint: Independently published

MY THANKS

To Claire for all her kindness and helping me in getting this story off the ground. Lots of love and light.

My Mum for always being there for me and being the rock of my life.

Thank you to Denise St Pier for her editing.

And last but not least to God and the Angels without whom nothing would be possible.

DEDICATION

I dedicate this book to Amelia, never lose your smile and always let your light shine and to David with love forever.

Amelia

GLENN WAKELING

From an early age I have always loved stories from classical to Si Fi and fantasy.

Such stories enriched my childhood and for an introverted soul as I was those stories were a refuge for me.

I also enjoyed writing stories at school as I loved expressing myself through the written word, not to mention making up adventures in my head and acting them out aloud.

Spirituality has always been important to me and over 20 years ago I trained as a Reiki practitioner, integrating my Reiki Master level by the time I was 20.

I had great faith but not enough faith in myself, yet through my spirituality I have come to believe in myself.

It has also helped me to deal with my learning difference of mild cerebral palsy which as I grew up affected my coordination.

Through my Reiki training I learnt many things, believed in myself and belief in a better world and this is what got me to write this story.

It has been a labour of love for me and I pray it gives some hope to all who read it.

May we all realise we are one and trust the light within us all and may we all know that we are loved and great enough just for being who we are.

Just as we are.

1

DAVID'S DREAM

David woke with a jolt. It was morning, 7:30am earth time, to be exact. Sitting in bed with a heart that beat like a thousand drums and a mind charged with excitement, the dream had been even more intense this time. It had seemed so real that the palms of his hands were now covered in sweat. David steadily removed himself from the refuge of his bed, and started to frantically pace up and down his bedroom as if he were a puppet being pulled along by strings, trying to make sense of what had happened during the night. He took three deep breaths in a bid to stop his racing heart. David fought to find clarity, but as much as he tried to centre himself, he could not shift the feelings of excitement and urgency that ran up and down the window of his mind like a giant clockwork spring. He felt as if a surge of electricity was travelling up his spine, making his skin emit goose bumps and disturbing his hopes of finding some sanctuary of calm and repose.

'Come on David, get a grip,' he tried saying to himself in a stiff upper lip way that was definitely not him.

However, after one or two minutes, although the feelings of bewilderment seemed to last more like two hours, David gradually became more relaxed and composed, as was his customary behaviour.

Sitting back down on his bed, feeling much more refreshed and in control of his thoughts, David attempted to try and make sense of what had happened whilst he had been asleep. He had dreamt that he had been standing in a void, which was completely black. It might have been outer space, he simply couldn't tell. He was not alone however, as standing beside him was an angel. David's expression changed from rigid tension and confusion, to one of hope and relief, looking up at the great pictures of angels on the wall above his bed, which he had collected through the years. He particularly held a fondness for one of his pictures, 'Awakening of a guardian angel', holding a rose in the palm of its hand, and clothed in a blue gown. Clearly it was his favourite. 'What did this dream mean?' David held a strong belief that dreams had meanings. 'Was he being told something? An angel beside him? A dark void? Outer space, or something else? Was he being warned, or perhaps he was just imagining things, as people had always said what an imagination he had. He'd been the writer of some very good stories when at school and college, attending angel workshops over the years, having had a strong belief in them since childhood. Were they now calling to him?' These questions and many more ran through the mind of the young man. 'I've got to remember more. Was there anything else I saw?' He laid back, closing his eyes, trying to visualise what else he had seen. The trouble with dreams is they come and go all too quickly. Then it suddenly came to him, the angel was carrying something; yes, a bird, a blue coloured bird that was native to this country. 'Oh, what was it?' The space-like realm had been very dark and there was this voice which seemed to be chiding him. He had been afraid, but the angel was encouraging him.

'Break it David, break it, break it, you can do it.'

The angel then showed David a candle and proceeded to point the candle at planet earth. The flame expanded, as it got nearer to the planet. David remembered in the dream how frightened he had been that the angel had set the world on fire.

'Stop!' David had yelled as the light had got brighter and brighter around the world. He had heard the angel say,

'Don't worry David, it's all for the good.'

He then awoke and found himself in his bed.

It was now 8.00am and David, hearing his Mum's footsteps on the landing, felt somewhat relieved and comforted by the sound of her voice.

'Morning Son, want a cup of tea?'

He went to give his mum a hug. He needed to talk, needed someone to tell about all that had happened. How could he tell anyone about this? Not so much the vision, but how it had made him feel, excited, frightened, overwhelmed and mesmerised, but perhaps, above all, needed. The dream had activated a sense of urgency, for what?

David pondered this thought for a long time, whilst bathing and getting dressed. Kneeling by his bed, his hands joined in prayer, David asked for guidance.

'Please God, help me understand what I've just dreamt. Angels, please give me clarity, help me realise what I've been seeing. Have I been shown something? Please tell me, I know you're not going to harm this world. I feel it's something very important, but I don't know what.'

'David, David,' called his mum from downstairs. 'David, stop praying and come downstairs, it's breakfast time.'

'Look, I must go now,' thought David, just a little irritated at his mums calling. 'Ok, 'I'm coming, keep your hair on, he called back. 'Got to go now, but I'll talk to you all again. Please tell me what all this is about!'

'Davviid! Come down for your breakfast now,' called his mum again.

'Honestly, you need the patience of a saint with parents sometimes,' thought David.

'Oh no, why does this toaster keep going wrong, what the heck's wrong with it?'

'I don't know, maybe your mouth took all the power,' teased the young man.

'What was that?' asked Mum.

The sun shone brightly its rays reflected through the kitchen window, catching the Swarovski crystals that hung nearby. The prisms caught the light of the sun allowing them to show their true beauty and in doing so radiated the colours to dance and flash across the room. It looked like a rainbow that had exploded into fragments and was now entertaining the human eye to a ballet of light and movement. David stared with innocence at this plethora of dancing rainbows. From childhood, as long as he could remember, he had loved to see colours. He could remember the TV series he had loved, one of the reasons being that he had loved the colours flashing, all the colours of the spectrum. Looking at one of his mum's crystals cut in the shape of a heart, it looked to him as if it was alive and pulsating rays of the rainbow. For what reason, your guess was as good as mine, as that was between the crystal and its creator.

'What were you praying about up there this time?' said mum 'I'm sure your prayers are getting longer and longer.'

'Nothing really,' said David, not quite knowing what to say.

A loving smile passed between the two of them, not only were they mum and son, they were also friends. His mum, Suzanne, and he had shared a very close bond, a bond that became even stronger when his dad and mum had separated when David was eight. They had certainly been through some tough times together, which had tested them both, but through it all they had come through unscathed. They'd survived and both had shown courage, not always openly but more so internally. They had their fair share of tears, but now they both lived their lives in the present moment, as much as they could. David's philosophy was 'change it around, it's them not you.' This was due to his Dad's own problem. which had led to his parents' divorce. David had also dealt with other hard times, it hadn't always been easy.

As a child, he had been diagnosed with mild cerebral palsy, although he saw it as mild autism. This was coupled with low self-esteem. He had gone to a school which helped children with learning differences, a beautiful place which David often referred to as 'a lesson within a place of lessons', where he had learnt a lot and had known some truly lovely people. Although he hated the stigma attached by society and the quiet looks and nods certain people gave each other when he said he had been to a 'Special School', David knew better, for he was a very spiritual person who knew only too well that such an experience had been to enrich him, not to label or shame him. Labelling and shaming came from the shallow judgements of people, fed by societal views, who saw things negatively. It wasn't their fault, as they did not understand, and were often fearful and a little ignorant. David's spirituality, which had been a part of him since he could remember, had enabled him to see things on a much deeper level. He realised that pain, happiness, joy and sadness had shaped his life in very profound ways.

By the time he turned Eighteen, David, on his own terms had pursued the healing art of Reiki, something that had helped him within and had sharpened his spiritual understanding, and taught his soul to fly. Reiki was divine energy that many who practised it believed came from God. It had been used in the great civilisations of Atlantis and Lemuria. Such wonderful things, but then are we all on the verge of discovering such great truths? His mum's voice once again broke David's thoughts.

'Are you alright darling? You seem to be lost in thought. There isn't anything wrong is there?'

Bless her. That was mum, always caring, always knowing, always showing that she loved him. Some people said she was too overprotective. Certainly, David had never felt overprotected in any way, she'd always encouraged him to be independent. The reason for this mistaken view of overprotection came from the experiences David and Suzanne had experienced together. David had been terribly hurt once and his mum had never wanted that hurt to happen ever again. She loved him.

'I'm ok Mum, really I am,' he replied, though his face seemed to suggest otherwise. He was falling into thought once again.

'Well, you seem to be worried. Tell me, come on David,' she said, placing her hand on top of his.

'Mum, I don't quite know how to explain. You see I'm not sure you'd understand this.'

'Try me,' was the reply.

'Well I've been having this dream and last night it was really intense. It was strange, it's odd how I felt about it. I haven't been able to stop thinking about it all morning. You see there was an angel floating beside me in this void.'

'Well that sounds like a lovely dream to me.' 'But there's more Mum, in this dream the angel holds this huge candle towards the earth, (in fact it looked more like a torch).'

'The earth.'

'That's right, Mum, but I heard this voice. There was something else with us, it was horrible. Its voice was chiding me, trying to scare me, but then the angel started to encourage me, telling me I can do it, I've got to break it.'

'Break what?'

'I don't know, I've just got to break it!'

At that moment, a cracking sound was heard as David's cup broke into pieces showering the table with coffee.

'Oh David!'

'It's ok Mum, sorry, are you ok?'

'Yes, I'm fine, I'll get a cloth. Well, it seems all those years going to the Mind, Body and Spirit festival and those angel workshops have taken their toll, not to mention the Reiki courses.'

'I've never had a dream that makes me feel so many emotions. So much happiness, wonder and excitement rolled into one. I feel.. I feel, Mum,' David tried to bring his feelings to the fore, but why was it so hard?

'It's alright David, go on, you can say it.'

'I feel that it's as if I'm being called to something, you know what you've always said to me.'

'Yes,' said mum, now looking as if the tale of this dream was starting to make her go into a state of contemplation. 'Yes, I know darling, but there could be a rational meaning to all this. Remember dreams are all made from things that we think during the day.'

'But remember how I felt the happiness, the joy, the fear and urgency?'

'You've always got angels on the brain 24/7. As for all the feelings, I just don't know. I wish I could help you more,' Suzanne said helplessly.

What could she say? What could she do to help her son work all this out?

'The more I think about it, the more it seems like it's meant for a reason, it's like a message or some sort of warning. I'm thinking of calling Elia and asking her what she thinks. Do you think she'll understand and won't pass it off as just an intense dream? It's more than intense Mum, it's profound, truly mind blowing and I need to find out more. I don't think it was just a dream. Such a dream could not make me feel so much, I mean soo much! When I woke up this morning, it was like something had opened within me, it was like electric was going up my back and my skin was going crazy with goose bumps. I mean, for a few seconds, it was truly like my mind and body had gone haywire.'

This dream had clearly made an impact on her son and Suzanne knew that she could not take this lightly. There was something in David's voice that had changed, perhaps something was going on. Suzanne had been a believer all her life, but sometimes looked upon things with an agnostic attitude. She was, like David, a very wise soul, more practical, perhaps due to her being a capricorn star sign. (David being an out of this world Aquarian), but also because she'd been hurt in life. Sometimes we can be overcome by the tides of life. We all need to learn how to ride with them, not against them. Suzanne had given so much in her life, that she'd sadly forgotten to give to herself. She was worried because David was such a caring soul and cared a lot for others, whether he knew them or not. However, he was also wise in so many ways, that she called him her therapist.

Suzanne knew deep inside this was more than a dream. She could either have said 'no it was just a dream', or she could let David face responsibility for what he had experienced. Trusting her instincts, she decided to follow the latter, not fight it, just accept it and, more importantly, trust it.

'Very well, you ring Elia and see what she says, but don't be disappointed if she thinks it's just imagination.'

'She won't, Mum, I just know it. Elia's becoming more evolved by the day. My Reiki Master has discovered so much within her own self that she wouldn't judge or discredit what anyone experiences.'

'But if it is just a dream, don't be upset, I know

you want to have a purpose in life.'

'Mum, please,' cried David in frustration, 'I know what you're saying, but if this means something, then wouldn't that be great? I know I've got a purpose, everything I've experienced in my life has been part of that purpose, somehow I just know.' He sighed.

'Have you got Elia's phone number?' Suzanne asked. 'Before you give her a ring, you stay right there and finish your breakfast, David Joseph. You're not going to find the truth about angelic dreams on an empty stomach.'

'Got you,' David said with excitement before delving into his bowl of cereal.

As soon as he'd finished his morning meal, he rushed to the living room, almost sprinting as if he had borrowed the sandals of Hermes to meet his goal. Rummaging through the cupboards with hands that shook, he found the address book and looked up his Reiki master's number. She lived a fair way from David's native town, but David and his Mum had taken a ride there many times over the past few years, in order to learn Reiki and to attend the many Reiki development groups. David dialled the number and, to his delight, Elia's gentle, yet business-like, voice answered. His heart leapt in excitement.

'Elia, hi, it's me, David. I'm so glad you're home.'

'Hello David, it's good to speak to you,' came the teachers welcoming response. 'What can I do for you?'

'I must see you Elia,' David said in a quiet, determined voice, with a slight coyness.

David had battled low self-esteem for many years, but now he knew he was getting better, although he had learnt early on that it was better to be true to himself, as he had never been able to put on an act of bravado to mask his feelings.

'You sound a little anxious,' the woman replied, picking up on the nervous undertone in David's voice.

'Please, I really do need to see you.'

'Yes, but what's the matter?'

'I can't explain it in length over the phone. Can I come over to you this afternoon, please? I think I'm being told something by the angels, but I don't know what.'

'Ok.' Elia said, now becoming interested in what he was saying. 'I am free today, so of course you can come over.'

David asked if she was sure, in his usual polite, cautious voice.

'Sure, I'll be glad of the company. See you at say, two o'clock?'

David felt excited, feeling somehow that Elia was not only interested, but seemed to be identifying with him also. Still, the questions raced through his mind. What would Elia make of the things he had seen? Oh, questions, questions!

'Patience, David,' a loud voice called from within him, but it definitely wasn't his own voice.

'Don't get excited, Davie boy.'

He'd had a lot happen to him in his life, now anything seemed possible and nothing impossible. He called to his mother and told her they were to go soon and to be there about two o'clock. They had lunch, and prepared to leave, dressing with regard for the rainy weather that had been forecast. David had no idea what to expect. Indeed, he had no idea what may happen in the next few days, for in his wildest dreams he could never have imagined what was coming his way.

2

THE FIGURE IN THE RAIN

It was a beautiful, sunny day. The sun's rays reflected through the leaves on the trees, just as they had done on the crystals, dancing rhythmically as if a myriad of fireflies had flown from the heart of the sun, to come to earth as if they had been sent to bless the skin of mortals. Winter was nearly over and soon it would be spring. David closed his eyes and held his head high as if to absorb the energy of the great star that had, for millennia, hung in the heavens, a great light that had given mankind hope for so long. A hope that has as much significance today as it ever had, perhaps in today's troubled world, even more so.

'Alright honey, let's go.'

David hadn't learnt to drive yet, it was just not the right time. As they drove out of the road, David glanced back at the place he had called home for many years, a place which held memories of great happiness and some sadness. He and his Mum only spoke to a few of their neighbours, but David smiled fondly and sent love to each and every one. It took quite a while to get to Elia's, but they finally arrived.

Elia Lotus was a wise and powerful healer renowned in her field. She lived very modestly, some would say monastically. Her house was tiny and made of white stone. Outside her door was the name 'Roseheart'.

'Such a sweet name,' thought David as he walked up to the door. He loved being in the company of this wise woman. She had helped him with so much. Perhaps she really could help him to make sense of the dream.

It was now just starting to rain slightly. Elia's door had a large glass heart cut into the middle, and a beautiful rose called 'Peace' trailed around it. David could see in the heart, the reflection of the houses opposite.

'So what?' you might well ask, but in the reflection he saw something unusual. It looked like a person, but who it was David could not tell, as the figure was covered from head to toe in a huge hood and robe, hiding its features, making any attempt at identification impossible. David spun around instinctively to see this figure and there it was, standing solemnly on the other side of the road. The figure made no movement whatsoever, it simply stood, not even its head altered in posture, seeming to be as still as a statue. David couldn't see its hands for they were also covered. Even though he couldn't see the eyes, hidden behind its long hood and veil, David sensed that he was being watched by the eyes of this soul. It was as though they were transfixed upon him.

'Mum, look. Look behind you!'

'What darling?' But as David's mum turned, somewhat startled by her son's surprised tone, Elia opened the door to greet them.

'Hello you two she said joyously, breaking the moment, which caused David to turn away from the figure.

Elia embraced them both simultaneously and, when David turned again, the hooded form was gone. But to where? It had only been seconds since he turned to greet his Reiki Master and he could see no place the figure could have gone in such a short space of time. This is truly mystifying, these past few hours were an enigma, there was no other way to describe this. It was baffling, to say the least.

'Come in,' Elia said. They were led through the hallway into the living room, a welcoming room, with sunrise coloured curtains and Buddhist orange walls which warmed and energised the senses in such a way that made you smile. 'Please sit down,' Elia said, lifting some new articles on meditation and something else, that couldn't be seen, off the sofa.

Elia was quite a picture herself. She was a short, yet voluptuous, woman, now in her middle years, and had been a real stunner in her youth and there seemed, even now she was in her sixties, an eternal agelessness about her. She wore hardly any makeup and possessed the most stunning olive complexion. Her hair was long and fell carelessly, yet immaculately, down to her shoulders. It was dark with a hint of silver now showing. She was clothed in a long flowing orange robe which seemed to match her home. Around her neck hung an ankh cross, the symbol of the gateway to life, in addition to a Rose quartz crystal, showing her love for all humanity.

'I'll make you both tea or coffee, or perhaps a fruit tea?'

David preferred fruit tea, but his mum liked her coffee. Whilst Elia went to make the drinks, helped by Suzanne, David looked about the room. There were many things that tickled his interest, a plethora of books on spiritual topics, ranging from life after death,Past Lifes, angel experiences and metaphysics to the Holy Bible. There was also a collection of spiritual figurines and ornaments scattered around, a long line of them on Elia's mantelpiece. He could clearly see: Jesus, Buddah, Quan Yin, Ganesh, Krishna, Mary with her infant Christ and St. Francis of Assisi, the patron of animals. Elia had collected these items on her travels to China, India, Israel and Italy. Wherever she had travelled, giving her Reiki courses she'd always been given something as a gift from a soul as a 'thanks'. A spiritual teacher had given her a crystal heart. Which David could also see on the mantel piece. The smell of incense floated across the room, gracing it with the aroma of nag champa, a beautiful herb grown in India and one of David's favourite scents, Elia had always had it burning during the Reiki courses. David scanned the articles which Elia had pulled out. They were interesting enough for anyone, regardless of faith or non-faith. That was interesting, a rare astrological event was soon to be taking place in the cosmos. What did that mean? A harmonic convergence? Scanning it further, his mind leaped in amazement. It was as though he had been guided to read it, it was strange how his dream kept coming up into his mind all day, but 'no', something else, but what?

His thinking was disturbed by his Mum and Elia returning with the beverages of raspberry fruit tea and coffee, which had been freshly made from the bean. He hoped they tasted as good as they smelled. When they sat down Elia looked with kindness and fascination into his blue eyes. Her beautiful almond shaped green eyes sparkled in the light.

'Now then, tell me what's going on,' she said with a smile.

Ever since David first took Reiki training, a few years back, Elia had always held a fondness for the young man, admiring his innocence and sincerity. He thought a lot of her too, for he had found through Reiki the path for which he was looking. Reiki's universal approach to all things had always appealed to him. It embraced everyone and everything regardless of race, creed or religion, from believer to atheist, all were one.

Within the time that followed, David related the details of his dream to his Reiki master. Elia listened intently as did his mum, who was sitting beside her son listening, trying to make sense of her child's strange dream or, dare she say it, his spiritual experience. David felt, however, that he couldn't tell Elia all the feelings he had experienced after awakening. He longed to, but struggled with it. Perhaps it was his natural shyness that stopped him, or maybe it was rooted in the fear that not even she would believe him. Elia stood up and walked up and down the room, just as he had done upon waking that morning.

'David, what you've just told me about your dream, it's very interesting.'

The look on her face said it all. It was as if she lacked normal expression, her eyes were now looking at him and Suzanne with wide-eyed wonder.

'Elia, do you know what I've been seeing? Please tell me that I'm not imagining all this, or am going mad. I've never felt anything stronger in my entire life.'

For a while Elia didn't say anything, she seemed not on this earth plane anymore. It was as if her mind had left her body and had been escorted to another dimension where she was joining some kind of enlightening insight. Her hands reached out for the pile of articles, but her eyes were still transfixed into space. Placing the articles on her lap, she sat down opposite David and Suzanne. She then seemed to gaze so intensely that one might have interpreted her look as a worried one.

'David, tell me, have you discovered anything about this?' Her finger pointed to a book. Its title read "Brave New World - SPIRITUAL EMERGENCY!"

David looked at the title. His heart leapt and you could be sure it had missed a beat.

'I, I'm not sure, no I don't think so,' came his response a little sheepishly. But it did seem, from the moment he had seen those articles, that there was some connection. 'It feels like I can identify with it for some reason, but I can't quite understand it.'

'Can it be?' questioned Elia.

'Can it be what?' said Suzanne, clearly irritated by this spiritual talk.

Ah, yes it was his Mum's practical nature kicking in again. She was such a kind soul but even she, at times, lacked patience. She liked to find out things quickly, there was a bit of her that liked to be in control, this more ethereal talk sometimes baffled her.

'Mum please have patience,' said David.

'I just want to know what all this is about so we can go home and recapture some normality.'

'I understand, Mum,' David said soothingly. 'Believe me, I do need to just go with it.'

'All right David, I know,' she said tapping her son's hand reassuringly.

Elia, on the other hand still looked like she was away with the fairies, or should I say, angels. She then dropped the article on the floor and ran, with speed and haste, upstairs.

'I'll be back, please wait. I'll be back!'

Another one blessed by Hermes. Elia returned looking much calmer, but still with excitement in her eyes. She held a box of angel cards, powerful tools that could help connect you with the angelic realm and could answer any question, big or small. David's eyes lit up, this was going to be good.

'Come over here David, we need to check this out, sweetheart.'

David sat beside her at her desk. What was she going to tell, or rather what were the angels going to tell him?

Elia selected four cards, she felt only four would be required. The first read 'prepare', the second 'journey', the third 'confront', something David had struggled with in his life, and lastly the fourth 'healed'. 'Journey' now seemed to stand out for him, but what kind?

'An inner one,' said Elia, as she had heard his thoughts.

David and his mum both looked at one another, then at Elia in awe, then at the angels' messages. David gazed at the beautiful pictures that decorated the cards. They'd been painted by a visionary a few years earlier and radiated pure love.

'You are being prepared for something, David, something quite extraordinary.' An angel standing in front of a young man enfolding him in its wings adorned that card. The 'journey' card, a rainbow bridge with a traveller, walking boldly. The 'confront' card, his least favourite, had this person outside a very large dark house looking afraid. The angel was there, but the soul didn't seem to know it. Somehow David felt this was to do with his dream. Finally, 'healed'. 'You've got to heal something, David, relating to both past and future. Most of the problems you once had have now been dispelled, but there is something that you still need to heal.' A picture of an archangel glowing with an emerald colour, showed it to be Raphael, leader of the healing angels. David had seen emerald circles above him during Reiki, indicating archangel Raphael was around and healing taking place. 'You're being prepared for some incredible work, David, I just don't know what it is right now, but it's very soon. That's it, very soon.'

David asked what the journey was about.

'It has something to do with the article over there,' Elia indicated.

'Elia, what does the 'confront' card signify?' he said, a little worried.

Elia stared again intently into his eyes.

'I am getting that you shall know when the time is right, but you've got to have courage.' David contemplated this in fascination. What was going on had become clearer, but it didn't really mention the dream, or did it? 'All I can tell you, David, is that you are very near to your life purpose and what you are going to do is going to make an impact on planet earth.' Elia's voice trembled with excitement and tears welled up in her eyes, which David had not seen before. 'Oh, I'm sorry sweetheart,' she said to herself, holding her heart to caress her Inner child within.

The wind and rain had now begun to gather in strength outside. It was now late afternoon. At least David had found out something about his future path. But what and how was it all going to come about?
Elia smiled, as if once again reading his thoughts.
'Please trust, dear one. Your angels will never let you down, they will show you what it is.' 'Thank you, Elia, so much. I'm truly grateful, I just wish I knew more.'
'Patience,' came the wise woman's reply. I'm sure you will know soon. All I feel able to
say to you is "be prepared", I really can't say any more.'
After embracing David and his mum, Elia showed them to the door. David suddenly remembered the cloaked figure, who had been watching him?
'Elia, do you know of anyone who dresses in a long robe and hood?'
'Not to my knowledge, why?' replied his teacher.
'Well before you answered the door, I saw this person across the road and he, or she, was covered in a long robe with the face covered by a long veil.'
Elia's face looked as baffled as David's mum.
'I'm sorry darling, I really don't know, there's certainly no-one up this road who dresses so you can't see them.'
'Ok then, don't worry about it Elia,' he said, feeling now just a bit silly 'It's probably nothing. Goodbye and God bless you.'
'Love and light to you, my lovely one, and to you Suzanne, honey.'
'Goodbye Elia, you too,' smiled Suzanne.

As the two of them left, Elia stopped waving and walked back into her living room. Sitting by the window, her face then turned to the rainy skies overhead. She spoke in a soft whisper.

'So it shall be, after so long. Oh bless you, my dear angel. It won't be long now.'

David and his mum were nearly home now, but the unwelcome visitors from the clouds pounded their droplets over the windscreen, making it hard to see.

'Are you alright, love? You're very quiet.'

'I'm ok, I did enjoy the visit. It was nice to see Elia again.'

'Sounds like you've got a nice destiny ahead of you.'
Suzanne tried to be cheerful but she knew that, when David was thinking, it was very hard to reach him. She would just remain quiet. David looked at the road signs. They were nearly home. It would be good to get in and get some dinner on. They passed local fields as they neared home. The area had once been mostly countryside until the forces of progress had insisted upon building on them. At that moment, in that very split second, as David looked at the rain ravaged fields, there stood the very same figure he'd seen at Elia's, still as a statue, he couldn't be mistaken.

'Mum, mum, look it's that cloaked person again!'

But how? How could that figure be here now? that would have been impossible. David's eyes froze in fascination. The figure didn't move, it just remained still, oblivious to the world around it, but looking at David with those hidden eyes. Suzanne slowed the car to see this mystery person.

'Tell me David, who is this you're talking about. Where? I can't see anyone.'

'But Mum, it's right opposite us in the field, can't you see it?'

'No I don't see it all,' she replied, straining her eyes in hope of seeing the mystery figure. 'I'm sorry, I don't see anything. Come on, we've got to get home, this weather's getting worse.'

David, realising that whatever he was looking at was, for some reason, failing to show itself to his mum, felt he couldn't pursue this matter further and, reluctantly, agreed to go home. He looked behind and the figure remained in the same position. The other curious thing was, despite the rain pouring down hard, with the sky looking as though Mother Nature had pulled a huge dark rug over it, the figure's cloak hadn't appeared to be wet at all. It had nothing to keep the rain off, just a hood. It was as if David was looking at something that was existing somewhere else, yet was standing on sodden countryside. David turned to face the front window, letting out a huge deep breath.

'What a day!'

All that had happened was so strange, yet had caused his mind to become so exerted he couldn't think about it anymore. He felt his mother's hand touch him reassuringly and then looked at her with a loving, yet tired look upon his face.

'It's alright Davie, I love you darling. You've had a lot on your mind lately. Now how about you just switch off? It's a lot for a young man to take on.'

'What is going on, Mum?'

'I don't know, all I know is that I love you and whatever happens I'll always be proud of you. Always remember that.'

'How could I possibly switch off all that happened at Elia's, all she said?' David stated in a desperate voice.

'Elia is just telling you what she thinks.'

'No Mum, she's telling me what the angels have told her.'

'Whatever it is, I think it's time for you to switch off now.'

'What about the figure in the field, and at Elia's?' asked David, his voice hoarse with anticipation.

'Oh, who knows who that was. Maybe what you saw in the field was a scarecrow and you mistook it for the person at Elia's.'

'But who do you think..?'

'Enough!'

That was that, one look from his mum and David knew it was time to stop. Perhaps he had taken all this too far. He had sometimes over-thought things in life and perhaps what he'd seen had just been his mind playing tricks. Perhaps. Yes, that's what it was. If only David and his mum knew.

They were home now, 7 Christ Heart Grove, home sweet home, thought David. It was getting near dinner time now, they had been out for nearly six hours. What a strange day it had been, be good to get some .... as they pulled up on the drive, they were greeted by their neighbour Rob, his face looking extremely concerned.

'Hello Suzanne, Hello David,' he called cheerfully, but with an undertone that reflected worry.

'Hi Rob, are you alright?' they replied simultaneously.

'Look I don't want to worry you, but we were walking the old pooch when I saw this on your wall.'

Rob walked down the side of their drive that led to the garden and pointed, gesturing with his hand. Suzanne and David followed, David walking faster than his mum, as if he knew it was somehow to do with him. They both stood, frozen with shock, their mouths open in astonishment. Written in the stone were the words 'WE NEED YOU'. There it was again, the dream he had the previous night, the mystery figure, all flashed before his eyes.

'I don't know how this got here, I really don't know,' said Suzanne, trying to sound as if she were in control.

David just continued to stare at the writing on the wall, his mind seemed suspended within time, his mouth could have swallowed a thousand flies at this point. He tried to speak, but to little avail, this was getting more surreal by the minute. Thinking quickly, Suzanne added,

'I guess it's some kind of joke.'

David looked at his mum, just a little hurt that his mum had said this was a prank when in all truth it wasn't, and they both knew it. Rob looked at David with a gentle reassurance, which made him feel that everything was ok. Within his eyes though, David sensed that Rob thought that this wasn't a joke at all and that, somehow, David knew about this.

'Look, don't worry David mate,' smiled Rob, 'You neither Sue, I think you could remove it but it looks like it's engraved in the stone.'

'Thanks Rob, don't worry, we'll get it off. We'll find a way, won't we Davie?'

'Oh sure,' came David's reply.

His tongue was still lost as he tried to understand all this.

'It's more like it's a message to you,' said Rob, as if he was trying to find out what it was all about.

He was a detective and was naturally used to asking questions. David had always liked Rob and had often wanted to help him if he was ever troubled by what he saw at work. He longed to tell him about the day that he'd had, but perhaps this just wasn't the right time.

The weather was horrendous as if some ocean in the sky had opened up and was now drenching Mother Earth in all its glory. Suzanne decided it would be silly for her and David to tackle the job now. They would try to have a normal evening. They graciously thanked Rob for his concern and, as Rob turned away, he tapped David on the shoulder, as if to say, it's ok mate, it will be fine. David responded by giving Rob a sincere smile.

'Cheers mate. I'll see you later.'

Throughout this time, the three of them had been unaware of a van that had parked opposite them. It was dark in colour, its windows equally dark, making it difficult to see inside. Its occupants were two men, both sinister looking, with monk-like cowls, making their features shadowed and hard to see. Inside, there was a surveillance-type screen. These men had been watching and listening to David, his mum and Rob, listening with interest and observing the writing on the wall. The driver pushed a red button on the console next to the screen, changing the image. Another similarly dressed figure, his face also in shadow, appeared. The driver spoke in a calculated voice.

'We need to speak to Lord Asphodel, there's something strange going on, he needs to be told about this.'

Within seconds, the van made a screeching sound before speeding off into the night.

The evening was a very quiet one to say the least. Suzanne had cooked salmon and rice, but what David didn't realise, was how quickly this quiet evening was going to change.

The clock chimed 10 o'clock, its pendulum swaying and tapping the wood of this small object. Gently swaying back and forth, the effects of this were almost hypnotic, it was like Father Time had slowed down the hours and was using the gentle ticking to send them into a relaxed state of mind. They would soon be making their way into the magical land of dreams. David decided to go to bed.

He made his way upstairs, his body feeling quite heavy now. The intrusion of the rain seemed to be somehow to do with this feeling. Cumulus and nimbus had been very unkind today, thought David as he proceeded to pull all the upstairs curtains. As he went to draw the curtains in his mum's room he glanced out onto the street, which he had loved to do since he was a child. He had always found this to be somewhat relaxing and would often see his neighbours, opposite. There were two boys, whose parents had split up, but their dad would come and visit. David saw this and identified with, and felt for them. Because he was a very intuitive person, he could often feel and sense things. He wasn't a nosy person, he was just very perceptive and thoughtful. Outside, everything looked normal, with not many cars about, making everything seem so peaceful. David exhaled a deep breath, welcoming the peaceful feeling. Lampposts lit the street, drenching the area with its yellow-green light. The lamplight was a reasonable substitute for the power of the sun, as it reflected its own fireflies of the night onto leaves and trees. Still, nothing could quite beat Father Sun.

David scanned the neighbourhood, staring at the long line of lampposts, shining their light on all sectors of the street. At that moment, something caught his eye. Standing right beside the lamp outside his house was undoubtedly the same, the very same figure in the long robe and hood, that he had seen twice that day. Once again, the figure stood still and silent, looking in his direction. Fear and fascination coursed through his mind, but what should he do? Should he attempt to make contact, or hide away within the safety of his home? It was at this point the figure started to move. It held out its arms to David, as if to beckon him to come out. The soul was clad in a robe of very unusual material, not cotton, wool, silk, or even plastic. It was more an unearthly material as if from another world. Transfixed by the figure and feeling that it was talking to him, David suddenly heard his mum's voice, breaking his time of visual contact with the hooded figure and when he turned back, the figure had gone. He scanned the street frantically, with his ocean blue eyes, but to no avail. It couldn't be that he was hallucinating could it? Maybe he was just imagining the figure, maybe all the excitement of the day had overworked his senses and encouraged the depths of his mind to play tricks on him. No, that wasn't it, it could not be. As excited as he had been with the day's events, it couldn't have made him see what he knew he had just seen. Once again, his mind flicked like a piece of elastic back to that same enigma where the figure couldn't have run off, no matter how quick a runner. David had only turned away for a couple of seconds, he surely would have seen it, it couldn't have eluded his vision in such a short space of time. What should he do? Well, if this mystery person didn't want to hang around for introductions, David concluded that there was nothing he could do. He casually drew the curtains and decided to let it be. He wouldn't tell his mum, it might make her worry. Was it wise, however, not to tell her? As long as she was ok, that was all that mattered. David began to wash. He was starting to feel very tired.

As he entered his bedroom, he made his way to his window. The rain had stopped and the clouds had cleared . Looking out at the blackness of night, made beautiful by her train of stars, that lit the night sky, shimmering like a multitude of scattered diamonds, David's eyes widened in dreamlike awe as he gazed up at the jewels of the night. No wonder mankind, since the dawn of time, had always looked there for truth, a truth that humanity perhaps will one day find. He looked down at his bedside table, where he had placed the crystals he had collected over the years, thus turning it into an altar.

David could hear his mum downstairs, locking the doors. Soon she'd be coming up to sleep. He hoped the next day would be much less strange than today. David was just dozing off when his mum came into the room.

'Goodnight love,' Suzanne said, 'Don't worry about anything, I suspect it's all to do with what you believe in, and, you know, the dream.'

Indeed, Suzanne had no idea how true that was.

'Goodnight Mum. I know it's ok really, I'm not worried. Today's been a long day. I don't understand it but I can't fight or worry about it either.'

David knew this was more than just coincidence, but he hardly had any energy now, and it was time for sleep.

3

THE CALLING

David awoke during the middle of the night feeling drowsy, but by no means relaxed, as his mind was still raging with questions about the previous day's events. He thought about the souls he had met and spoken to during the day. He thought about Elia and how she'd looked when he told her of his dream. He thought about what she'd said to him during the angel reading. The mysterious figure continued to rampage through the eye of his mind. Every time he thought about it, the more of a mystery it all seemed to be. Who was it? What did he or she want with him? David could, at times, hear little noises going on outside, it was only badgers and foxes in the garden. Other than that, everything else was hauntingly silent throughout the house and, indeed, next door. It was both haunting and comforting at the same time.

Unable to contain his restless fidgeting any longer he got out of bed. He hadn't been asleep long, say two or three hours at most. Looking out of his window, he could see the sky had become even clearer, in fact there was no cloud in the night sky. The moon spilt her milky coloured light onto David's face making him feel refreshed and slightly more relaxed. The garden had been invaded by the badgers. They'd knocked down some flowerpots on the patio.

'They are getting brave,' thought David with amusement, 'but just wait till mum catches them.' Hopefully. they weren't making tunnels under the garden! He turned to look at his clock. 'What's going on?'

Instead of giving the correct time, his clock showed 7:11am, David tried to alter the device, thinking the batteries were low. He was unable to change it. It seemed to be frozen in time, as if something didn't want David to change the numbers. 7:11am it read and 7:11am it wanted to stay. 7.11 that means the merging of Heaven and Earth said David to himself. Suddenly, a gentle voice spoke as if from nowhere.

'David.' He spun round, circling his bedroom. Where was it coming from? What in heaven was going on? He started to shake. 'David, please don't be afraid, it is I.'

Whatever, or whoever, it was, it wanted his attention. He decided he needed to communicate.

'Who are you?'

'I am your guardian angel and one of many who stand beside you. We are so glad to have been able to get through to you, dear one. Your nervousness made it very hard for us to reach you, but The One was adamant, and made it very clear to us.

'The One?' said David.

'Yes, we think you know The Creator very well, not to mention Archangel Michael.'

Archangel Michael had often come in to Elia during Reiki healing, in which he would impart profound messages.

'What was The One adamant about and what did he make clear to you?' queried David, now beginning to feel excitement on a great level.

'That you, upon special invitation, come with us this night to the realms of the divine.' David's heart was now starting to leap.

'The realms of the divine? Why me, dear angels?'

'It is your destiny, and by slowing down our own frequency, we have been able to show ourselves to you.'

David watched in awe as something extraordinary began to happen. A tiny speck of light appeared directly in front of him. And David felt his Third Eye the energy centre in the middle of his Forehead begin to open up. It hung in the air, very much resembling a star, Spherical in shape, it grew bigger in size and beauty. The room became brighter until the whole room was flooded in brilliant light. The sphere embraced David, immersing him within. He felt no fear, in fact he seemed to deal with what he was seeing with an acceptance quite unusual for many people, for he felt warm, safe and completely shielded within the beautiful cocoon. The great centre of the sphere, like a pulsating crystal, now seemed to form an actual shape. David couldn't help but stare, transfixed, at this incredible manifestation. Who wouldn't, I ask you? He had been told at his Reiki courses that he had two guardian angels, as did everyone. Now, as he looked face to face with one of them, he felt this angel was representing both entities, and this was truly awesome.

The angelic being was truly a sight for blessed eyes. The face was soft and appeared to be glowing. It was difficult for David to see the facial features, as the light around them seemed so bright, pulsating, making them even more supernatural. The angel was glowing with golden yellow light whilst also emanating a silver white energy. Its aura was a treat for the eye, impossible to describe how lovely. The angel was clothed in a robe of liquid light and its wings sparkled like shimmering gossamer.

At this point, David became aware of a plethora of angels within the orb, enfolding him with unconditional love. They were smiling sincerely, whilst stroking, touching and caressing him, particularly around his head. They were all his angels they loved him and he loved them. The unearthly beings stood three foot taller than him. Their feet were hidden under their robes of light, but their most distinguishing feature was the great light that emanated from the centre of their chests. David had a million and one questions that he wanted to ask his heavenly friends, but his mind now felt calm and free of the anxiety that he had earlier.

'Are your wings made of gossamer?' he asked.

'Our wings are our auric field, but people, over time, have called them wings because they depicted our energy as this. Our light was made by the Creator at the time of Creations birth.'

Intrigued, David couldn't help noticing that the great light seemed to be getting stronger.

'What is that light radiating from you?'

'This is our heart, it is the heart of the Divine. You, and all people and creatures on earth, have this light. The spiritual among you call it the heart chakra. Within this light is the greatest power you all have - love.'

The angels mimicked this by placing their hands where the light was.

'How beautiful,' David thought.

He was more enraptured by this supernatural encounter than overwhelmed by it. It was as if he had met very close friends following a long absence. Did these wondrous beings have names or were they simply to be known as his guardian angels?

'Do you have names?' David asked cautiously. 'Is one of you called Angelica?' This was the name Elia had mentioned, when treating him once with Reiki.

'Yes, darling, I am Angelica,' one of the angels spoke in an excited, childlike voice.

The angel David had seen first seemed to be the one who took prominence over all the others. It replied instantly and with such great kindness.

'My name is Nada, we have names that are earthly and ethereal, It makes no difference to us. I was given this name by The One, as it represents the true nature of heart which is pure and beyond lower self.'

David could detect a very sweet smell about the angels. The scent was almost indescribable, but like honey and roses. This was a smell he had noticed before, during a Reiki session.

'David, are you ready upon this night to come with us to the realms of Eternity?.

David nodded a little gingerly, but then hesitated, as if in doubt. He couldn't leave his mum. She needed to come with them, she should see this.

'No, David,' the angel spoke as if Nada could hear his thoughts, 'it only needs to be you.'

'But my mum is a good soul too, please let her see this,' he pleaded.

'David, hear us,' said Nada calmly, with absolute love, 'You are needed. This is your path, dear one, for what you are going to do shall benefit countless souls, such as your mother. You are going to make the world a better place for all. You walk the path of love, Blue Robin.'

'Who, what did you call me?' David replied.

Nada gave a knowing look.

'You won't be leaving your Mum she will be with you throughout this journey.'

'Wha....what do you mean? If I am going with you, how can I still be with her?'

'Look upon your bed, David,' came the reply.

David did so, still enfolded within the angels' orb. Suddenly, he let out a great cry.

'What on Earth, What's going on?'

There, lying on his bed, he saw himself, looking as if in deep peaceful, sleep. His angels flocked closer around him, using their energy to comfort and relax him.

'Angels, what's happened, have I had an out of body experience?

'Yes,' came the reply. 'In a way, you have. You see, sweet one, where you're going can only be possible if you ethereally travel. You are now in your true self, your higher self. By coming with us you will be bio-locating. Yet, as you have not properly left earth, it not being your time, and shall not be for many years, you will still be connected to your physical self. All souls experience this when they dream. Their souls travel to the many realms, just as you have. We are, however, bending laws of physics with you, yet this is how it's meant to be, and one day all shall experience their highest selves. By coming with us you will be able to witness your higher purpose.'

The angels seemed to speak in unison. David examined his new form with fascination. It was similar to his vessel of flesh and blood, legs, arms, head. He certainly was no orb. He was completely unclad, naturally; pyjamas, they were of the physical world. His skin glowed with a white light, his hair was still fair, but seemed even more so and glowed, just like the light around his body - his own aura surrounded within an even more beautiful aura of the angels. His blue eyes sparkled, lit by the torches of his soul. His entire form seemed almost animated. He felt free and light and more joyful than he had ever been in physical form. Most interesting though were the glowing, spinning balls of energy stemming from his crown, his forehead, throat, thymus, heart, solar plexus (his gut), his sacral, sexual organ right down to the root. His heart being the brightest, in conjunction with his spinal cord.

'These are my chakras, my wheels of light,' said David, as if to himself.

'Yes, indeed, they are dear one and whilst you operate within this form, your earthly self,' (indicating the vessel of David in the bed), 'will function as normally as you do on earth, but in a soul-induced sleep. There are many different levels that humans are made of, David. The one you know in life on earth is just one layer of the many bodies you have. This night, it gives us great pleasure to tell you that you shall be travelling in a body as light as the air, yet far stronger than any earthly one, to journey with us to the realms of light.'

'You mean I'm going to see Heaven?'

'You see it every day, dear one, all people do. They just don't realise. But yes, you are going to see Heaven, as many humans call it, in all its true glory. Now you are in your highest form, you shall have the spiritual sight that allows you to see all things of the highest truth - love. You will see what most humans don't. From this night onwards you will see paradise.'

The angels stopped talking and turned to look behind them, as if they had heard something, turning back, nodding to each other as if in acknowledgement of something or someone.

'The One is calling, it rings the bell of destiny to us. It's time David.'

'Please, before I go, I must check on my mum. I know I'll always be with her, but I'd like to see her.'

'Very well, but destiny's bell asks you to have no fear and to love with us.'

David knew it would be foolish at this point to argue with such beings of light. He found himself walking through the wall, into his mum's bedroom. Now, what a blast that was! Throughout this time, he remained enfolded by his angels within their orb. He gazed at his mum's sleeping form, and to his delight he saw that she lay enfolded in her own orb by her own angels. There were four in total, almost like his own in beauty and radiance. They smiled, whilst nodding to Nada and his other angels, not speaking, but David heard them through his mind, as in telepathy, and in a more loving way than any language spoken orally. David placed his hand upon his mum's head caressing both her and her angels.

'I've to go now Mum, but hear me. I need you to know, I love you and, although a part of me is going, I am not leaving you. I have to do this now. I'm going to be safe, with my angel. Nada will take care of me.'

He kissed his mum, knowing in his heart that she could hear him. The angels smiled at each other, and then

David found the orb floating back to his bedroom, just as Suzanne spoke softly in her sleep,

'I love you David. The One awaits you, as do we all. You must go now.'

'Return to love, David, it is so easy. Feel Heaven calling you. You don't need to bring anything, just your own sacred soul.'

'Well, I always have liked to travel light,' David said with a smile.

He'd heard that angels had a great sense of humour and, indeed, he could hear the infectious laughter of his guardians clearly, within him. The looks on their faces said it all.

The angels held both his hands with a gentle, yet steady, touch. He now heard the bell, the most beautiful tinkling sound, seeming to be coming straight from his heart, getting louder and louder.

'Heaven is truly within you all,' they said, as a spiral formation leapt from David's heart centre, forming itself into a giant-like tunnel, unlimited by space or time, until it was as big as the angel orb itself. David, felt a warmth as if blessed with pure love.

'Are we going through the tunnel?'

'We are going to defy gravity and walk on the wings of infinity.'

On saying this, the angels, David and the orb passed through the tunnel. The formation then faded, no tunnel, no orb, no angels and no David, just his vessel lying upon the bed. The room was now empty and silent, disturbed only by the voices of the night.

4

THE TUNNEL

Within the tunnel it was dark, yet not eerily so, as the angels' light illuminated the long winding passageway. Inside the orb, David felt calm and at total peace, cocooned within the angels' wings. He felt so warm and protected, like a baby in its mother's arms, yet more so, like a little soul still within the womb. His whole form seemed to be floating with the angels through the tunnel, suspended as if on cushions of air. The walls of this tunnel were not solid, it was hard to describe exactly what they were made of. It was like energy in some animated form, truly incredible. His angels, with beaming faces, communicated via telepathy.

'You are in the passageway between worlds, a bridge between the physical and spiritual. All souls come through this way and all souls return this way.'

'How can you do this?'

'We told you, dear one. The One gave us the power, which allows us to transcend and defy the limitations you humans feel exists. Everything on earth is on a very low vibration. Your earth is of a lower dimension. It is so easy for us, of the invisible higher realms, to walk through your world, but because we are on a higher level, our frequency is much stronger and lighter than yours, making us invisible to the eyes of mortals.'

'So, you're always with us, all of you, so close to us? Why don't we feel your presence?'

'We cannot come into humans lives if we are not asked, sacred one. That is due to the law of the universe. If people accepted us more and invited us in, then we could. However, that time may not be too far away.'

'I do hope so,' thought David to himself.

The angels floated onwards, the sound of destiny's bell still tinkling in the background, more rhythmically than before. Suddenly, David saw a beautiful, piercing, White light in the distance, it was the eye of Eternity. As they got nearer, the light grew brighter and bigger until they reached it.

'What's on the other side?' David croaked with an emotion and excitement he'd rarely felt, since childhood. His angelic friends laughed with equal excitement, as if touched by David's wonder, which was so infectious.

'Well, why don't we find out?' they replied just as they all passed through the light and into Eternity.

'Oh, my goodness!' cried David, as Nada kissed his forehead.

'Welcome home. David, our dear one, Welcome home.'

5

THE GARDEN

They stood within a vast, beautiful, green meadow, the air so clean and fresh, so different from planet earth, with its man-made smog and pollution. Butterflies of all varieties and colours, some golden, fluttered gracefully to and fro amongst the flowers, the likes of which far surpassed those on our planet filling the air with their sweet perfume. There were trees too, some bearing luscious fruits, standing tall and strong with feathery singers nestled within them, filling the air with birdsong. They, too, were of all varieties, robins to sparrows, finches to blue-tits. It filled the young Mans, soul with a tranquillity he had never felt in his physical life. It was as if he had discovered rare treasures, so precious you'd never wish to part with them. Davids eyes scanned the vast landscape, to his left, not far from where they'd entered there stood a marvellous domed building which was Greco-Roman in style, with ornate pillars. A stairway led up to it.

'That which you see there, dear one, is the Hall of Wisdom, where the scanning machine resides. The Scanning Machine replays events that have taken place during your Lifetime on Earth as well as beyond. It gives you your Life Review. That is where you go when you officially come back here,' said Nada, pointing toward it. 'It is synonymous with homecoming.' David also saw two other buildings close by these were The Halls of Justice a building of Impeccable design surrounded by Fountains that graced the outside of the Grecian building with its vast White Marble dome. And The Hall of Records a vast edifice of Spectacular carved columns and a dome of sparkling gold. Every soul in the Universe visited this place and within it contained every work of art, literature and historical piece ever written not to mention the complete written knowledge of the mind of God. Beyond that stood Two very high buildings , so high they very nearly pierced the Sky of Heaven, made entirely of shining blue glass these were known as The Towers, this was the place all Souls would go to prepare for Incarnation on Earth.

'I feel I've seen it before,' said David.

'Of course you have. You have had so many Lifetimes so naturally you have frequently visited here, playing amongst the marble pillars with your soul family, who have often travelled here too.'

'David, David.' The young man looked up.

There, standing at the top of the steps at the entrance by the door, of The Hall of Wisdom a plethora of souls, each one accompanied by angels, started to run towards him. These were the relatives from Davids current Lifetime in addition to every loved one from every Past Life his Soul had ever lived. Mothers, Fathers, former Brothers and Sisters, Aunts , Uncles, cousins and close friends. Plus every pet he had known and loved as well.

'Nada, it can't be.'

'Oh yes it can, dear one.'

Each of the souls threw their arms around him, hugging and kissing him repeatedly. And David remembered every single one. Like his two grandads, Ted and Eric, plus his nanny on his mum's side and Auntie Muriel and Uncle Ralph, who had passed some years ago. A corgi came running up to greet his former master, with love and licks.

'Sammy, how are you boy? How are you doing? God, I've missed you.' David's eyes were now filling with joyous tears. 'I think of you every day. Not a day passes when I don't'

The angels, of which there must have been well over a Thousand, along with his loved ones, smiled thoughtfully at each other. His loved ones wore flowing gowns. Uncle Ralph wore a very striking blue gown and they all looked so much younger. David had read this, that when you returned home, you went back to being young, about thirty years old.

'We've watched you grow every day, old boy,' said grandad Eric. 'We want you to know how proud we all are.'

'Thank you, grandad, I really don't know what to say. All I can say is it's glorious to be here and I can't describe how I feel. I don't quite know what's going on, but, but....'

'Don't worry. Just know that you are surrounded by love,' said Auntie Muriel 'Love of the purest kind.'

His Uncle Ralph smiled and nodded slowly. Always a placid man, Ralph was a gentle soul who'd never said a bad word about anyone. On earth, he'd been married to Muriel for over sixty-three years. They had lived not far from Elia, in a tiny bungalow which David had often visited, playing imaginary games at the bottom of their garden, which backed on to a railway line.

'Come on, old Sam, give your master a rest' Ralph said. 'I always look after him, he's never alone, we all walk together in this meadow the gardens of eternity. His loved ones each gave David a final hug, waved him goodbye and left saying,

'We'll meet again, David, it's now time for you to meet with your true family.'

As brief as this meeting had been, it had been so special, so wondrous and assuring as he knew that all who had passed were in such a special place. If only his mum and dad could have seen this.

'How could anything top this experience?' thought David.

'Oh, but it can,' said his angels, once again reading his thoughts. We are going to take you to Shambhala the dimension of the Highest Consciousness to The Temple of Truth 'And Look who's come to escort you there.

They pointed with glowing hands towards the Azure coloured skies. David found it quite difficult to make out at first, then 'Hang on, they looked like, no they couldn't be, surely. Oh, yes they were.' David had to blink to see if he was dreaming, but no, coming straight towards them, were a winged herd of flying horses, no they were Unicorns led by one that was blessed with the purest white coat. The Unicorns of the air approached David and his angels, gracefully landing a few feet away. They were equally as majestic to look at as the angels, a beautiful sight, to be sure, especially their leader with eyes the colour of amethyst, who was truly magnificent. It's pure, white face emanated kindness with a beautiful Silver Horn that stemmed from its forehead. David felt so closely connected to this awesome creature, he wanted to embrace it, which he did, placing his arms around its neck. It seemed to respond by gently rubbing its head against David's face. Nada and the other angels smiled at David's unconditional ways and gentle manner. David felt he had come home to a family he had not seen for a very long time. Nada was the first to break the silence by introducing David's new friend.

'This is Pegasus. He is your animal guide or totem animal.'

Pegasus. This was just getting too cool for words. Ever since David had been a small boy, he had loved the stories and been fascinated by the legend of Pegasus. Many called it a myth, but David had always believed in the truth of these stories, as if by some inner knowledge. His motto, 'never say never to anything, for there might be a grain of truth in it.' He always loved the story of Pegasus and how he had helped Prince Perseus in his mission to rescue the Princess Andromeda.

'It's ok David, it's all true. Pegasus exists, as do many creatures who are regarded as myth, on the spiritual planes. Unicorns, Merpeople, Dragons, griffins and all elemental beings Elves, gnomes, fawns, fairies, sprites and sylphs, and all animals, return here, when their time on earth is at an end. Not to mention dinosaurs. All have a place here, but don't worry, the only thing that's extinct about them is their ferociousness.'

'Oh, I'm glad to hear that. This isn't my imagination.' but he stopped at the thought, 'This could only be a dream.'

'We assure you it is not, though it has to be said, your strong imagination and innocence has allowed us to come closer than to a lot of mortals. You see, when children go to school at the age of four or five, they are taught to conform and do well, with emphasis on competition and success. As a result, they tend to lose their spiritual awareness and their natural innocence starts to become clouded, blocking the mortal's ability to communicate between the two worlds. You are someone, David, who has maintained their true power, thereby helping you to remain open to us. That is how we were able to reach you.'

There were so many questions David had, but as if in response, Nada floated over him once again, encasing his form in its beautiful orb, placing its hand upon his forehead.

'Be calm David, the more still you are, the more you will be able to hear us.'

David felt the nervousness of his mind calming, feeling at ease once again, relaxed as if through some gentle hypnosis.

'Pegasus, just like us, has been your friend, but your connection with him, as with us, goes back through the ages of Millennia, back to the last great golden age of earth when men and women of peace led each day of their lives with pure love. It is for this reason that you have been allowed access here before your time on earth has properly finished. Tell us, David, can you see yourself as you were?'

David nodded, he remembered Atlantis, walking amongst the people of this beautiful continent, conversing so clearly and freely with Nada and many other spiritual beings, other angels and fairies and riding daily on the back of unicorns with such confidence. The visualisation, strong as it was, seemed to then fade, leaving David with just a taste of the world he had loved. It had been disturbed by Pegasus nudging excitedly at his friend's head.

'David, would you give Pegasus the honour of riding through this realm? He, not to mention us, wants to show you the gardens beyond. He has asked us if you wouldn't mind.'

'Mind? No, of course I don't mind. I'd be delighted,' the boy said, surprised such a great being of light would be so humble as to ask a mere mortal to ride upon his back. 'The visualisation, I saw was Atlantis. You were right, it was such a wonderful place.

You have much to know and much to do. You will see Atlantis again, but the Creator wishes you to enjoy yourself first, to adjust to your surroundings, even though they are familiar to you. It has been a long time measured by your earth's clock, since you were last here.'

Turning back to meet Pegasus' perceptive eyes, David attempted to speak, but so in awe at being in the angels', not to mention Pegasus' presence, he found he could only speak in a meek whisper.

'I'd love it Pegasus,' he said, pressing his face against the noble animal, with a tear forming in his eye.

The winged Animal seemed to smile, and gave a gentle nod, as if to say, 'I'm ready' as David climbed up onto this wondrous creature. As he did so, all the other winged Unicorns began to take off, with Pegasus the last to do so, high into the air, so graceful and gentle, almost balletic, up, up and away. The angels followed now, no longer in need of their orbs to travel in, they were home and free to fly and float amongst this heavenly realm.

'We know where to take you, David, the Creator wants us to take you to the sea of Compassion. There is someone waiting for you, someone you know quite well we think.'

The Unicorns were soon joined by other angels, many in the form of cherubs. They continued to veer upwards, onwards, high above the fields of golden flowers, across the sky towards the light of the great central sun. David had never felt happier in all his mortal life, never felt such elation and bliss. It was truly beyond description. They were now so high up, they could see the great horizon of Heaven. There were no cars, no roads, no pollution, just endless landscapes of emerald green fields, and lush gardens interspersed by paths of pebbled stone, on which he saw many souls, probably once human, walking, some leisurely, some briskly, some were with family whilst some were not. Some Souls acted as gardeners and loved tending to the beautiful gardens, and everyone had their Guardian angels with them. Others were running or jogging, or playing sports, others with animals such as dogs and cats, whilst in the fields, there were shepherd-like souls who tended their flocks of sheep, lambs, cows and horses. They were grazing, all existing in complete harmony. Looking down at the pebble pathways, there were white marble benches about the place. Some were occupied by souls who seemed to sit cross-legged in meditation, whilst others just sat, resting, reading books, playing musical instruments such as harps and guitars or chatting with each other. Some souls would look up and wave or smile at them, even calling to them and whistling.

'Look, there's David,' one said, while others looked and smiled, before returning to their business.

Just as on earth, some souls are loud, some quiet and reserved. Everyone was kind, nobody judged anyone here for every soul was happy within themselves. There was no need to compare, all were one and all knew they were unique. There were also houses, some beautiful thatched cottages with pristine gardens, spacious homes with glorious Swimming Pools and some houses that seemed to be made from quartz crystal, which used the energy of the light to supply their resources. There were also grand fairy tale castles that looked like they had jumped out of your favourite storybook, complete with drawbridges and moats.

'Here, in life eternal, a soul can decide where they choose to live,' said Nada. 'Some wish for the place they could only dream of in physical life'. She made a notion with her hand to the grandiose castles. 'Others prefer to live in exact replicas of those they once had on earth.'

Below them, in the fields baby unicorns danced to the music of a fawn's flute, producing the sweetest melody. Little children of all ages who had just finished 'ring-a-ring-o-roses' rushed to join in the dancing, before finally losing interest and running back to their beautiful abodes, one or two looking as if they were made from candy canes and chocolate.

'Ha thought David, 'some things just never change.'

From out of the land and sky, came the blessed elementals known so well through folklore. Fairies in beautiful gowns covered in flowers, with wings like butterflies, greeting David and the angels with kisses and special blessings, fluttering and flitting, before moving on to see if the unicorns wanted to play. This life eternal was very different to the Heaven most people thought was above the clouds. This was an actual place, a world, a universe, where literally anything seemed possible. Beyond time and space, defying the limitations of logic, a world where dream and reality intermingled, where innocence dwelled, alive and well, and happiness was the universal language. David studied the other Unicorns, Whereas Pegasus was pure white, his companions were the colours of the rainbow, and gold and silver.

'How does it feel to see the gardens of Eternity again, dear one?' asked the angels out of curiosity.

'It feels wonderful, just like it's the best feeling I've ever had.'

'In these gardens, innocence and the dreams of childhood become reality once more. This is also known as the "seventh heaven". Come, the sea of Compassion is not far away now.'

'If Mum could see me now,' thought David.

It was morning back on earth. The ripples of sunlight peaked through the curtains of David's bedroom.

'Davie, I've brought you some tea.' David's mum was at the door with his favourite beverage, but there was no answer,'David, come on, wake up darling.' Still nothing.
Feeling slightly troubled, Suzanne entered the bedroom, David looked as if he was still asleep, stretched out upon the bed. She looked at her son with eyes of love, just like the angels had, not so long ago. Aware of his unusual stillness, Suzanne tried to wake her son by nudging him.

'David, David, come on wake up love..... DAVID wake up.' Fear gripped Suzanne's mind as David continued not to move. 'Oh God, could my boy be..?'

She hurriedly checked her son's pulse and, to her relief, she felt his heart beating as normal. But why was his body not responding? Why was he not hearing her calls? Why wasn't he waking up? Suzanne started to panic. What should she do? Call a doctor? Perhaps David could be in some sort of coma. Her racing mind was disturbed at that moment by a knock at the door. Whoever it was, they continued knocking. Irritated and flustered, Suzanne quickly ran down stairs, ready to confront this most annoying early caller. As she opened the door, a familiar voice greeted her. Suzanne's mouth fell open and her mind quickly changed from panic to relief. Standing in the doorway was Elia Lotus with a kind smile upon her face.

'Suzanne, I've come to see you and David. I know what's happened, so if I could please come in?'

'Please do,' said Suzanne in desperation.

Very calmly Elia entered and was ushered quickly up the stairs by the anxious woman, who began telling Elia how she'd found David, how she'd been unable to wake him. Elia saw her fear at being powerless to do anything for her son, lying in this coma-like state, her grief at not being able to control the situation.

'I had a dream very similar to David's, Suzanne, and I saw him literally leaving his body on some level and being in the presence of angels.' Elia stopped, observing Suzanne. Perhaps it was too soon to be telling all she knew. The poor woman must be going out of her mind. Dressed this time in a long white flowing tunic, her shining long dark hair hanging carelessly, but neatly down to her shoulders in a youthful way, she looked at least fifteen years younger than her years. Elia possessed a calm and ethereal manner as she entered the bedroom and calmly walked up to David. She used her hands to scan David's energy. Her relaxed attitude and gentle presence had eased the strain Suzanne felt, and had filled her mind with small, but powerful, tinges of hope. Elia was the best tonic for any tense situation. True, Elia was not a doctor, but she was a healer and could see things on a clairvoyant level, something the more "black and white" mind of a physician just wasn't trained to do. Elia had had many ups and downs in her incarnation, once describing her life to someone as being like a rollercoaster, but a wonderful experience. She'd known great happiness and great sadness also. She'd once loved a man but they had parted ways. What, or who he was and why she'd lost him, she'd never told, perhaps somewhere deep down it still hurt. Following a bout of internal despair, Elia had nearly given up on this tumultuous journey of life, when she had an epiphany, a realisation. Her Guardian Angel had appeared to her and led her on an Incredible Inner Journey into the Universe, helping her to never be afraid, the angel helped her to realise what it was she had to do. It led her to India to study Meditation, and Angel Therapy. This led her onto her path with Reiki, in which she combined all these things to help others to heal and find themselves again. She was also highly intuitive and naturally clairvoyant since birth. She had helped so many, but could she help in this? Elia stopped her scanning and walked over to Suzanne, her face filled with realisation. 'David is okay,' she said soothingly, gently touching Suzanne's shoulder.

'He is working on an enlightened level, which means that a layer of his consciousness is working elsewhere, hence the reason for his comatose, physical state.'

'But why? Why now, Elia, and how long will David be like this?'

The beautiful healer sighed before saying in her rich accented voice,

'It's difficult to know how and when, but whilst I was scanning him, my angel, Christia, came through and said you mustn't fear, and that it's vital that you let this process continue for as long as it is meant to.' Suzanne looked both thankful and perplexed. 'David is working, not in this reality, but in another dimension, the seventh heaven, "home" to be exact.'

'Seventh heaven? But why is all this happening now, Elia?' her perplexed side now coming to the fore.

'He has been assigned by the light itself to go on a mission of great importance. It's so imperative that we look after his physical form, as he can still feel things. I cannot emphasise this enough. Although working in another realm, he is still connected to his physical self.'

Suddenly Suzanne caught on.

'This is all to do with what he was telling me yesterday, and why he came to see you at your house of white stone.'

'Yes, and last night I had a dream, as I was saying earlier. I woke up realising that this was a premonition. I'm sorry I didn't call first, but I knew I had to get over here as soon as possible.'

Feeling a need to refresh herself, after the whirlwind events, Suzanne gave a wary nod to Elia, before embracing her.

'Darling, we need to leave David as he is. He's fine and will return to his physical body but, until then, we can't let anyone know. There are - let's just say - people out there who try to control us, Magicians. They lurk in the shadows scheming, plotting, selling us lies of freedom when they know only too well that it doesn't exist, unbeknown to but just a few of us.'

'You say they are in the shadows? Who are they?' these Magicians? asked Suzanne.

'Well they are hidden from the rest of the world. We never see them and that's just the way they like it replied Elia. They have powers, and are advanced in ways that would oppose David's mission of the light.'

'What should we do?' asked Suzanne.

'We must stay as silent as we can and protect our minds by thinking only positive thoughts. As the angels say "if you cultivate flowers then weeds cannot take hold". Tell no one about this event, Suzanne, not a soul, for whisperers lurk in the shadows. Nobody must know, you understand?'

Suzanne humbly nodded. The day had begun like any other, yet now all that was normal had been pulled from under her. There was a certain dread in Elia's face as she spoke these words, so Suzanne knew it was not to be taken lightly. Elia then lightened up, her eyes now widened in a cheeky fashion.

'Now, how about we have a nice cup of tea?'

'I'd prefer a stiff drink' said Suzanne.

'Very well, I'll agree with that. Remember honey, shaken not stirred.'

Suzanne only smiled faintly. Despite the arrival of Elia, she still felt instinctive love and protection for her son.

Kneeling beside David's physical body, she gently kissed his forehead before whispering in his ear,

'I love you David, come back to me soon, darling.'

Then she stood up, brushing away a tear from her eye. Elia smiled, and turned back to David.

'God bless you, sweet angel and may peace and light go with you, wherever you are now. Remember, just trust.' Thank goodness for Elia being there. They would be safe now, surely.

'I may be able to link with David, so I can see where he is and what is happening.' stated Elia.

'Yes please, Elia. If you could, that would be wonderful.'

'Okay, I shall place my hand over his heart to link, with his soul, and we shall see.'

As she did so and closed her eyes, a knowing smile flickered over her face, for Elia could see where David was, and who he was with, as if observing from a scanner Screen.

'Well what can you see Elia?'

'I see home,' came her voice. 'I can see home.'

It may well have been an hour or two since Elia had arrived, but in the realm of seventh heaven, only a few seconds had passed since we last saw David fly with Pegasus, Nada and their entourage, over the gardens of Paradise. Time in life eternal didn't exist as it did on earth. The concept of it simply didn't matter. You could, for example, leave a loved one to incarnate on earth, but whatever age you lived to, it didn't matter, as it was only a few seconds in life eternal that your loved one would have to wait before seeing you again. It was such a tempting thought. David would have loved to stay in this realm, to run, taste and smell the sweet air of eternity, to fly with Nada and Pegasus, and all his angels. How good that would be. How selfish - he had a mum and dad back on earth, not to mention others who loved him. Why would he think like that? Nada once again answered his thoughts.

'It's normal to feel like this, David. Once a soul feels and sees its true home, they never want to leave and some never do. But you must, as it is not your time yet and you are here to fulfil a part of your life purpose. We need say no more.'

They passed over more splendid gardens filled with flowers of every colour - red, pink, orange, yellow, blue, purple, green, white, violet and gold. A treat for the heart, not to mention the eye. The flowers were tended by fairies, who hovered over them, along with the butterflies and bumblebees.

'These flowers are magnificent, brighter than any flower I've ever seen on earth.

'They are grown by the goddess of the rainbow, Iris,' Nada replied. 'Every month, she comes and feeds them with the elixir of the spectrum, ensuring their survival for ageless eternity, whilst our beloved friends, the elementals, tend to them on a regular basis. See how they work so hard.'

As David continued to gaze at the pastoral beauty, he could also see more cherubs tending to the emerald trees and playing with the Fairies amongst the gold and rainbow flowers, their faces emanating the richest of smiles. At that moment, several of the cherubs flew upward to David, stroking his head and then mischievously getting in the way of Nada and the other angels. David, who loved being in the company of these winged rascals, let out a peel of laughter. The cheeky cherubs, and all angels, are so good at giving joy to others. Nada, however, made it known when playtime was up, with a slight brush of her hand. The cheeky cherubs retreated with a look on their faces which seemed to say, "okay back to work, or the boss is going to find out we're playing up." David's heart once again leapt, his spiritual body felt strong and some of his chakras had now opened up like the petals of flowers, especially his heart chakra, whilst his soul bathed in the honey of happiness. He was very moved by what he saw - a winged Mother horse teaching her young to fly. The colts were adorable and like Pegasus, and friends were all different colours. They flew so close that David felt he could touch them. He wanted, so much, to reach out and caress their soft furry bodies, or stroke the tiny wings of these coloured colts, but Nada urged him to respect their space, as they were still pupils of flight. Reluctantly, David agreed.

They passed over vast Forests, Mountains, and winding rivers, which cascaded along the valleys below filled with the sound of flutes and gentle singing, before coming to a magnificent turquoise ocean, where sunlight splintered across the surface like dancing diamonds. At this point, each of the flying Unicorns started to swoop downwards, nose-diving towards the glistening water to a perfect landing. The poise of these creatures was phenomenal as they glided along the surface, their wings folded behind their backs, resembling the agility of swans. Pegasus had landed like this too, with David obliged to hold on tight, and yet feeling completely safe. The coolness of the water was refreshing, as Pegasus floated upon its shimmering surface. Nada had also touched down, gliding, resembling a skater on ice, her long robe of light billowing out upon the ocean. They had been joined by David's other angels, and the cherubs, who couldn't resist jumping in and getting themselves wet trying to imitate the beauty of their wiser counterparts. Being of a more mischievous nature, they were less successful, splashing around and struggling to tread water, their innocence and sheer love of fun made them even more infectious to be around. The water was decorated by an abundance of lilies, which floated upon the surface giving it an almost ornate feel. One of the cherubs, the self- appointed leader, pointed to a group of lily pads floating nearby.

'This will do,' they thought, and they hovered over to their new forms of transport, seating themselves upon the lilies, using them as you would use floats at a swimming pool. It should have gone smoothly, but for the odd one or two, who seemed to want the biggest pad, therefore simultaneously trying to push the other off. It was a scene that would have put Laurel and Hardy to shame. Nonetheless, this debate was soon remedied by a gesture made by Nada, resulting in a truce between the two cherubs. One would push the lily from behind, legs kicking, while the other, the calmer of the two, would sit on the pad and paddle with his hands, giving directions to his friend to steer.

'Nice work, fellas.' David grinned, applauding the cherubs for their teamwork.

If only human beings could work together this way, we could see the fun in life more than we do sometimes. Not being afraid to play like children, sometimes helps to lighten life. If we could only share more, the world would be a better place.

They had come to a giant waterfall. Mermaids perched on nearby rocks, others swam under water, their glowing velvet, finned tails and soft radiant bodies, so streamlined and graceful, performing an aquatic ballet to which all fish, dolphin and turtle were invited to join in. They beckoned to the angels to join them but Nada knew they were here for another reason and politely declined.

'This, David, is the sea of Compassion, the ocean of consciousness. So many dreams are made here, and wonders lie untold.'

The sight of the waterfall was truly spectacular, as it seemed to resemble liquid light falling, as if in slow motion, onto the blue below. Beyond this point, it veered off in all directions in the form of flowing streams, trickling through the emerald meadows like veins of light.

'Nada, why does everything from this realm seem to glow?'

'Glow?'

'Yes, it's as if everything is extra bright. Even the water here is not like it is on earth.'

'That is because in the higher realms everything resonates on a much higher vibration, so nothing is dense or heavy, as all is closer to the Creator replied the angel. That's why all you see here emanates with light, the vibration of love.'

They had now come to an oriental setting with trees of cherry blossom which swayed over the water lazily in the gentle breeze. An amazing huge Rainbow extended from the water right up to the sky.

'Why have we stopped here?' enquired David, gesturing towards the waterfall, its beauty sending a wave of peace through his soul.

'We have come here to meet the goddess of Compassion, the Bodhisativa herself, dear one.'

'You mean Quan Yin?' David fell silent for an instant.

A voice softly called his name.

'David, David, our dear one, so lovely to see you again in our realm.' David turned.

Coming towards them, as if out of some dream-like mist, was Quan Yin - she who hears our weeping world and the cries of all who call upon her. Quan Yin was sitting within a giant floating lily pad, riding it like a boat. She was truly beautiful. She wore a gown of the purest silk, the colour powder blue. Her hair was black as ebony and her skin of purest snow. Just like the picture of her in Davids room, Quan Yin held a golden vase in her left hand and, in her right, a lotus flower. She was the eastern counterpart of Mother Mary and held great love for the earth and all within it. Her Light shone out melting into curling Clouds around her.

'I have come with true compassion to bless you, David, just as I did when you were a humble student of Reiki. This gift I wish to bestow upon you again, our beloved.'

David remembered that March, that warm day, his Reiki one and two course. During the attunement he had felt the wonderful sensation of water being sprinkled upon his head, and him not wanting it to stop. Although he'd never doubted, this confirmed his faith in God. Elia had no access to water during the attunement, which made the experience of it even more profound. Now he could see Quan Yin, in the flesh, about to bless him again with her dew of compassion. What a treat! Nada and all the other beings watched in awe as the Eastern Divine Mother glided nearer to David, upon her lily boat. They bowed their heads slightly, as her gentle presence came upon them and David, who also had bowed his head, for he knew he was in the company of one of Divine Mother's many forms.

'My sweet dew shall cleanse your mind of any fear and raise your DNA to an even higher frequency then what it already is. Remember David, though you are now working with your spiritual body, you are, by spiritual law, still linked with your physical one. It will only change on the day of your passing. Only then shall you truly cease contact with your earthly form.'

David nodded, his highly evolved spiritual understanding helped him to trust Heaven implicitly and, before he knew it, Quan Yin was scooping the dew from her vase. The senses of the young man seared through his entire being the instant he felt Quan Yin sprinkling the dew upon his head, flowing down over his shoulders, in a surreal way. Every drop was ecstasy to David. The sensation, the taste, the smell, truly delicious nectar for the soul. He didn't want the purification process to end and, as with the Reiki attunement, Quan Yin seemed to know this and deliberately prolonged the experience for David's pleasure.

'Ah, enough for now, my beloved. More for later times, as my sweet dew is like the realms of Heaven, it lasts forever.'

'Thank you, Quan Yin. Just feeling that again, but this time seeing it also, is wonderful.'

'It is my sweetest pleasure, dear David. The hearts of all those who are humane and humble, no matter what creed, race or religion, fills my own heart with light. You do not know what good your sweet nature does to your world.'

'I am humbled just being in your service, Quan Yin. I will remember and treasure your words always.'

The Bodhisativa smiled, then slowly rose, standing upright on her lily boat. Pointing to the Sky, to the Golden Clouds that David could see high above.

'The time is now ripe for you to taste even more sweet fruit. Time for you to come to the Temple of Truth, to see Shambhala, child of light.'

'The Temple of Truth? The building which was talked about when I first arrived here, do you mean?'

'Yes, David. You are now ready to journey there. Do you now hear all the Ascended masters calling you?'

David could indeed hear voices calling him, some male, some female, some he wasn't even sure what they were. This was interceded by the chimes of destiny's bell. It was now time for the meeting to begin.

'Archangel Michael is so looking forward to seeing you again, as are all the archangels. Everyone is going to the Temple of Truth. I will guide you there. I, who am also an ascended master, sit as one of the boards of light and take great comfort in knowing that this time has come.' Quan Yin called to the skies of Heaven. 'Father, Mother, send me my transport. Come, Fire-Cho, my beloved dragon.'

As if from nowhere, a dragon, big and powerful, appeared and came down along the Rainbow to the sea of Compassion, beside Quan Yin. He was a magnificent sight. His nostrils breathed clouds of smoke, yet his eyes were kind. The dragon paid little attention to David,

Nada and Pegasus, for he only truly had eyes for his mistress.

'Meet Fire-Cho, my loyal pet dragon.'

David should have been aghast at this moment, but had seen so many miraculous creatures that nothing much surprised him anymore. The wonder of realising that such creatures existed, alive and well in life eternal was going to stay with David forever. Stepping up from her lily boat onto her dragons back seemed so effortless for Quan Yin. She did it with such ease and grace. Standing upright, with nothing to hold but the dragon's ears, Quan Yin was completely unfazed. We shall Ascend to Shambhala across the Rainbow Bridge that you see before us .

'Come, let us go up, up and away.

On that command, Fire-Cho rose up into the air with the gentle treasure that was the Bodhisativa , balanced and just as comfortable as she had been on her lily standing on the snout of Fire-Cho. Nada touched David's arm and, along with Pegasus and all the others, left the shimmering sea of Compassion behind them.

'Quick Pegasus, follow that dragon,' said David excitedly as they sped like bullets over the Rainbow Bridge heading straight up towards the Golden Clouds.

They raced on, trying to keep up with the dragon and Quan Yin. They were going so fast, but Fire-Cho was going even faster. They would have outraced the fastest formula one cars, at this rate.

'How does Quan Yin manage to stay on that thing?' said David.

'Anything's possible when you believe, dear one,' came Nada's response.

'But she's not even holding on. She's not even being rocked about.'

'It is because she trusts. Her heart is in complete synchronicity with Fire-Cho's, so she has no need of fear. Like all the masters, long ago, she realised that fear was but the product of illusion. However, many of you have not learnt this. That is why we want to help you all.' They drew nearer and nearer until at last they were at the top of the Rainbow passing through the Golden Clouds.

It was then that David saw a golden light shining, getting closer. He recognised it. Had it been in a dream? Had he indeed been here before? He suddenly became conscious of many other entities, some looked like star-shaped objects, whilst others were spherical, like the angels orb he had been enfolded in. More of these beautiful beings appeared. Splashes of geometrical brilliance flashed across the skyline, making their way towards this great place.

'What are these shapes, angels?'

'Many, that you recognise as orbs, are the angels, beloved one. The archangels and most of the masters have already arrived. The other star-shape beings are members of the Intergalactic Council, the members led by Commander Ashtar, all part of the Great brotherhood and from all different galaxies; Sirius, Arctaurus, Andromeda, Orion and Paleidian systems. They are all here for this very special occasion.'

David would soon find out what the occasion was.

6

THE CITY OF LIGHT.

The light drew nearer and nearer, shining more brightly. David had barely time to blink, for at that moment, they all passed through the light to a place even more stunning, ethereal and surreal, like entering into a dream. It was Paradise itself. David felt the warmth of love pulsating through him. Wrapped in a blanket of protection, all feelings of fear had left him, all sadness and worry had completely dissipated from him.

'You are now on the highest realm, David, hence you feeling our love for you so strongly, more powerful even than you felt it on the seventh dimension.'

'The highest realm. So which dimension is this?'

'The twelfth, any higher beyond this great light is the source of The One.'

They were flying above a vast golden city. Some buildings resembled Greco-Roman in architecture, just like The Hall of Wisdom, whilst others Indian and

Egyptian in style. Sensational to behold, so magnificent, this entire realm glowing like the rays of the sun.

'Welcome to Shambhala, the Kingdom of the angels, archangels and home of the ascended masters.'

'Wow, this is where you guys live?' exclaimed David.

'Yes, this is the realm where all Paradise is personified.'

David had often heard of Shambhala through his spiritual teaching, but to have a glimpse of it was something beyond comprehension. Yet why did this all seem so familiar? Could it be that he was one such soul who had been blessed and able to walk amongst the shining streets below, or to have lived in one of those divine buildings and had rubbed shoulders with angels or archangels, to have walked hand in hand with a master? Strange though it was, it seemed to be becoming more recognisable. He noticed a crystal-like building. Yes, he had just flown past the Crystal Cathedral, but how did he know that? He recalled he used to play there, play hide and seek through the streets with Nada. He recognised other structures, the Cathedral of Sacred Heights, a beautiful domed building where he had sung with a chorus of divine beings, sung praises of peace to the Creator, with Nada and his other angels. His recently salvaged memories of Shambhala were interrupted by Nada pointing ahead.

'Look David, there is the Temple of Truth.'

It was an extraordinary sight, resembling that ancient building in Greece, the Parthenon. Its exterior walls shone with golden, white light emanating warmth, decorated with roses and bougainvillea, which hung in garlands around it. It stood perched upon a hill, overlooking the beautiful realm of Shambhala as if it were a beacon of hope for all its souls. David could now see that, aside from the orbs and other star-shapes, there were chariots, pulled by multi-coloured winged unicorns. Their drivers appeared to glow, but were too far away for David to see who they were. They seemed to come from the great central sun destined toward the great Temple. It was a spectacular sight. Quan Yin was first to arrive at the entrance on Fire-Cho, greeted by two shining beings. They ushered her and her beloved dragon into the glorious building. The other angels and masters followed, pursued by a glowing Violet crystal pyramid. One by one they entered; orbs, chariots, multi-coloured unicorns and the crystal pyramid. In they went to the Temple of Truth. David and his friends settled at the great steps. He felt excited but was filled with some trepidation. What would the masters do? Would they judge him, look down on him? His angels guided him to go forward, up the great steps. Nada caressed him lovingly and he heard the gentle voice say,

'Don't fear, dear one. We want you to know there is no judgement here, no condemnation. You are loved, and love shall never hurt you.'

The steps were vast, there must have been at least ninety. It was strange being so high up, how big it made him feel. The Temple was huge, its walls and glowing pillars at least one hundred feet in height had been forged by Light. The sweet aroma of the garlands of flowers made David conscious of a thousand memories, each locked within his mind, of a peace long since forgotten to him in mortal life. The entrance was encrusted with many jewels of ruby, emerald, sapphire, fire opals and pearls. A giant diamond, at least ten thousand carats in size, was centred in the middle, just above the entrance, its many facets glistening in the light. Engraved in the language which David recognised as Gods own words were engraved upon a Crystal Tablet next to The Shining Temple.

'What did they mean?'

'It is written in Aramaic the universal language of our Father and Mother. "We see all whosoever enters here. Come in peace and ye shall know only peace. Do good unto others and ye shall have good done unto you. Come like the lamb and ye shall go like the lamb. Love and light to all God's children."'

'Beautiful,' thought David.

He heard a noise behind him, and looking down, he saw a tiny lamb, its face the picture of innocence, staring intently upon young David, who was unable to resist the little creature, scooping it into his arms.

'Gosh, he's so beautiful, is he coming in with us?'

'That he is, he always likes to be near his master,' the angels said, pointing upwards to a little white dove perched upon the roof of the building. It then flew into the Temple, beckoning, and in a voice so familiar,

'Do come in, sweet lamb. You're so welcome.'

At this, the two glowing figures came towards them bowing graciously.

'We are the shining wise ones. Welcome to the Temple of Truth. Come, the Brother/ Sisterhood of Light is expecting you.'

David took a deep breath, as he made the steps into truth. The first thing he noticed was a marvellous statue of marble and gold.

'This is Azna, the feminine embodiment of the Creator,' said Nada. 'Just as God is OM father, masculine, so too is he mother, feminine. This statue represents that side of our Creator.'

It clearly was amazing to look at.

'The Creator deemed it far more comforting for his children to see his divine mother form, because when you come into the earthly realm, you are greeted by the face of your mother who nurtures you,' added his angels. 'We think the Creator knew this and wanted you to feel safe and secure when you returned home.'

'Good idea,' David said, and they proceeded through the Corridor of Light.

Angelic soldiers stood in a long line either side of the hallway, each one holding trumpets of gold which they then started blowing as if to announce the coming of the young man and his lamb. They made their way to a giant door of shimmering glass. There was music coming from within. Fragments of light dotted and danced throughout the hallway, like splinters of tiny mirrors reflecting and deflecting back and forth, tinkling like the sound of tiny bells.

'Come in, come into the light,' cooed the Dove.

The great glass doors opened. David, still holding the tiny lamb, with his angels, Pegasus and the other winged Unicorns, followed the dove through the door. His mouth fell open at the sight before him. The vast chamber in front of him was, like its exterior, a wonder to behold, golden in colour, with pillars of white alabaster and marble, decorated with hanging baskets of flowers. Once again, the architecture was Greco-Roman in style and seemed to resemble a church or cathedral, Interlaced with its framework of arches, pure crystal pulsating with light, whilst Torches of violet fire adorned the walls. A giant starlight at the top of the temple flooded the great hall, the source of all its beauty. A sparkling blue pool with an ornate fountain, in which swam a horde of multi-coloured fish, their species hard to tell, was situated in a corner at the right side of the temple. The sound of powerful yet sweet voices singing, echoed throughout the hall.

'What is that song?' David whispered.

'The song of the Seraph,' came Nada's reply. 'They have sung the timeless sound of the Creator since the dawn of existence, and shall continue to do so for eternity.'

The sound was so sweet - paradise in notes.

Back on earth, Elia could also hear the music, as she tuned deeper into David's soul, a small tear forming in her ocean green eyes.

An awesome sight, the ascended masters, bright, pure, peaceful and powerful filled the hall, their beauty overwhelming David. The little white dove landed gracefully at the feet of the masters, and started to grow, rising upwards until it became the size of a man. Its wings became arms and its torso changed into a white robe with a blue cloth draped around it.

Its neck, head and beak grew into a handsome, kind face of a man, with a beard and a fine head of auburn hair falling around the shoulders. His eyes were the colour of crystal blue, his face smiling at David, as were all the masters. David felt the comfort you felt from a loving parent. The master held out his arms and David ran into them.

'It's you, isn't it? It's you, Jesus! I have missed you.'

'Ah there, dear one,' came the kind, gentle voice. 'Yes, it is I, your friend. I am here, we are all here.'

Tears ran down David's cheeks, unable to contain his emotions any longer.

'Please do not cry. Why have you missed me? We have always been here with you.'

'I know that. I just wish I could have known it more in my heart.'

Jesus tenderly continued to hold the child within his arms, as all the masters kissed and stroked David's head.

'Welcome home, welcome to the Temple of Truth. We are the Brother and Sisterhood of Light, also known as the Council of Love. We preside over all Heaven carrying, as do the angels and archangels, the unconditional love of the Creator, directing light out into all the cosmos, never stopping, never faltering until all hearts are touched by the sweet light of all source.'

The lamb, which had been huddled within David's arms the whole time, had started to feel a little uncomfortable and squashed by all the heavenly bodies, and bleated in protest. It lent its head directly upon Jesus's heart, which glowed with the pulse of sunlight, the tiny creature's eyes looking straight into his masters, as he put his soft lips to the little lamb's forehead and gently kissed it.

'He really loves you,' smiled David, his voice still quaking with emotion.

'All animals here are loved, David, from big to small, the fierce to the meek, and all that fly, swim, walk or slither, all are loved here in Paradise. No one is ever left out, human or animal, insect or plant, all are seen within their own sacredness,' said another master, oriental in creed and dressed in a robe of glowing gold.

This was Lord Gautama, the Buddah. The Buddah, forever awake to the light of all life, enlightened by the great truth he had found so long ago under the bondhi tree, smiled with compassion. He stood beside Quan Yin, her vase of healing water held in her hand, for she who heard the weeping worlds was the feminine counterpart of Buddah. She stood, once again, upon a beautiful giant lily the colour of pink, with golden pearls studded upon the petals, floating above the ground. Her beloved Fire-Cho was sleeping behind her, curled up.

'He rests from all his travelling, carrying me upon his back. He will soon be replenished, and back to his fiery old self,' she said.

The masters and angels, gave a little chuckle, observing the pun. The time is now ready. Archangel Michael, as our host, shall guide us through our meeting. Let us assemble,' said Jesus.

'Come and sit here, David. As our guest, you can have a special place,' said Nada, as she ushered David to his seat, a marble bench which felt so comfortable. 'Please, dear ones, take Pegasus and all our Unicorn friends out for some refreshment. I'd recommend the zianga fruits from our forests of Shambhala.

'A good choice, my dear Lady Nada' smiled Jesus, or Sananda, as they called him at home.

'Lady Nada, of course,' David said now looking at his beautiful angel. 'What an honour, I have Lady Nada, who is also an ascended master, as my guardian angel, as well as the twin flame of Jesus. Lady Nada, why didn't you tell me who you were?'

'I thought I'd keep it as a surprise. You would have found out sooner or later,' she replied with a little wink, as she held her dear Sananda's hand before kissing him upon the lips.

As the winged Unicorns and Fire-Cho were led to their treats by the shining wise ones, each of the masters formed a huge circle within the air. Level after level was filled with hundreds of masters and angels, glowing in brilliance, their bodies lighter and more luminous. The masters had each lived as one of us in our world, and other worlds. There, they had reached a level of oneness, where their true selves knew and saw life for what it truly was. All were happy, they knew they were one. For they had all attained Self Mastery.

Each of the masters had a halo directly above their heads symbolising their Christ, Buddah unity of the Divine. Sananda had a pure golden halo, just like Buddah, for gold was the colour of love and wisdom, a brother/sister energy. Lady Nada's was pink, the colour of love and peace. Quan Yin's was pure white, whilst others were blue and green, the colour of healers, or orange, yellow, violet and purple. The great gathering of masters and angels was amazing, whilst in the centre stood a wondrous woman dressed in a blue and white robe. Her hair was long and she wore a silk headdress. Her beautiful face, radiant with a complexion that took your breath away. She wore a crown of pure gold and her dress glittered, as if a thousand stars were embroidered onto the fabric. Her energy, so pure and gentle, she was Mary, queen of all angels. She held, within her two hands, a sphere. In fact, it looked like a miniature replica of planet earth.

'That's a ball made to look like earth, isn't it?' David said in a puzzled voice.

'No dear one, it is Mother Earth,' said Nada, as she and Sananda exchanged surprised glances.

'This is incredible,' David thought.

He, the masters and the angels stood looking with love at the planet, like giants amongst the stars. The world, that was indeed his physical home, had up until now, always seemed so huge and vast, but here was no bigger than a beach ball, dwarfed by the beings of light.

'We must seem so tiny and so insignificant to you all. ,' said David.

'Tiny, yes. Insignificant, No,' answered Buddah, calmly. 'But, if you knew of our greatness and realised the infinite love that is truly around you, that could indeed help you. Instead of focusing on your problems, you would realise just how small those worries truly are, for The One holds you all, as represented by dear Mother Mary. That is why she is called the mother of the world.'

It was a curious thing and David himself wasn't sure about this, but it seemed that this whole room seemed to be melding into the great starlight at the top, as if the Temple was connected to it. It was almost as though this building of Heaven was coming from the light. The great rays of light seemed to become the pillars and vice-versa. Could it be this great domain was getting its power from the light? Was this powering the crystal pillars, making them glow and pulsate?

'Yes, dear one,' came Nada's response. 'The light is the Temple's power source and is the source of power for us all. It is the light of creation, the realm in which The One resides. Its light has been the spiritual link to everything on earth, and the entire universe, since the dawn of time.'

David continued to gaze at the great assembly of ascended masters, who had each seemed to find their perfect place, floating within a circle so vast. Yet the Temple could, indeed, accommodate them, as it was transcending the very laws of space. The huge hall seemed bigger on the inside than on the outside. There were so many, David couldn't even begin to count them all, although he knew a great many of them. Some he had heard about through his Reiki training, and others via reading spiritual books, and some in his RE lessons at school. He named them all in his mind. Melcheizedeck, a great wise and powerful being who'd never lived or died. Sananda, when he'd lived as Jesus, had been a priest in the Order of Melcheizedeck. There was Sanat Kunara, one of the great guardians of the universe, El-Morya, Lord Kuthumi. Ascended Master Afra a powerful master stood next to his Lion Sampson strong and tall. Lord Mattreya, was the essence of loving kindness, in the form of the laughing Buddah, not Lord Gautama, but another being who'd achieved Buddahood, and was, indeed, a very short chubby and happy little soul. Lanto, the great Chinese master, who'd also found enlightenment to such a degree that his heart centre shone like the sun, making him one of the brightest masters there. His face glowed with contentment and, like all the angels and masters, he emanated peace in its truest form. Serapis Bey, the great master, whose energy was linked to the cosmic computers of Egypt, the Pyramids, which had originated in Atlantis, was also there. There were the avatars of India, Lord Krishna, and his twin flame Sophia, goddess of wisdom. Ganesh, the beautiful elephant god and remover of obstacles was smiling sweetly, his little trunk swaying in an animated way. Lackshimi, lovely goddess of inner riches, Pravarti, the beautiful spirit of motherhood, with glowing babies surrounding her, was also there. Sita, another famed avatar, who was known as a goddess of Hinduism, and Shiva, seen as a god of the universe, and was indeed very powerful. His energy was strong, fiery and intense, which filled David with awe. There were others, such as Vishnu, and the Tibetan goddess, Tara, in all her forms - white Tara, green Tara, Red Tara, who sat in a tiny circle of three on soft lily pads, very much like Quin Yins, as did avatars like Ganesh and Lord Mattreya. Then there were the High Priests and Priestesses of Atlantis, who had been called gods and godesses, famed throughout ancient Greece. Ascended masters Zeus, Hera, Apollo emanating a sun-like aura, Aphrodite and her Venusian counterpart Venus. Poseidon, looking quite like the famed sea king of old complete with trident. He was, in truth, an Atlantean who could use his Mer-like abilities to possess a sparkling green fishtail. Hermes, also known as Thoth, also had Mer-like abilities to transform into anything from the ocean and could fly through the air, with wings that grew from his feet, thus he could either sprout gills when he swam, or wings when he flew. His name was a play on words, meaning Hesmer. Then there was Jupiter, the most ancient of the masters, and one of the most respected. Both he, and his brother Zeus, were surrounded within their own energy by bolts of thunder and lightning, surging through their auras, representing how powerful they were. The beautiful goddess of wisdom, Pallas Athena was also there, clothed in a long Grecian robe the colour of gold, her eyes the colour violet. She wore a belt of sapphire with a rose quartz crystal in the centre. She carried a shield called the aegis, made of pure crystal. Could that have been the very shield that she gave Perseus to protect himself from the snake-like Medusa? Perched proudly upon Athena's shoulder was a sweet little owl, who'd nuzzle her cheek from time to time. Of course, the owl was her special or 'token' bird, as owls were known to possess great wisdom. She'd given her feathered friend, the owl, to her dear friend St Germain when he had incarnated as the wizard, Merlin, in England. He had called it Archimedes, but Athena just called her little friend 'Owl' - all wise and all knowing. She nodded respectfully at David who had loved her ever since he was a child when he had read the stories. The other High Priests from Atlantis consisted of Ra, Osiris, Horus, Matt and Isis. Moses stood nearby, the rays of God shining from his head. He, like Sananda, was dressed in a robe of white, and in his arms he held the Tablet of The Ten Commandments. Next to him stood the great King Solomon, who possessed the wisdom of all the ages. Masters of the laws of alchemy, Master Hillarion, stood close to King Solomon. He was a great healer and was clothed in emerald green. St. Germain, master of the violet flame, also known as the wonder man of Europe, was a powerful alchemist, and stood beside him. The violet flame flickered upon his forehead, whilst his aura, also the colour of violet, burned around him. There was also the goddess Liberty who held a great glowing torch and wore a Crown of Crystals upon her head, wonderous to see who stood beside Portia the goddess of Justice. Along with Artemis the goddess of the Moon. Hippolyta queen of the Amazons, and her twin flame Heracles. The Council of Elementals led by the Green Man the wise being of the Forests, The Fairy Queen and King, and Pan the wise spirit of Nature who held within his hand a Flute which sounded like the music David had heard earlier in the Gardens of Eternity. In addition to many Saints and teachers from Christianity and every Religion, Abraham, St Francis of Assisi and St Clare, St Teresa of Avila, Mohammad, Lao-Tsu, Babaji, White Eagle, Yogananda, Mother Teresa, Mahatma Gandhi and Confucious . The gentle Tibetan Saint Djwal

Khul was also there as was the joyous being The Spirit of Christmas.

Iris, goddess of the rainbow, so beautiful, so pretty to look at,. Her entire form was a rainbow organza, floating gracefully and hovering from one space to another, sending rainbow Reiki out to David and to all her brothers and sisters of light and mischievously showering Shambhala in rainbows.

'I have fun doing this all eternity,' Iris said, as she decorated the Temple with colour.

'She never can help it,' Sananda spoke, lovingly.

'Oh, my dear, how can you help but not love receiving such a blessing from the rainbow goddess? We forget just how important its significance is to our realm, but also to the entire universe,' was Nada's response.

'Ah, indeed you are right, sweet Nada, oh how you are right.'

Iris eventually resumed showering everyone in colours and left a gorgeous rainbow next to the Light of God.

The great crystal Pyramid, that had entered the Temple, had now rested upon the ground and started opening, automatically revealing shining beings, different from the wise ones David had seen earlier. These beings were clad in silver space suits like uniforms, their entire forms fantastic to see. It was like watching the best sci-fi movie, awesome, just totally mind-blowing. Their leader was dressed in a tunic of starlight, its face was friendly and benevolent, its eyes like the other masters, clear and kind, and he was totally bald. This somehow added to its great beauty. The awesome 'spaceman' led his fellow beings towards Sananda, Nada and all the other masters and angels, with each being having a look of great fondness, love and respect. Especially Sananda, whose face was glowing as the extra-terrestrial approached.

'Welcome back, my dear friend,' Sananda said, before embracing him lovingly. 'I'm so glad to see you again brother of stars'.

'As am I, my dear Sananda,' responded the benevolent being, before placing his silver gloved hand upon his brother's forehead. This was done in response to Sananda's hug in alien-like affection.

'David, I'd like you to meet Commander Ashtar, head of the Intergalactic Space Command, child of Orion and one of our closest friends of the light.'

Commander Ashtar turned to the boy and held out his hand, shaking it.

'Welcome, David. I am so pleased to see you here. It's been such a long time, since I last saw you, when you lived upon my planet. You were one of my finest cadets.'

'That's interesting Co...Commander Ashtar.'

'Please, call me just Ashtar.'

'Oh, ok then, Ashtar. My Reiki teacher told me, through a reading once, that my energy was from another planet.

'Yes, your name was Trolon when you lived in that life with me. We had so many adventures together, and saved an entire populace once, do you not remember?'

He had indeed heard of Ashtar and had always felt this strong connection to the stars, often feeling different from those around him, but he didn't mind that because it was cool to be different. Here he was, talking to one of his heroes, as if they'd been friends forever.

'How is it you can speak my language? You all talk to me in colloquial english.'

'Because we can, we can speak any language in the entire universe. You, in your mortal life, could not know or understand the language you once spoke, but I can speak earthling as easily as I can speak my own language, even though it is very different. My entire Starfleet has been watching your foster world of earth, watching and protecting it for aeons.'

'Seriously?'

'Yes, without our help, your world might have destroyed itself long ago, but our Starfleets were able, along with each master and angel that you see, to stabilise the Earth Mother, preparing her for this great event that is about to open before humanity. The mothership has been waiting, whilst hearing the cries of your Mother Earth. Now it is time for the crying to stop.'

He spoke these words in a tone far more firmly than he'd spoken before, it sent ripples of thunder through the young man's heart. The sound of trumpets was heard once again and David, along with Ashtar and his Intergalactic Command, found their places near Nada and Sananda in the great circle of angels and masters.

David knew something was about to happen but he knew not what. Gazing upwards, as all the beings were doing, he noticed fifteen golden thrones floating in the air, just a few feet under the great light and in direct alignment with Mother Mary, who remained standing in the centre of the room, still holding our beloved Mother Earth. Her gentle hands caressed, and sometimes stroked, our lovely world. Suddenly, all the chattering stopped, and there was silence until you could only hear the gentle flutter of an angel's wing. Something was about to happen. Then they appeared, coming from the great light above, directly from source itself - the archangels. Each one was emanating a colour. David recognised them all, as did Elia, who was on earth tuning into David, whilst her eyes filled with tears. Archangel Uriel, Archangel Jophiel, Archangel Chamiel, Archangel Zadkiel, Archangel Haniel, Archangel Ariel, Archangel Raquel, Archangel Azrael, Archangel Christiel, Archangel Raziel, Archangel Raphael, Archangel Gabriel, Archangel Mariel, Archangel Metatron and his brother Sandalphon. They were a splendid sight to behold and were far taller than the other angels present. David had often heard this about Archangels. They each made their way to the thrones, each possessing a colour based upon their function. Raphael's was the colour emerald green, the colour of healers and he was the Archangel of healing. There was one the colour of violet; Archangel Gabriel's copper; Jophiel, a brilliant yellow; Ariel, pink, as she was the Archangel of love. Chamiels, the colour of orange; Christel, gold, and as bright as Sananda and Buddah. Archangel Mariel was ice blue, but Raziel's was an amalgam of all the colours put together. Like Iris, he shimmered with rainbow energy. The Archangels made their way to the thrones, but someone was missing, Archangel Michael. Archangel Raphael acted as spokesperson for them and addressed the great hall. He was looking straight at David and his presence had a very soothing effect on the young man.

'Dearest David, dear Sananda, Lady Nada, masters, fellow angels, and family of the stars. The Creator welcomes you here upon this momentous time in earth's history. It is of vital importance that you have come here David, but now it is my great pleasure to introduce your host, long has he wished to speak to you and now he can finally do so. I give you the prince of light, champion of peace and hero of God, behold Archangel Michael.'

A great cheer was heard throughout the ethereal chamber as the great archangel made his entrance from the light in grandiose fashion, met by the cheering crowds and to the sound of the heavenly trumpets. The feeling of excitement and energy that exploded within David's heart felt stronger than a supernova and yet as peaceful as enlightenment.

The eyes of everyone followed this awesome being, as he floated gracefully to take his place in the centre of the air. Archangel Michael smiled at David before raising his right hand, putting a stop to the rapturous applause that had serenaded his entrance, gently nodding his head as if to say, "Thank you, all is well." Michael stood upon the air heading the Archangels who had come before him, his hands calmly clenched. He was a truly magnificent sight, clothed in a long robe of purest white, which, like his fellow Archangels and Masters appeared to glow. His robe was covered by a long blue cloak which was trimmed with gold, and he also had about his waist a lustrous belt shimmering with sparkling crystal and gold.

His hair was golden blonde, flowing down past his neck, and he held an exquisite balance of masculine handsomeness and feminine beauty, with eyes the colour of amethyst equalling the beauty of Pegasus. His wings, the largest of all the angels, glistened white, like sun shining on snow. The feet of this being were laced in bronze sandals, the sort a Grecian soldier would wear, giving Michael the look of a warrior. He wore two gold bracelets fastened on his wrists, and carried a great shining sword.

'That must be the Sword of Truth,' thought David.

Indeed, it was. This sword never harmed anybody. It was used to prick the conscience of humanity or to cut away the chords of disharmony in people's lives, if only they would ask. The sword floated by the archangel's side and was not held in its place by a sheath, but supported instead by some supernatural power, controlled by Michael or the Creator. What was even more fascinating to behold, was the light which emanated around him of blue and purple, fluctuating in a brightness that sometimes surpassed the brightness of Michael's pure white robe - before becoming clear again. This only accentuated the majesty of the archangel's glory. Viewing him in all his splendour was so powerful, it was the sort of presence that could make a woman swoon and perspire and a man drool with envy and admiration. The Spiritual feeling that was being generated was, in short, beyond perfection itself. David's heart and mind were, by this point, undergoing some sort of transcendental bliss, for he was no longer his familiar self. All his perceptions about who he was, just fell away. All the hurt and sadness was just a drop in the great ocean of life. The judgements and opinions other people had thrown at him were just so small, so tiny compared to the true greatness of who he truly was. He knew somehow that he was going to hear something that he had wanted to know all his life, through all his prayers, deepest wishes, dreams and longing. Turning to David, the great archangel smiled.

'Welcome Rainbow Child welcome.'

Michael, who glowed like star fire, but twice as beautiful, spoke in a voice so kind that David felt his heart chakra completely open. He felt a power he had rarely felt on earth, this was his true self now beginning to shine. Archangel Michael flew down, and stood face to face with David. It was typically humble of Michael to do this so that David would not be overwhelmed or fearful of the great Archangel. He seemed to possess a manner that merely wanted to be a friend to David and somehow an equal instead of being a great master. The other Archangels stayed upon their thrones, each one emanating a great love, only surpassed by God.

'David, my dear friend. I welcome you here on behalf of all of us in the higher realms, and the Creator Father Mother itself.' Archangel Michael's voice was gentle but possessed an authority that sent empowerment into the soul. 'I, as prince of all the archangels, have been asked to represent the board of light to tell you why we have called you here. We know that you have called us in your prayers, you and many other earth angels who wish for peace upon your world. You, Blue Robin, have been chosen to come here representing the light as our chosen emissary for all your brothers and sisters on earth. For an old chapter is about to close, and a new one is about to open, a new glorious dawn waits upon the horizon of dear Mother Earth. That is why it is so imperative for you to listen to this.' David nodded his head cautiously, detecting the gentle but firm energy. The great hall of light was serenaded by excited chattering amongst the many masters and angels. Michael raised his hand indicating the need for silence, to which every soul simultaneously quietened upon the instant. 'Dear one, what you are about to hear will probably be one of the most important things you will ever hear. Your world now stands at a crucial turning point, for the prophecies have now reached fruition. The prophecies that have been told and taught from the mouths of our brothers and sisters, the masters. Since the beginning of time, The One has always wanted your world to be a place of love and light and for a time that's just what it was. Please observe, dear one.' Archangel Michael pointed with his great sword, all eyes following, to the tiny planet earth which Mother Mary still tenderly held within her hands. An image appeared within the sphere of a world long forgotten. It was of a beautiful city, part of a great continent, shining with light. In fact, its radiance was nearly as great as that of Shambhala. 'Do you see it David?'

'Yes, I see. It's Atlantis.'

'Indeed, it all began here during the era of Eden,' said Michael. 'Atlantis was a civilisation that surpassed the world you live in today by millions of years, both in technology and in mind, body and soul. It was a golden age upon your world, where men and women lived in greater understanding, greater compassion and greater capacity for goodness.'

As he was speaking, images continued to appear upon the globe of the souls who had lived there.

'People walked around in robes and tunics, whilst emanating peace, even though they are but shades of the past, their energy still exists and is preserved safely here in Shambhala,' Mother Mary added. 'Their goodness is still strong, hence why we can all feel it. For many, many years, your world lived like this in complete peace, love and pure happiness. No-one and nothing was judged. No-one was hurt, because people knew that if they hurt others, they would ultimately be hurting themselves. Everyone existed to be good and to live in the here and now.' It truly was a Golden age on Earth.

David gazed lovingly at the Atlanteans. They truly were happy; not wanting; not hating, but doing unto others as they would wish to be treated themselves. Just living in the present. It all seemed to come back to David as he remembered the spirituality, the kindness surpassing the doctrine of religions today. He remembered also the crystal-like technology that was used to power buildings and used to perform profound forms of healing. While some people, like the great priests and priestesses, could actually fly unaided as they lived at the highest level of endurance. They flew, levitated and teleported to wherever they wanted to go. Oh, so many memories had been unlocked by his subconscious and were now flowing freely within him.

'However,' came Archangel Michaels voice, breaking David's revue and etched, it seemed, with some sadness. 'Things did not remain that way. The balance of good and evil had always been there and due to the misuse of free will, which was The One's great gift for you all, life in Atlantis started to change for the worse. One individual the King of Atlantis started to use his gifts for the dark, becoming greedy for power. He eventually turned against his fellow Atlanteans, and against God succumbing to cruelty, breeding hatred.' The very mention of that word sent a cold shiver across the heavenly assemblage, and this was something David could never have thought possible in this beautiful realm. Archangel Michael then took a deep breath, as if to compose himself before continuing. 'This Atlantean succumbed to the temptations of lower self. He even convinced others to do the biddings of the ego, turning against his love, the fair queen of Atlantis, who, like yourself the high priests and priestesses, tried desperately in vain to maintain the purity. But by this point it was too late. A new hostile energy had come upon Atlantis, known as duality. This duality gave birth to the offspring known as Illusion.' David looked at the images of earth's long past, and gazed in sadness at the horrors of what he saw, as this soul's pursuit for control and power had taken him to the depths of lower self, forgetting the most important thing of all, which was to love others and to treat everybody as you would want to be treated. There were sacrifices, supposedly undertaken in the name of God. People began to be cruel to others, whilst there was dishonouring of women. Disagreements resulting in wars and divisive factions, bringing the end of this once peaceful civilisation. Within the course of a few years Atlantis had moved from light to dark, and a bleak mist engulfed Atlantis, enshrouding it in despair. David could see this image on the earth. Each master, angel and archangel shed a tear in sad recollection. 'You see, David, because Atlantis was chosen by the universe to represent Shambhala to be a beacon of love for your world, when it started its downfall it made Mother Earth sick through all the horrors that were occurring, and so in the end she could no longer withstand it. Under the surface of the sea, there was a great earthquake, resulting in a huge tsunami which drowned Atlantis, engulfing it beneath the waves. In one sad moment Atlantis was gone, at least on a physical level. It was a tragic day for all of us , as indeed it was for our brother, Lord Poseidon.' Poseidon gently acknowledged this by giving a mournful nod. 'But there were those who held strong and who did survive the cataclysm. There were those who, as you've recently discovered, could breathe under water by morphing into mermaids and mermen, whilst others could transform themselves into dolphins. The fair queen and yourself were of these souls. You and she, like

Sananda, Lady Nada, Athena, Poseidon, Hermes, Aphrodite, Zeus and Hera and others, were the pure ones. On the day before the destruction the Creator called you to come together for one final time, using the last ounce of Pure energy that remained under the guidance of the One you created a marvellous Crystal ;The Genesis Crystal; unique within its beauty as it held within The Seeds of New Earth. For the One had long foreseen the fate of Atlantis and also the time when Earth would be ready to return to Peace, that time has come. You entrusted The Genesis Crystal to Akash the most ancient and wisest of the wise to keep it safe in the realms of Light until the day when the guardianship would be passed onto you. And so it was on that next fateful day you, the Queen and those you see before you were allowed to survive. For you had preserved the flame of truth, the essence of the universal heart, and you then went to many different lands throughout the mother's globe - Greece, Egypt, Australia, New Zealand, Peru, Mesopotamia, Ireland and Britain, where you took your divine knowledge, passing it onto those who could see and whose hearts were open.' A beautiful image then appeared above the earth, which was shimmering and glowing with a pink coloured energy. All the masters, angels and archangels held their arms outwards as if to embrace it. 'This, David, is the universal heart, the essence of all truth.' David wasn't sure but he could not hear the beating of it. 'You won't hear it, dear one. The universal heart is sleeping, carrying within it the love of all Heaven, but it wants to awaken so it can shower the world in all its truth.

'What truth is that?' David quietly asked.

'Connection, that we are all connected, and all facets of the Light. So then the Soul can become whole again. It will only awaken when mankind has let go.'

'Let go? What from? Hate, fear, pain, loss?'

'Yes, from the Illusion that has blindfolded your world for so long. You see, dear one, when the corrupt did what they did in Atlantis, they created a cycle of Wounds. This vicious cycle feeds off the negativity of people, which keeps much of humanity in a perpetual state of duality, thereby feeding the Illusion that rules over the Wounds. The cycle has continued to remain intact for twenty-six thousand years, thus allowing Illusion to spread like a cancer, infecting governments, corporations and religions with its stain of corruption.' Causing man to hate another and to see another as different from them.

David looked at all the masters and angels who all stood together hands joined together.

'I've noticed you all hold hands. You all seem like a great family, all of you are best friends.' You hold my hands also.

'That's because, David, in the truth of the Creator, there is no war and no difference between us. In truth, we are best friends. All the religions in the world are one, just like the flowers of the fields, all may be of different colours, shapes and sizes, but all are still flowers, and so it is for all humanity, all are part of the same great light.' The great archangel then spoke in a melancholy manner.

'The Illusion has distorted the truth in your religious leaders' minds, making them think one belief is right over all others. This is feeding one of the Wounds of ignorance. It is creating duality, thereby killing and starting terrible wars in the name of The One.' Each of the great masters, upon hearing this, bowed their heads in considerable sadness. 'It is during this rolling chapter that we seek to rectify this terrible misguidance that the Illusion has done to you. All God's children are connected. You are all brothers and sisters, as shall soon be realised.'

It was a truth that struck home within David. There wouldn't be any war if these world leaders and religions only knew this truth, how different it all could be.

'If only humanity listened to what we tried to say. They would realise that this is how the song should be sung,' echoed the soothing voice of Sananda. 'All we wish for is to work for the good of our Creator. We are all on the same journey and it is no less true for all humanity.'

David bowed his head, as if slightly ashamed of what his people had done by inflicting and inciting pain and war upon others, and in the name of God. If only they knew and could see what he could see. His thoughts were interrupted by the tender look of Archangel Michael and a gentle touch of Nada's wing, indicating that all was not lost.

'You are all so powerful, so bright and pure. Why can't you not stop Illusion, thus preventing these wars?' asked David. Over the years many of us have returned to the earth to try to awaken our sleeping brothers and sisters answered Sananda, I myself have had many lives both on Earth and beyond before I reached my enlightened state in the life where all knew me as Jesus. David smiled as he remembered having spent time with Sananda in quite a few of those lifetimes, often as one of his disciples. Every Master that you see around you in this Temple are in their ultimate enlightened bodies, that goes for you as well David. But continued Sananda, no matter how much we all tried to awaken the light within it was not without a cost, by then Illusion had contaminated so many minds and poisoned so many hearts that we knew that there would be opposition as the world was now rife with duality thus there were those who could not be reached and tried their upmost to slander or harm us, just as the Illusion intended. So what we had to do all of us was to teach by example, but it was never easy.

'The Illusion placed a veil over your physical world, making it harder for us to communicate with you. In fact, there was a time when contact between us was extremely rare, although we tried desperately to reach you all. We can only come through if asked. If you do not give us permission, we cannot break the veil. Oh, but how we long to. There are some things that not even we can transcend. To come in uninvited would be breaking the law of the universe and the gift of free will. But,' said Michael, 'in the last two or three decades, as is measured by the earth's clock, more souls have elected to come onto the earth plane to help bring the light back onto your world. Souls like you and Elia, who are Incarnated angels, and who lived in golden Atlantis in many other lifetimes and you whose Soul is in truth from Shambhala. You knew that the vile times of Illusion were numbered and that the timeline of old would soon come to pass. It will soon be in the new chapter, and you shall indeed be forces for the change that is coming.' David remembered the day some loving representatives of light came upon him in the beautiful garden that he dwelled within, asking how he felt about leaving to reincarnate to help bring the love back to earth. 'You could have stayed safely within our realm, dear one, but your adventurous side soon got the better of you.'

'Yes, from what I remember, initially I was quite reluctant to go back, I so loved it here in Paradise, yet I agreed to carry out this exciting task along with many of my fellow light workers.' I knew there would be challenges along the way, I knew I would know heartbreak and from a young age. I knew that the vessel I would choose would have a learning difference, and would find some practical things hard. But my higher self trusted and knew that through it all everything would be alright in the end. My Life has been a journey not a walk in the park, but I have learnt to trust myself more over the years, thanks to all of you.

'Already, your love has been doing so much good, amongst many, spoke Archangel Raphael others have started invoking us in ways that once could never be imagined. Slowly but surely, Illusion is weakening, yet is stubbornly holding on like a petulant child, maintaining the exhausted Wounds within their cycle. You have the power to break this cycle, your innocence of spirit is key to this. Illusion has kept humanity in chains for centuries but now the chains are ready to be broken.'

'But is there a way to destroy this vile entity?' asked David.

'Oh, you can't destroy it, you have to heal it. By healing the Wounds, you break the cycle, cutting the Illusion's power over humanity.

'Hello David,' said a voice.

David looked around him but all the angels, archangels and ascended masters were looking towards the earth. It was a serene, yet powerful voice.

'It's Mother Earth, she is talking to me.'

Then, in complete awe, David watched as a beautiful face appeared within the sphere of blue and green.

'At last, my darling child, it is time for you to hear me, for I have heard your words of love and encouragement carried upon my winds, carried by the elementals, as you walked upon my soil, sat upon my grass, and swam in the waters of my heart.'

David watched as the face of earth grew larger and larger, coming out of the sphere, until David could see the Earth Mother's entire form.

'David, please meet Lady Gaia, beloved earth herself.'

The wondrous Earth Mother held her arms out wide bathing in the great light that lit the Temple, and soaking up the love energy that flowed from the masters' hands to Gaia, for she had been lovingly created from the day existence took its first breath. She had loved her Father Mother as they'd lovingly created Gaia in the image of Heaven.

'I have known so many times, seen so many things and felt so many emotions - joy, happiness, peace, war, sadness, hope and despair, nurtured so much yet cleansed in equal measure.'

Lady Gaia's form was blue and green in colour, whilst the long hair that trailed behind her was the colour of harvest gold. She was completely supported by Mother Mary, who, with complete ease, held the Earth Mother as easily as she'd held her in spherical form, within her hands. Gaia possessed the wings of a giant butterfly, complete with markings, for she, also born of the light, was from a realm of angels whom the Creator had chosen to enfold all of the beloved planets called the Thrones. David gazed in fascination at Gaia. Flowers of all types were draped around her head, but perhaps most surreally, her body seemed to contain or show every living creature that lived upon her. In an almost three-dimensional way, all creatures of earth would move in and around our Mother's entire body. From the butterflies that danced upon her, forming a necklace around her neck, to the lions, tigers, pandas, giraffes, elephants, monkeys, dogs and cats, who walked upon the green of her land. The whales, dolphins, turtles, seals and fish swam, jumped and splashed within her azure blue. They, like us, were the children of this kind and devoted Mother, who for countless ages had provided food and water for all of us who lived within her heart.

'Lady Gaia, I don't know what to say. It's mind blowing,'

'And believe me, so are you, David,' the mother of earth replied, picking the young man up in her arms. 'You, sweet soul, are so blessed, your light filled me with joy the day you entered my womb to access me. I need you David, you and all your kind, to come together, to heal me and save all my children from the plague of Illusion that, like a foul fog, still permeates me, still likes to hurt me.'

'There are many who are willing to heal you Lady Gaia. The soul pod that David comes from, lived in the times of Atlantis, and are now ready to bring that golden energy of the universal heart back to you, so that you shall know and feel the pure and true power of love once again,' stated dear Archangel Michael. 'The Atlantean queen herself has also come into one final incarnation to help usher in the new dawn that lies just upon the horizon.'

'You mean the one who had bravely led the expedition out of Atlantis? Am I to see her again?' asked David.

'Yes, she will be revealed to you very soon. Her presence upon this earth is aiding all our earth angels, and with her help you shall soon see the love of the Divine said Sananda. 'So, dear one, do not fear and do not anger. Just for today, be happy and rejoice for Azna,Om because God in feminine and Masculine form is returning to Gaia.'

'Azna Om.' David felt a tingling sensation around his back, as if a ball of fire was travelling up his spine.

'Yes. God is coming as that is what is needed for the new age of Aquarius. Love, empathy, compassion is about to sweep through your world, all the qualities the heart possesses are about to open.'

'Michael, you said that Atlantis' downfall was caused by the King and then others followed, and they inadvertently then caused the destruction of Atlantis. Are they still upon our world.' David asked, but he knew what the answer would be.

'Yes. Sadly the King and all those who were corrupted also escaped during the deluge, the Illusion offered them Sanctuary within the dark realm in exchange for their Souls, here they reside within the shadows gloating, hidden from the rest of your world controlling it with Illusion as their master and so it has remained for many thousands of years. They are known as the Magicians and they worship the Illusion. The Magicians are the tricksters of your world, who seek to suppress and oppress the children of light. They hoodwink the mass populace of Gaia by feeding you their homespun lies of freedom. Freedom does not truly exist upon the earth, it never has. You're just being deceived to think that it does. Freedom and truth shall only become reality when the Illusion and its Wounds are healed, and then you shall

TRULY know what truth is. Until now, it is nothing but the product of a sick fantasy, created by Illusion and orchestrated by the magicians. Mother/Father and Gaia can tolerate this no more, we cannot emphasise this enough.'

'Look here, David,' said Gaia, 'Behold.'

The boy looked, as the Earth Mother pulled back her robes of blue and green to reveal a tree, its roots connected to her planet earth. David nearly looked away, almost disgusted by the sight, for, instead of being lush and green as he'd expected, it was brown, with some parts even black. Its branches were decaying with no sign of health at all, no leaf grew upon it, and it looked as if it had been attacked by the harshest winter. David could smell the rotting odour. This the only awful sight since his arrival in this beautiful place. Michael touched the boy reassuringly on the shoulder, half whispering,

'See, the price of corruption, a tragic symbol of the Illusion's handiwork.'

'That absolutely reeks!' came David's response.

'You smell the rotten odour of corruption, dear one, the stench that has plagued the earth for twenty-six thousand years. Each root is linked to Lady Gaia and humanity's emotions.'

'It was originally so beautiful back in the days of light, in the era of Atlantis, but after the downfall when the Illusion and the Wounds gained in power, they influenced the cruelty of Man, so triggering violence and wars. The magicians seized control. As a result, the roots of the once great Tree of Life have become rotten and are rapidly decaying. No rains can bring nourishment to the old roots anymore,' said Gaia as a turquoise tear fell from her eye.

'You mean to tell me that this Tree of Life was once great but is now dying, all due to the hatred of Man? Is there nothing you can do?' asked David, in a sickened voice.

The old tree is ready to go, along with its rotten seeds. They shall be replaced by the seeds of new earth, where the roots of integrity, truth, divine justice, mercy, wisdom, love and intuition shall flourish in accord with the frequency of the fifth dimension, the kingdom of Love.'

The faces of Sananda, Mary, Nada, Buddah, Quan Yin, Moses, Soloman, Mother Teresa, Zeus, Athena, Ghandi, Ganesh, Krishna, Sophia and that of every master started to, once again, brighten.

'Everything is starting to shift, raising in vibration,' Michael continued. 'That is why so many things scandals within politics, crimes committed by your current monetary systems, and all places of power, are being unearthed. Expect more of this to come as the corrupt can't escape the wave of light that is coming onto Gaia. Nothing is accidental. All corporations that operate from greed and avarice; monetary systems who inflict power, over others, are starting to collapse because of the rotten roots; rotten governments who create war feeding off the vulnerable and who put money before saving a life. All shall be swept away as the light of Azna/Om shines the truth upon all who take, and are crooked and cruel. It is time for the children to sing and for the people to take back their power. Azna/Om shall separate the liars from the truthful, and those who are still operating with vested interests, like the Magicians, from tyranny and control shall be exposed. The truth shall set them free.' At that very moment, the Temple of Truth was filled with rapturous applause for Archangel Michael's stirring speech. The great Archangel, so modest was he that, as if slightly embarrassed by the applause, quickly turned once again to David. 'So, you see David, the new era shall be based upon love, which is why you are here. You have the power of love within you and you are one of the physical hands who can change things.'

'So, what needs to happen?' pondered David.

'You, dear child, are the Blue Robin.' That name again. 'It is your sacred name, it means he who comes in darkest winter shall prepare for the new spring, for you are not just an Incarnated angel, you are a Rainbow child, whose place is to plant the new seeds for all humanity, thereby saving your Earth Mother. It is time for the magicians to leave Illusion and come out of the darkness, their world needs to crumble. Your heart shall light up the dark so that love, can return.'

David's face started to become wrinkled with worry.

'That means facing these magicians, doesn't it? Even the Illusion?'

'Yes, it does, dear one, sooner or later, to heal. You will have to.'

'But who am I to face the magicians. In this life I'm just a boy. I grew up with mild cerebral palsy and autism?'

'You mean "AWEtism", smiled the archangel. 'David, don't you realise it's that which makes you different; is what makes you special. Your attention has always been dialled into higher dimensions, hence why we have been able to come so close to you, to show you this event. You're not going to be alone, dear one, all of us are going to be with you. Your love can heal the Wounds inflicting humanity.' David, at this point, knew it was unwise to argue with an Archangel, especially Michael, but certain doubts were starting to rush through his mind. 'You and Elia are the bridge, dear one.'

'Elia, will she be with me?'

'Yes, she will.'

'Thank goodness,' David thought to himself.'

'That will allow Heaven to come unto earth. This is all part of the Divine plan, for we are preparing the rays of the great central sun to penetrate the earth. Your heart and Elia's shall merge with this light creating the bridge between Heaven and earth. All creation will then make the giant leap into the fifth dimension, thus bringing a new era of light, and Paradise will once again shine upon dear Gaia. Divine Mother/Father shall raise you all onto this level of zealous compassion and once earth is freed from suppression, Illusion can be completely dissolved for ever. The new tree shall be born from the seeds and then Harmony's Doorway shall open for you all.'

'Is that like some kind of spiritual gateway?' asked David.

'It is the new chapter for earth. It's the doorway, metaphorically speaking, a transitional shift allowing you to truly pass into the fifth dimension. But now I feel it's time to prepare, and as the saying goes, "no time like the present". You are going to be wonderful, dear one, but beware of the magicians,' said Gaia.

David watched as the beautiful Earth Mother shrunk in size before returning to spherical form, as Mother Mary lovingly kissed her before smiling with great serenity to David and her brothers and sisters. David suddenly felt very tired, he is weary even in his enlightened state said Sananda with a kind smile upon his face. Take him to his

Sanctuary Nada he needs refreshment and rest, before the next phase of his mission is to begin. Nada took David in her arms and floated out of the Temple to a beautiful abode to prepare David for his journey.

'Fear not, David, you shall not be alone. 'said Lady Nada.

Archangel Michael, Sananda, Mother Mary, Buddah, Quan Yin, Krishna, Ganesh, Lackshimi and all the beings of light, watched as Nada flew out of the Temple with David and his other angels in tow. Sananda looked thoughtfully at Michael approaching, as both their great auras met.

'Do you think David will be alright, my friend? He does have doubt within himself.'

'I know he will be, my Sananda. You know how hard it was for you when you inhabited your physical vessel as Jesus of Nazareth.'

'Indeed, I do,' came the ascended master's reply.

'David assigned himself to this mission, choosing to live in a mortal vessel, he knew that he'd have to confront fear and doubt.'

'Yet all clouds, no matter how black or grey, can always be pierced by sunlight, allowing the blue skies to come through,' came the wise words of the Buddah.

Archangel Michael proudly smiled at his golden brother and to all his fellow archangels and masters. David has the wings he just needs to fly.

'I know this is a great step to be taking, my friends, but with love and perseverance David will free his fear and fulfil the first steps of his life purpose, shining like the angel that he truly is; the fact that he feels afraid comes from living on a realm filled with Illusion. When all souls on earth realise that this is all that fear truly is, they shall all shine, and David's mission is to show this to his brothers and sisters, whilst guiding them out of winter and into eternal spring. We must all prepare for this great happening for the Creator has set the stars in alignment within the galaxy, ready for this historic moment.'

'I will situate my fleet around Gaia, and the light of the mothership shall filter its rays upon the planet, allowing you steady access upon her, puncturing the veil that little bit more.'

'Thank you, Ashtar, dear friend. I feel we will need it. The Illusion will soon know what is happening and shall make things as hard as it can, for it will not give up its dark easily,' said Michael.

'Nor shall we give up our light, or compassion,' spoke Quan Yin defiantly.

'Indeed, sister, the Illusion and its magicians will do anything to hold onto the Wounds, but the tricks of the dark and its falsehood is no match for my spirit of truth and wisdom,' answered Athena staunchly. 'If it's a battle that Illusion wants, it shall be of no match for me as I am invincible in combat of any kind. I prefer to use wisdom though as it is this that will be the Illusion's downfall,' she said whilst she caressed her beloved owl.

'Aye, sweet Athena, as shall my light of liberty, as I shine my great torch upon such troubled entities, melting the dark of such lost souls,' returned the Goddess of Liberty.

'Indeed, sisters, for there is no question that divine justice coupled with such liberty, wisdom and compassion shall be done,' replied the Goddess Portia.

'So, let it be, my family, for the winds of God favour our course and this time there shall be no excuse not to let love, The One and absolute truth in,' spoke Sananda, who had picked up the little lamb that had sat next to him the entire time. Cradling it within his arms.

'Great brother Michael, you must let the Queen of Atlantis come in to help him,' said the emerald Archangel Raphael.

'Yes, this I shall now do, Brother.' Michael looked downward, his eyes gazing upon the little ball of Mother Earth, smiling at the beautiful face of Gaia, who looked back at the Archangel with such hope. 'Elia, we know you have listened to us, dear one, so you also know that we need you. Please answer me.'

'Yes,' came the excited voice of Elia, who now could be seen clearly within the planet.

'Elia, so good to see you again.'

'As it is to see you, Sir,' came the reply.

Elia was by now sitting cross legged in her favourite lotus position, her beauty almost as radiant as an angel.

'Elia, you, like David, have been called at this great moment in Gaia's history due to your divine heritage and connection to Atlantis.'

'Yes indeed, my lord, you wish for me to come to Shambhala to be with David. Shall I come immediately then?'

'Yes, immediately,' came the Archangel's reply.

They spoke to each other through telepathy before Elia faded from the globe and returned to the features of Gaia.

Elia's eyes opened wide with excitement, yet still sitting perfectly calm, she turned her head slowly towards Suzanne, who was sitting upon a chair next to her. Elia's hand remained upon David's heart, whose vessel still lay upon the bed. Suzanne was reluctant to disturb Elia's meditation, for she seemed so calm and tranquil, surrounded by her aura of peace. Why could Suzanne not be like Elia, so relaxed and internally contented?

'Are you alright? You seemed so at peace that I didn't want to disturb you.'

'Yes, I am. I was speaking to Archangel Michael. I wish you could have seen it; the love, the light, the hope. It's all true, so beautiful, it's.....'

'Yes, but what did archangel Michael say to you?'

Elia couldn't help but feel a tinge of annoyance at this mortal woman's impatience, but Suzanne had not seen the glory that she had so, sensitive of this, she replied,

'I've got to go, I have to go to Shambhala, Suzanne. David needs me.'

A slight jealousy roused in Suzanne.

'He needs you?'

'Yes. It has something to do with our past life connection in Atlantis. We have both been chosen to represent the light workers of earth and David, the Blue Robin, is one of the Rainbow children. His heart and soul are far more angel than human, just as I have always said. His heart has always been lovely. He is not of this world, he is from Shambhala. I have to go now Suzanne.'

'Wait, Elia, please. What will I do? How long will you be gone?'

'How long, is not important. I could be gone days, weeks, months, yet it may only seem to you like the blinking of an eye.'

'Thanks, but that isn't much help, Elia,' Suzanne said in a deflated voice.

'You must not leave this house. I am being told you must carry on as normal and to be as silent as the night that has just passed, to keep your thoughts positive or the Illusion and its magicians will find out about this. They have been spying on you already. Last night, they saw the writing upon your wall.'

'The writing on the wall? Only our neighbour Rob was with us. Is he somehow involved, do you think, with these magicians?'

Elia paused for a brief moment, listening to what her angels were telling her.

'No, Rob's genuinely a good man, but he, like all his colleagues, has no comprehension of the magicians. His superiors, like all our figures of authority, are being dominated by them. No, there were two of them in a vehicle, resembling a van, they spied upon you and are reporting what they saw, perhaps at this very moment. Just keep your doors locked and do not open to anyone, for the magicians know so many tricks.'

Suzanne's recollection of the previous night was so hazy now, such a lot had happened within that space of time that it seemed like an eternity, but thinking hard, she could recall seeing a van inside of her peripheral vision, although she'd thought nothing of it at the time. There were many vehicles that parked in their road. She turned to say this to Elia, but the healer was once again within the deep recesses of meditation. Suzanne then saw two angels of glowing gold, lifting the spirit of Elia from her vessel. Her mouth fell open,as she watched as they smiled and then vanished with Elia's soul body, waving goodbye. Suzanne suddenly felt warm and safe, and, falling back upon her chair, she saw a plethora of giant golden butterflies, dancing around her. These beautiful creatures fluttered back and forth, floating across the room, as their bodies quivered with an energy that she felt to be their life force. She watched in fascination before hearing a voice,

'It's okay. David will be fine. There is no need to worry.' The beings generated a great sense of comfort, for they were Suzanne's guardian angels. They were just letting her know that all was well. 'Your third eye has opened, Suzanne, hence why you can see us in a shape-like form. We won't be able to maintain our visual form much longer but the more you talk to us and ask us to come into your life, the stronger we will be in helping you and your loved ones.'

'I want you to stay with me so I can see you forever,' the child within her said.

'The more you let go of fear, worry and control, the stronger your third eye shall be, the more we will be able to assist you. We are always with you, Suzanne, always believe us.'

Suzanne felt a golden ray hit her forehead as her third eye pulsated with life. She then became conscious of a loud banging at the front door.

'Who was that? Could it be one of those Magicians trying to get in?'

A familiar voice soon put her fear to bed.

'Suzanne, can you hear me, are you there, and David?'

It was Jonathan, her ex-husband, David's father. David had been due to see him around about now. She looked to her angels.

'Should I not answer? Perhaps he will go.'

But knowing Jonathan, he would persist until he got an answer.

'Answer it. Jonathan has a right to know what's happened, for these events concern him as much as you. He is the Blue Robin's father.'

Reluctant to leave her blissful environment, for she could have happily sat with her angels on that chair forever, Suzanne left the bedroom, went down the stairs, and hurriedly opened the door to pull her former husband into the house. Jonathan, surprised, wondered what on earth was going on.

'Are you okay? What's the matter with you?' he asked, observing Suzanne's nervous behaviour as she quickly locked the door behind them.

'Umm, hi Jonathan, how are you?'

'I'm fine. What's the matter? I've been knocking for over five minutes.'

'I'm sorry, a lot's been going on this morning.'

'Well, as long as you're alright. Where's Davie? I was wondering if he wanted to go swimming today.'

Jonathan had a tired, almost worn out look upon his face, and a soul which harboured the stresses of life, which he rarely could shut out from his mind, much to David's chagrin. Jonathan was a chameleon, had been throughout his life, a good man in many ways, but also one who had been hurt and knew how to hurt. Yet there was still love there and flashes of wittiness that David had always enjoyed. Jonathan had loved both of them and still did love David, but the hurt within him caused him to sometimes carry out actions which had affected them both. David saw past this and always looked to the light that was within his dad. Thanks to his spiritual understanding, he loved and accepted his father for who he was.

'Jonathan, there's something I need to tell you, you'd better be sitting down.'

'Suzanne, please tell me what's going on. Ever since you opened the door, you've been acting strange. What's the problem? You can tell me.'

'Well, you see it's very complex. I don't even know if you'll believe what's happened, but it does involve David.'

'David? Well what's he done; knowing him it can't be anything too bad or serious.'

'Well no, it isn't anything he's done wrong, but something has happened to him. You'd best come upstairs and I'll explain everything to you.'

Suzanne led the way with David's dad following with some hesitation. What Suzanne was saying was making him feel uneasy. On entering the bedroom, he stopped in surprise on seeing the bodies of Elia and David laying in there. Unfortunately, the angels could no longer be seen, and Suzanne thought this a shame as they may have been able to help explain things to David's father. Or maybe they might have just finished the old man off for good.

'Sit down, Jonathan.'

'No, David, David no, what's wrong with him?' he shouted, his voice quaking. He didn't need more stress.

'No please listen, Jonathan, listen. Sit down and let me tell you everything.'

7

BORN TO SHINE

In the meantime, David had been led by his angels into another beautiful place, smaller than the Temple of Truth, and more like a house with its exterior made of white marble, and pillars adorning the entrance. Inside, the room was exquisite, well suited for any healer to live in. There were vases of flowers, picked fresh from the gardens, with a heavenly scent, upon the windowsills, below the windows of stained glass. There was the soothing scent of nag champa, as in Elia's abode. Gentle music, like Gregorian chants, played in the background. He could not tell where the music came from, possibly the Cathedral, which he had seen earlier. He sat upon a very comfortable bed shaped like a huge star. Its pillows and satin sheets had been made up immaculately to accommodate the young guest. He felt like royalty, feeling humbled by this experience and he just being a mortal. Archangel Michael had insisted, for all God's children were special; human, animal, extra-terrestrial and were treated as such.

It hadn't taken David long to realise this beautiful abode was the place he had lived in whilst in Shambhala. The memories had literally flowed back into his conscious mind, as he remembered how he had lived, working in his garden, which his angels tended with him, as he learned about the sacred energies which flowed around him; all the holistic arts that he'd participated in, running so freely, with his beloved angels beside him. This was something he'd loved to do on earth, especially on cool summer evenings. He held a crystal goblet filled with a delicious drink, which was considered a delicacy on Shambhala. He had forgotten just how good it had tasted. It was pink in colour, with bubbles popping on the surface. Its taste filled his palette with satisfaction. It was made from the juices of roses that grew in the gardens tended by Mother Mary and which were often said to be visited by Azna herself. Nada sat beside David. Her glowing form fanned out like a swan upon the star like bed, whilst his other angels and guides hovered like satellites around his energy. They were now in their most pure, powerful form, emanating in golden light, and basking in the great love. They orbited the young man like the planets, around a Sun, as if sensing that he was in need of comfort and reassurance and indeed, something was wrong. Although he felt the love around him and bathed within the ecstasy of this truth, David's face now showed signs of doubt and a little worry. Nada gazed upon this expression creeping across his face, and enfolded her wings around him.

'What's the matter, David? We see your worry and we know what it is. We just want you to tell us. Do not be afraid, for as you know there is no judgement in love.'

'It's just,' David started, feeling unsure how to put this, 'it's just that I don't know if I can fulfil what you want me to. I'm not sure. Can't another earth angel or light worker perform this task?'

'David, you elected to take on this assignment to help bring Heaven to earth, and believe me, we are not mistaken in our minds. For it is you who can break the cycle of Wounds and end the Illusion's reign upon your world. We know you better than you even know yourself. For it is just the Illusion speaking through you now, filling your mind with lower feelings of doubt, trying to make you feel that you are not good enough. Well, believe me, you are!'

Nada's voice, though so loving and kind, now showed an undertone of steel like a strong mother bear encouraging its cub.

'We know that you still have fear within you, David, but your soul knew it would have to work to overcome this negativity. We also know what it is you are frightened of, and it is not that you are afraid of not being good enough, but rather you are afraid that you ARE good enough. Hear us, dear one, it is your light, not your dark, that frightens you. You've asked yourself all your life "who am I to be great, successful, beautiful and wonderful?" but let us ask you "who are you, not to be?" You were born to shine like all Gods children. It is your birthright. Playing small won't help the world, dear David, for there is nothing enlightening in shrinking, just so others around you won't feel insecure. In time, you will help those around you not to feel that way. You must confront and heal your fear, that is why you are here.' David continued to listen, as his body leaned back against Nada's wing, soothed by these words. His other angels continued to caress him as he soaked up their energies. 'Upon that day when humanity passes into the new earth, they will need souls like you and Elia to guide them, for there are many who do not see or feel us and who lack understanding. They may even be afraid of the great change that is gradually happening now. You will need to teach by example.'

'Perhaps that is one of the things that I'm also fearful of. What if people don't believe me?'

'Your fellow earthlings can fear the unknown and we know that some still live within the illusion of hurting others, but rest assured that each soul's consciousness is rising slowly but surely, to the level of the fifth dimension, the frequency of pure love. Those who are still killing, suppressing and trying to dominate with fear, have made themselves slaves to the Illusion and are working for the magicians darkness will find their corruption crumbling around them. There will be no stone left unturned in preparation for this great moment, as God, in the form of Azna/Om, shall elevate all and everything to the next level.'

'Then I must simply not fear,' said David in a peacefully chilled voice.

'Never, beloved one, never,' replied Nada, before kissing him upon his crown chakra. 'You'll teach them so much, send out so much.' Gesturing towards his heart, 'You will help others to trust again. Azna will free humanity from their troubled sleep Om shall help them to find their true strength, and thus the Illusion's nightmare shall come to pass, awakening all to the truth that is love.'

'Is Azna/Om close to the earth now?'

'Closer than anyone knows. Gods already there.'

David drew in a deep breath at these words. 'The One, just needs you to help it break through the veil.'

'These magicians sound terrible, Nada. Why do this? Why instigate and cause so much suffering?'

David trembled, half remembering them from the last days of Atlantis.

'Because they succumbed to the dark, forgetting that all were one, causing more duality, lifetime after lifetime. They have fed the Illusion, instigating their games of control and inadvertently causing more wars, such as the two world wars of your twentieth century. Helping men to hate and to kill others just because they thought they were different . They are just lost, David, their leader so very lost and very hurt, but there are many who are ready to see us and know Azna/Oms's love. Although the Illusion will try to cling on to control and keep trying to spread the lie of hate, the light shall triumph over it.' Nada then paused, 'And When all its darkness is swept away like dust, it will be a new age, a golden age where the universal heart shall awaken, shining within all for coming eternity. From the ashes of Illusion, a new world will be born.'

'Nada,' came an excited voice. It was the voice of Sananda. 'The time has come for David. Elia is here.'

'Excellent. Come, it is time. We will be meeting with Archangel Michael and the others at the top of the rainbow bridge.'

David could have stayed basking in the light of his angels forever, but before he knew it, he was once again flying over his home, the great rainbow bridge just ahead, just beyond the Temple of Truth. It was such a beautiful vision. Every part of the bridge is linked to a multitude of worlds, universes, creeds and races. The rainbow reminds us that no matter how multifaceted every being in the universe is, we are all one and the same, nothing is just black and white. We are all connected, part of the Oneness.

'Such beautiful philosophy,' thought David, as he watched archangel Michael, and his fellow archangels, standing with Sananda, the Buddah, Quan Yin, Mother Mary, Krishna, Ganesh, and every other master standing together on the vast rainbow.

'Welcome, once again to the Rainbow bridge David, Sananda said warmly. We the Masters call it the bridge of Worlds, David. It is this that we ride upon to access dear Mother Earth.' And every other world, or dimension in Creation.

A familiar voice came from the crowd,

'Hello, young man.' It was Elia.

'Elia, how wonderful to see you here,' greeted David to his friend and mentor. The two healers embraced, and David noted that she was dressed in a splendid gown of golden cloth. Like David, Elia's chakras were visible and glowed as brightly as his. 'What are you doing here?' asked David, bewildered.

'I was called to come here, so I have bio-located. My earth body is alive and well, just as yours is, but in deep meditation.'

'What, in your house?'

'No, in your bedroom to be exact. I know your mum's okay. When I left that realm, your mum's guardian angels made themselves known to her and they seemed to be able to put her at ease. I think, from what my angels told me, your Dad is with her.'

What a relief it was for David to know that she was okay, and that Dad also knew what had happened.

'I'm here to assist you with your journey, David. Nada, and dear sweet angels, it is an honour to be in such company,' said Elia humbly. She'd already said such things to Sananda, Michael and the others.

'As it is for us too, Elia,' came Nada's response.

'You are now ready to begin your journey, David,' said Michael. He held out his hand and presented a gown of deep purple and a cloak of royal blue. 'These are for you, dear one.'

He gestured to David's angels, who took the handsome cloth from the archangel and proceeded to dress the young man in the purple gown. The tunic felt comfortable, the material unlike anything David had ever worn and it had been made by Michael himself. Emblazoned upon his chest was the emblem of the Robin, in flight representing his sacred name symbolising all that was hope. The Insignia was embroided in gold cotton.

'The colour of the tunic represents the spiritual frequencies and the emblem, the gentleness of your soul, the truth of your higher self.' Michael then placed the royal blue cape around David himself. It felt comforting and the young man felt protected. 'This, David, is my cloak of protection, a replica of my very own. It will shield you from psychic attack, and all forms of negative energy. Use it well, but always remember to call my name and to use these words to invoke me, "Archangel

Michael above me, Archangel Michael below me, Archangel Michael in front of me, Archangel Michael behind me." The cloak is ingrained with my own energy. It will protect you and your loved ones from the Illusion, shielding you from its darkness.' David felt like a superhero with his cloak and tunic, while Elia looked like a goddess incarnate in her golden gown, her energy so evident, with her long hair flowing down her back. Upon her head, a tiara of gold and silver, an emblem of half Sun and half Moon at its centre. 'The symbol you both have is the balance of masculine and feminine energy, the sun being the male and the moon, the female. By possessing this, you are both honouring the balance within you,' stated Michael. David was also given a headband with the same symbol upon it, representing the right feminine, intuitive brain, the other was the left, masculine, logical side.

'Dear Michael, please guide us to where we must go.' said Elia.

The archangel pointed to one of the rainbow paths.

'That colour leads to your destination.'

Elia and David observed this path. It led downwards, and they both gasped as they saw it lead into the shimmering sea of compassion. Was this to be an underwater adventure?

'You want us to swim to this destination?' David asked.

'This will take you to Atlantis. Atlantis but it was destroyed wasn't it? said David. But here at home everything exists in its most pure state, nothing is ever spoilt, and all the places that are extinct upon Mother Earth, are preserved in complete perfection replied Michael. You shall return to Atlantis completely protected beneath the sea of Compassion. See, you are expected.' The two souls gazed downwards at the sparkling ocean as two dolphins came to the surface, ready to escort them to the fabled civilisation. 'Your dolphin guides will take you to Atlantis.'

With that, each of the masters began to fly back to the Temple of Truth, waving goodbye to them both.

'Michael, wait,' called Elia. 'What should we do once we are there? Who should we go to?'

'You must seek out Akash, keeper of the seeds and historian of all karmic records. He is the book of life itself.' Akash so we are to see him again, Elias voice could not help but sound excited. 'He is very wise and powerful one of the wisest beings in all Creation second only to the Creator. Oh of course David you already know this how silly you were there with me. He holds the story of all your lives within his soul said Archangel Michael. That is whom you must seek. God speed you both on your mission, endless blessings unto you.'

Michael then flew off, leaving David and Elia alone with their angels upon the rainbow bridge, whilst below the two dolphins seemed to be beckoning to them both with a mixture of clicks and noises as was the norm in dolphin 'language'.

'I think they are growing impatient. Come on, David, we must trust that we are safe,' said Elia, raring to go, always the adventurer.

'Nada, will you all come with us?' asked David hopefully.

'We are always with you or have you learnt nothing from us so far,' said the angelic being. 'We are personally assigned to you for your entire life. You are never alone.'

Before David could answer, Elia had taken him by the hand and pulled him down the rainbow slide, and they descended in slow motion, landing in the turquoise water with a splash. For a moment, they both bobbed upon the sparkling surface like tiny corks floating, whilst they treaded the water. The two dolphins approached them and guided them down into the vast blue, down to Atlantis.

8

AKASH

Holding tightly onto the dorsal fins of their dolphin friends, David and Elia couldn't have felt more at ease, as they swam beneath the azure surface into a world where its depths held the greatest mysteries of all. The dolphins, who loved to be playful, began corkscrewing, somersaulting and rolling, performing the most beautiful ballet, but mindful all the time, and gentle so that their charges would not fall off and be lost in the vast blue sea. It didn't matter, as Elia and David felt just as at home here swimming in the sea of Compassion as the dolphins did. They now both sported fish tails instead of legs.

Many Atlanteans had this ability whilst they swam in the oceans. It was like being in a beautiful dream as their souls floated within a transcendental tranquillity within this ocean of consciousness; totally happy and soaring in the joy. To his wonder, David found that he could breathe under the water, completely free and unaided. His mouth seemed to be sucking in the water whilst breathing air through it. It was as if their whole physiology seemed to have been altered to adapt to marine life, yet it all seemed to come so naturally to him, as if he'd always known, but just forgotten how. He felt like 'Aquaman', whom he'd loved since childhood, a great aquatic superhero who was also the king of Atlantis. He could converse with all sea life. Elia swam with her dolphin just a little ahead of him, her long golden gown billowing around her completely unspoilt by the water, her tail also golden, and her long mane of hair swirling in the gentle currents. David's own tunic of purple, and long blue cloak, seemed also unspoilt in the surreal ocean.

'Elia, we can breathe under water,' David said, calling to his Reiki master via telepathy.

'Yes,' came the healer's response. 'Remember, David, we who once walked among Atlantis could swim under water without protection. We were just as at home under the sea as we were on terra firma. Our subconscious minds have always known how to do this. It's our stubborn conscious minds that tell us we cannot.'

The dolphins seemed to reciprocate what Elia had just said to David, answering now in a series of whistling sounds which made them all the more endearing. Their very presence brought warmth to the heart and huge smiles to the mouths of David and Elia.

'Dear dolphins, I can't tell you how much this means to me,' said David joyously. 'I've always wanted to swim with your kind, it's been a lifelong dream. Apart from seeing you from a boat off the coast of Australia some years back, this is the first time I've swum with you, perhaps it will be my only time. Thank you so much. I'm never going to forget this, you truly are the angels of the sea.'

He found himself becoming emotional. Elia smiled thoughtfully at the young man, remembering his sheer appreciation for all things good which had been one of the things that Elia had found so endearing about him the first time they'd met on the Reiki course. The dolphins turned their rubbery smooth heads to gently nuzzle David, nudging him to show their appreciation.

'May all your kind find peace upon our earth,' said Elia tenderly before kissing them both upon their heads.

They had come to a beautiful coral garden, inhabited by a range of creatures, who, like their land dwelling relatives, seemed to glow, their tropical colours magnified even more radiantly. There were all species of tropical fish, turtles, manta rays, octopus, starfish, polyps, sea anemones, seahorses, stingrays, dugong, manatee, more dolphins, seals and sealions, crabs, lobster and Peaceful Whale sharks, all living peacefully here with not a sign of hostility, just like in the gardens above. A vast clearing lay ahead, coming out of the endless blue like a rare, long forgotten jewel, there stood the great city of Atlantis. Cleansed by Water, preserved by Compassion.

'Elia, I can see Atlantis.'

An excited eagerness filled David's mind as he looked upon the glorious civilisation, so wondrous to the eye, and just as he had always remembered it. But it was now protected by a huge dome of crystal glass that encased the entire city. Elia had tears in her eyes as she hugged David, remembering Atlantis', former glory. As they approached with their dolphin guides, they were greeted by a gathering of mermaids, whom David had seen earlier with Nada and Pegasus, and who'd tried so hard to beckon him beneath the waves. The mermaids swam around the two lightworkers, handing bouquets of sea flowers to them both, to welcome them back to this wondrous place that they had once called home. David seemed to recognise each one clearly. He now remembered how they'd lived amongst the mermaids who were Atlanteans, some of whom had elected not to return to earth, but chose instead to live within Atlantis, preserved in its original form by the crystal dome, venturing out to play in the sea of Compassion and tending the coral garden.

Elia spoke for both of them as she received the lovely gifts.

'Thank you Anana, Tulista, many thanks Astara, Adria, Ocra, thank you, so lovely to see you all again.'

'The pleasure is all ours, your Majesty, their voices like liquid velvet.

'Your Majesty? Then it is you Elia, you are the queen of Atlantis,' uttered David.

Elia gave a very modest look, whilst the mermaids bid the dolphins forward, carrying Elia and David into an area of the dome, shaped like a shell. This began to open revealing an underground water tunnel.

'Please pass through this passage, sweet queen and dear Blue Robin. Akash has been expecting you.'

They both entered the passage, along with their dolphin and mermaid friends, whilst David looked back at the vast coral garden that sparkled like treasure, as the panel closed behind them. They swam along this winding tunnel. Its walls either side seemed to be made of amethyst, and then their friends veered upwards vertically, swimming towards the surface as if beckoned by some force. As their heads and bodies broke the surface, they found themselves within Atlantis. Looking above, they could see the crystal dome coating the entire civilisation, like a vast ceiling with the deep blue sea of Compassion beyond. It reminded David of the Eden Project in Cornwall. Cornwall! All that seemed such a world away. There was a Shangri-la atmosphere, not unlike Shambhala and very nearly as beautiful, with waterfalls flowing like crystal liquid into the turquoise waterway from where they had just emerged, whilst the landscape bore beautiful trees and flowers. Looking about, David gazed in awe at the amazing buildings made entirely of crystal, adorned with vast columns and pillars. Some of the structures were round, whilst others were of Greco-Roman design, as Atlantis had based its architecture on Shambhala and after its physical destruction, the survivors had styled all architecture on Atlantis.

'Oh, there's no place like home,' grinned Elia. 'How does it feel to be home, at least to our former home?'

'Like being in Paradise, just like I was in Shambhala,' his voice was quiet, as he took in the delights of this watery world.

They proceeded to swim along the surface of the waterway, pursued by the mermaids and frequently greeted by their fellow Atlanteans who wore robes and tunics of white with golden rope belts. Many had long dark hair, similar to Elia. In contrast, David's fair hair stood out like an oddity. Their feet were large and some of them were finned. Just like Elia and David, all these citizens could morph into Merpeople whenever their bodies ventured into the ocean. They were delighted to see their queen and Blue Robin, but for David, just sensing their great love was enough. The water was warm but temperate and they could feel the tingling of bio-electrical currents generated by the dolphins highly evolved sonar energy, rippling through their bodies into the marrow of their bones - as the dolphins can see into all creature's bodies. They were at this point sending great healing, mastered from the star energy of their origin galaxy, Sirius, into their very souls.

'Elia, I can feel the dolphin energy flowing through me, it's just like ultrasound, but ten times as powerful.'

Elia was looking straight ahead of her, riding regally upon her dolphin, like a proud monarch upon her horse, with her mermaid tail draped down its back. So impeccable, she looked absolutely magnificent. The entire sight was breathtaking. If only David had his camera with him, although he knew no photograph could ever capture the beauty he had seen.

'David, look. That is where we are going,' Elia said, pointing straight ahead of her to the Akashic.

They had come to a huge, obelisc-shaped building made from amethyst, with an exterior engraving resembling that of a honeycomb. Twice the size of Ashtar's starship, it must have been at least eighty feet high. At the top of the stunning structure was a pulsating gem which seemed to act as the power source. Elia noticed the wonder in David's face and his fascination with the sparkling jewel.

'It is powered by what you see. The crystal of Poseidon. It serves not only as a beacon of power for the Akashic, but as a power source for the entire city.'

As they drew closer, they could hear the rhythmic pulse of the magnificent crystal, like the purring of a huge cat in peaceful slumber.

'Do you not remember how all Atlantis was powered by this light, David, and how we all once bathed within its glow of infinite warmth, reminding us all of the great sunlight that also shone within? Oh, how those days held no dark cloud of fear to penetrate us, nor any magician to rob or corrupt us!'

Elia shone, her face bore an expression of ecstasy, bathing in the memory of a world lost in the annals of history, so far away, yet so near that we may well be able to attain it again. David felt both the sadness and the joy, as his soul's memory continued to open. The mystical waterway ran through into the Akashic via an entrance carved within the wall which was shaped like a triangle. The dolphins and mermaids excitedly approached this awesome structure whilst ushering David and Elia ever nearer, briefly passing under an ornate crystal bridge. The blinking light of the Akashic reflected upon the water like a thousand pieces of a mirror. The purring sounds of its crystal generator vibrated within David's being, sending him into an almost hypnotic state, as they passed into the domain. The walls of the interior sparkled, just like the exterior, of beautiful amethyst. It seemed they had approached a corridor or passageway.

'We have arrived. Come, we must walk from here.'

'Walk? Elia, we are still mer-like!'

'Not to worry, just know that we can walk, picture us with legs, and it will be so.'

Indeed, as Elia's dolphin drew close to the side, allowing her to pull herself onto the floor, she reverted back to having legs. How had it happened? There are some things in Heaven and earth we may not understand. Miracles should never be questioned, just accepted. David's dolphin did the same for him and he also found himself back with two legs, his fishtail gone.

'Start getting used to our mer abilities. Once you start accepting them, and when you start saying "I can" instead of "I can't", anything is possible.' Elia placed her hand over the dolphin's forehead. 'Thank you, dear brother. Thank you for carrying us here.' before tenderly kissing it.

David did the same to his dolphin, cupping his hands around its head.

'I love you. Thank you so much, that was such an awesome journey.'

Elia nodded.

'They will wait for us.'

'Oh, thank you so much.'

At that moment they were interrupted by a beautiful sound, a voice, or should I say song, a whale song.

'Elia, do you hear that?' said David in a quiet, excited voice.

'Yes, indeed.' They waved goodbye to their dolphin and mermaid guides who looked on with equal excitement and anticipation. Again, the beautiful song was heard. 'It comes from this way, we must follow the sound, David.'

They began to walk down the amethyst corridor, staying together all the while allowing themselves to be guided by the sound of the whale song, it seemed to be calling to them, it was not to be ignored. As they walked, the song got louder, and David and Elia's hearts were swelling with anticipation. They were like children, entranced by this enchanting voice, their inner child must have been dancing at this point. They could see what looked like a giant sea anemone straight ahead, its tasselled body opened, revealing an entrance into a vast chamber, from where the song was coming.

'Is this where we're supposed to go, Elia?'

'Yes, I do believe it's the centre of the Akashic. I think we will find who we're looking for here.' They held hands, and Elia held her breath, as they passed through the huge anemone. Its long tentacle-like senses seemed to float effortlessly in the air, just as if it was underwater. The chamber they found themselves in, was vast. It was an amazing place, looking like the inside of a giant honeycomb. The walls were also made of amethyst, but interlaced with a golden structure, shaped all around it. The pulsating sound was just as powerful and even louder than on the outside and David could see the great crystal right at the top bringing life and light to the entire civilisation. 'David, look,' gasped Elia, in quiet astonishment.

Centred in this vast chamber was a shell throne, upon which sat a huge whale, a great humpback to be exact. David, in shock, stared at the sight before him, his mouth open. The whale song suddenly stopped. Without effort, the huge whale lifted itself from its shell-like throne, floating upon the very air it breathed, just like in the ocean, and it started to swim towards them both.

'Welcome, dear queen, and welcome, dear David.' The voice was deep and quite old, yet wise and kind. 'I am Akash, I have been expecting you.' The mighty mammal swam very close to them, its big, wise eyes looked straight into theirs, seeing so deeply into their hearts, as if reading their souls. It was such a powerful moment. Elia, though in awe, seemed to be less surprised than David. She had spent a lifetime preparing for this moment. If she had any trepidation at all she certainly didn't show it, for she possessed this innate calm which had helped her through the tough times in her life. David heard a "Wow" utter from his lips, as the great whale floated in suspension within the air. He'd only seen whales in documentaries, so to be this close was beyond imagination. You have no idea how many suns I have seen rise and fall whilst waiting for this great moment said the wonderous creature.'

'I am sorry it has been so long Akash, so many of us on Mother Earth have only just started to wake up to the great love and yet many more remain asleep, aware only in their subconscious of this,' Elia said in a regretful way.

'There are far more than you give credit for, my dear Elia. So much of your humanity have started to raise their energy to such an extent, that the veil that blocks us from reaching you has slowly started to weaken. It may be but a little time until all have fully awakened to us, my brothers and sisters, the angels and masters.' The kind eyes then focused on David. 'And, as you have been told, that is why you are here, dear Blue Robin. Your mission of peace is to bring and spread our light far into the earthly realms. You may both have questions to ask at this moment so please do so.'

'How old are you?' David said.

'Mother Father created me the day the first ever star was born. I have seen many born since then and the rise of every sun, planet and moon. My age exceeds them all, for I am of the kind who knows every secret of the universe. I am as old as Father Time himself. I came into being on the morning of all Creation. Only Melcheizedeck of the created, equals my age.'

Remarkable, thought David.

'Tell us, why or how can you speak in colloquial english?'

'Why should I not?'

'Well with all due respect Sir, you are a whale.' David said, starting to feel embarrassed.

Elia smiled, sensing the humour of the situation.

'My kind, who came from Sirius, just like the dolphins, know your mortal language as the angels do, due to our time spent with you here in Atlantis, where we co-existed together. We learnt and mastered the art of communication between the species, so to this day we all understand what you say but your kind have just forgotten how to speak back to us. We are all so close. You humans still know this on a certain level, that is why you gasp, you smile, you cheer, you weep, you laugh whenever you see us from a boat; from your shores and within your entertainment devices.'

Elia and David felt such love for this mighty mammal in all its benevolence. They held their hands out to the gentle creature, rubbing their hands along its wet rubbery skin. Akash, in return, nuzzled them both with his head despite his ability to talk human, he still continued to make the profound noises of a whale, gentle whistles and clicks, coupled with sonar-like sounds which send electrical currents into the body. David and Elia felt tingles surging through their beings. It was once said that to swim with a whale was akin to swimming with God, and they both truly felt this while gazing into the great eyes of this ancient being. He had seen and felt so much, during his lifetime.

'Akash, we know that you oversee the paths of all souls,' spoke Elia. 'Your own heart is the greatest library in all the cosmos. You are also the keeper of the seeds. Please do you have them.'

The great creature veered his head upwards towards the top of this great obelisc, swimming vertically, still upheld in thin air, right to the top where, upon raising his flippers, he retrieved a glowing spherical orb, which was situated just under the pulsating crystal of Poseidon. As Akash did so, he fell backwards, just like a whale breaching in the sea before diving down to meet his awestruck friends.

'Will you just look at that, David,' said Elia.

'Cripes, it's absolutely amazing,' said the stunned David, enthralled by the scene.

Akash gracefully approached them carrying the fascinating object within his flippers. It seemed to be alive. It glowed and shone with the colour of Golden Light. The source appeared to pulsate within, like a beating heart, steadily pumping life to its physical casing. The beautiful orb floated from the flippers of Akash, simply resting in the air. Observing it more closely, David and Elia could see that its crystalline membrane was patterned just like the Akashic, thus resembling a honeycomb.

'Take it, beloved ones. You are its new custodians. It wishes for you to safeguard it in time for the preparation.' It gives me the finest pleasure to be returning this to you thus to all humanity, this that you so lovingly created from Light itself such aeons ago.

The wondrous sphere floated nearer until it moved back and forth between the two healers, as if not knowing which one to go to.

'Uh, Elia, since you are the queen you'd better take it.'

Elia humbly smiled but then looked thoughtfully at the boy.

'Thank you, but why don't you take it, David?'

'Me?'

'Yes you, for you are the Blue Robin. Please, I insist.' The boy held out his hands, albeit with trepidation. 'It's okay David, don't be nervous. Be your usual gentle self. That's it, there you go.'

The beautiful orb of light rested comfortably upon the young man's palm. It was the size of a Grapefruit though light in weight considering, and looked as healthy as any seasonal fruit, good enough to eat.

'Very pretty thing, isn't it, David?' Elia whispered into his ear.

'Yes, it's extraordinary. It's like the rarest jewel and far more precious than any diamond.'

David held the magnificent orb a little higher in his hands, as if admiring its full glory. He could feel the pulsating heartbeat within, coursing through his hands into his very blood, sending waves of energy through his veins like tiny torches. He also felt much more centred and grounded than he'd ever felt his entire life. He felt rooted and as strong as a tree.

'What you now hold within your hands, is the answer to all mankind's ills, physical proof for positive change upon your world,' said Akash. 'It is the Genesis Crystal that with purity you created and within are the seeds of new earth preserved and protected now for centuries, safe from the clutches of Illusion and its minions.' David and Elia both gazed into the bright light within. They could see the seeds , zig-zagging back and forth like dancing entities, cocooned, nestled within their sacred container. 'Each of these seeds are of the fifth dimensional frequency, the level that golden Atlantis was on. They are the blueprints needed to take your planet, Mother Earth, back into this vibration transcending darkness and into the light. Just as you've been told, the new world will rise from the ashes, full of love and hope, opening the doorway for the new dawn to come through. Within the crystal are the memory banks, Atlantean codes, which can be accessed and which will enable mankind to rebuild golden Atlantis, once more, upon your world. This will be downloaded into humanity, as soon as the crystal is opened and the seeds of new earth are planted. This great knowledge will be revealed to every soul who comes from loving intent. You hold the beginning of an entire world upon your hands and, this time, the Illusion will not be able to break through. You will make it a better world than the first, with the help of the angels. For thousands of years, golden Atlantis thrived until its end, but now peace will prevail forever.'

'It is imperative then, Akash, that the magicians must not get their hands on it,' said Elia.

'Yes, indeed, dear queen, for if they do they will suppress and keep it hidden from humanity, unless the cycle of Wounds is dissolved.'

'If they do, what then?' queried David.

'History shall repeat itself, continuing in sickness, poverty and war. Now is the time to end all this. Time is ripe for the new era to be ushered in.'

'And then?'

'Well, let's just say the biggest miracle of all shall happen.'

'What will that be, Akash?' they spoke in tandem.

'You will know, when the time is right. It is now time for you to return, beloved ones, back to the surface, ready to return to earth.' David didn't want to leave his true home, yet within his heart he knew this was imperative. 'You are frightened of the dark, David. Don't let it overpower you. Remember, it will try to embrace the light. But it will never eclipse it, never ever.'

'You protected this crystal,' said Elia. 'You guarded the seeds, ready for this moment. I feel your love Akash, it's almost God-like.'

'Thank you, my queen. Yes, the day you entrusted the Crystal to me I ascended back to the Light along with all the creatures whom you have met, where I have lived beneath the Sea of Compassion. Where Atlantis lives in its original form safe and protected unhampered by the forces of darkness. Ever since then I have safeguarded it under these holy waters, awaiting the time when you and David would incarnate again in your present forms, ready to help bring Heaven back to earth. You must go now. They await you above, as does every soul on Gaia.'

As these words were spoken, Elia and David began to float back into the passageway through which they had entered.

'Akash, will we see you again?' they called.

'Yes, and remember, the Genesis Crystal contains my consciousness, so you can contact me through it.Remember David make it a better world than the first. Love and light my beloved ones, love and light.'

Elia and David found themselves back where they had started, on the backs of their dolphins, who had waited patiently for them. They dived back under the inlet, into the sea of Compassion, before making their way to the surface, and on to the rainbow bridge. When they reached the rainbow after bidding their dolphin and mermaid friends goodbye, they could see Nada, Christa, Angelica, Archangel Michael and all their other angels waiting for them upon the rainbow bridge ready to fly them back up to Shambhala. They'd certainly had a "whale of a time!"

David still held the Genesis Crystal in his palm. Both he and Elia had become Merlike upon leaving Atlantis, and human once they had reached the rainbow again.

'Nada, you missed so much. We saw Akash. He's a huge whale. He gave us this, which can help bring about new earth!' I remember the day I made this from the power of God.

'Yes, we were with you and Elia the whole time.'

'But how come? I didn't see you.'

'You didn't need to. Your mind was strongly focused upon Atlantis, but we were with you. Even when you cannot see us, we are all still there, remember that.'

David, not knowing what to say, just broke into a huge smile, hugging his angels while Elia proudly hugged him.

'It is time for you to go back to the world of earth, to send love into the world, David,' beamed Elia.

David gently nodded, looking down upon the Genesis Crystal within his hand. He remembered Akash's words, "make it a better world than the first, David." He would not forget this, it would stay within his heart forever.

David held the Genesis Crystal close to his breast, nurturing it as if it were a child, feeling the great love reciprocating back into his heart chakra.

'I promise, Akash, dear friend, that this time it's going to be different, I swear it, I know it shall be.'

Elia stood beside him, holding his arm.

'Are you alright my friend?'

'Yes, Elia, I'm fine,' David answered, lost in thought, for he was so entranced by the divine crystal. 'I can't quite believe what I'm holding!' again after so long.

'Yes, it's quite extraordinary, isn't it? The days of duality are nearly at an end. Soon, humanity will discover the most important truth of all. All hearts are one heart, David, and one heart is all hearts. That is what we must know.'

As David turned in response to his wise Reiki master's words, the surroundings of Shambhala and their heavenly friends started to fade, although they heard the voice of Michael and Sananda echo around them,

'We shall be with you. Do not be afraid, trust us.'

These were the words of all the loving masters.

Spiralling back through the passage between worlds, their angels beside them, they found themselves back in David's bedroom. The sensation, likened to awakening from a lovely dream, was tinged with slight disappointment at being back in the everyday reality. They were still in their spiritual bodies, their true selfs, their earthly vessels were exactly where they had left them, on and beside the bed. His mum and dad next to them, looked like they had been in deep discussion. David knew that worried look all too well.

'I'm not sure I can accept all that you are telling me Suzanne.' David's dad said.

'David had this dream, then we saw the words "we need you" painted on our wall. I don't know how it got there, so please don't ask me. Now I can't wake David up. Elia showed up to explain what's happening. I know it sounds crazy Jonathan, but somehow within my heart, I can't help but believe it to be true.'

'Now she's away with the fairies,' came the cold remark from David's dad.

Oh, how typical of his old man, thought David. Well-intentioned, but just a little tactless at times.

'Then there were the angels who surrounded me. Oh Jonathan, it was like a love I'd never felt before. It was like I was suddenly loved just for being me. Apart from the love I feel from Davie, I've never felt anything like that my entire life.'

David's father was looking down carefully, taking on board what his former wife had said.

'It must have been lovely,' came his soft reply.

'It was.'

'I wish I could know love like that.' came Jonathan's reply.

'Perhaps you can. Maybe if we stopped what we were so caught up in every day and just gave the angels a chance to reach us, we would all be happier and content within ourselves. Maybe we can all try to let them in.'

David and Elia listened intently to the pair. In Elia's face, there was fascination due to all her years as a therapist and in David's, there was hope.

'Yes, that's right. Go on dad, give it a try,' he thought to himself. 'They can help us all so much.'

'Elia, can mum and dad see us?'

'No, dear one. They cannot see us clairvoyantly yet, but they may well be able to hear us. Let me try something.'

'Then they can't see the crystal or any of our angels?'

'No, but they will. One day, everyone will.'

'Okay, let's think about this,' said Jonathan, turning business-like all of a sudden and trying to sound in control. 'What about this writing on the wall. "Blue Robin" What does Elia think that all means?'

The wise woman seized her chance.

'It means the merging of Heaven and earth, darling.'

'What? Who said that?

'It's Elia,' cried Suzanne excitedly. 'She's come back. Elia can you hear us?'

'Yes, Suzanne, of course I can hear you, sweetheart. Just as I thought, David, although they may not be able to see us, they can hear us on a clairaudient level, one of the different forms of clairvoyance.'

David's face shone with joy.

'Elia, is David there with you?' asked Suzanne, anxiously.

'Yes, I'm here mum. Please don't worry, nor you dad, I am with you.'

'Davie, oh Davie darling, I'm so glad you're alright.'

'Alright,' came his dad's agitated voice. 'We can't even see him. Why can't we see you, you little whatsit?'

'Because, David said in fondness of his dad's ways, which always made him laugh, Elia and I are in spirit form, or our higher selves if you like, and you are not developed clairvoyantly enough to see us. I have been on a fantastic journey with Elia, I've seen Heaven, things you're not going to believe, but we hope you will. We've got something that was given to us, something that's so important that will help transform our world and all mankind.'

'Tell us David, tell us. I've been trying to explain to your dad,'

As Suzanne spoke these words, she felt David's arms embrace them both in a loving hug, tears flowing down their cheeks as David held them tight. Elia smiled, she was now holding the Genesis Crystal within the palm of her hand. Every angel that was present, soaked in the warm energy of love, bathing in the sweetness of this moment.

Outside, the weather was clear, a mixture of cloud and sunshine. Birds sang in the trees and the hope of Spring was just around the corner. The birds were not the only things in the sky that day, something far more sinister was lurking. A metallic object, closely resembling a drone, hovered nearby. It was dark in colour and at its centre was a lens-like eye similar to that of a dalek. It was watching Jonathan and Suzanne, its powerful lens/eye flashing as if it were photographing, with its hi-tech computer system recording every last detail. Suddenly the flashing stopped and the menacing eye-like camera went back into its metal structure, safely tucked away, its work complete. A voice, calm but emotionless as if dead to all feeling, came through its high-tech system.

'Orwell, return to Erratus Manor.'

Obeying the command of the sinister voice, Orwell, without haste, sped off through the air unnoticed by anyone. It travelled up to a hundred miles an hour going back to those who had sent it to do their dirty work. It was returning to Erratus Manor, the abode of all that was corrupt, the house of the magicians.

9

HOUSE OF THE MAGICIANS

Erratus Manor stood alone and completely hidden from any soul from the outside world. Orwell had now left all suburbia far behind, as the digital spy sped down a disused road before reaching a long winding lane. Hardly noticed by day and carefully avoided by night. Its speed now slowed down considerably, as instructed by its computer navigation systems. It eerily floated down the long and winding lane. Orwell completed its last phase of the journey, coming upon a mist-like vapour, which engulfed the cunning drone, swallowing it up within its pea soup thickness. It seemed to act like a barrier blocking what lay beyond from any connections with the outside world. This was the veil that sought to block any vestige of light from passing through. Inside the mist were many glistening angels, with sad faces, as they could not get through. They stood with their hands held in prayer waiting for the day when the veil would be lifted. Orwell, drifted through the mist and out the other side, he was now in the dark dimension, directly facing Erratus Manor, its exterior dark and gothic, standing alone like some poor lost child who'd never seen the sun. It seemed isolated, as if trapped by the ghost-like mist of the veil. It was always night here, never day. The garden, if you could call it a garden, was messy and overgrown, resembling a jungle, it swayed as if in slow motion. In the centre stood a large tree, rotten and decaying. Its roots, long since deprived of light and the nourishment of rain, had died. The branches seemed to ensnare the house like spindly skeletal hands, holding the house and its residents captive. Rotten apples, long since fallen from the once flourishing tree, lay strewn across the ground, as maggots crawled over them. The face of death was chillingly etched into their once sweet flesh. Reaching the entrance of this dark abode, Orwell gave out a sound like a police car siren, its noise so loud and fearful. This was followed by an eerie silence before the same voice came through.

'Enter, Orwell.'

The huge black entrance opened and Orwell went inside, as the doors shut behind it. The surroundings, once again, fell as silent as the grave. The treacherous drone hovered within a huge dark chamber. This place was born to darkness. No light lived here, not even the flicker of a candle. Orwell remained undeterred, making its way across the hallway to an entrance known as the left door. Again, the metallic antennae camera lens came out of its metal body and proceeded to push a button on the doors right hand side. Then, with a humming sound, the left door opened, revealing a flight of stairs, leading into a vast impressive control room. The control columns were, without wanting to give the magicians too much credit, sophisticated to say the least, with computers, not of this world. They were made from a black crystalline substance and looked alarmingly similar to Atlantis, but more mechanised. The magicians sat around these controls calmly and cunningly activating the dark crystalline panels. Here, all control was carried out upon the earth, feeding her populace with their fiendish lies, spinning all sorts of corruption, deceitfully disguised. The justification, the cover up of crooked monetary systems, the dependency on drugs, oil and genetic modification, and the slander of those who were innocent, the cruel cover up of murder - it all happened in this control room. They wore dark gowns, covered from head to toe, their hands covered by black gloves with monk-like cowls upon their heads. Their faces were suppressed by shadow, eyes as if shut, or blind - but from what? They were unperturbed by this and seemed to glide across the chamber like Phantoms without any difficulty, as if they could see clearly.

At the top of the control room, floating menacingly in a huge circle, were six utterly horrid creatures, spectral in form and looking like they had come out of some hideous nightmare. These were the Wounds. They made our dear Mother Earth ill and kept the threat of all war in their vicious cycle intact. They made strange wailing noises, coupled with cruel, hateful insults, which they spat out at each other and sometimes just out to the world and everyone. Their cruel wailings and ramblings hurt dear Gaia (Mother Earth). Each wound was the manifestation of Mankind's lower self. The result of every warmonger, hate preacher, terrorist and corrupt leader had empowered these Wounds and given them power. First there was Hate, a fanatic, carrying a gun, laughing cruelly every time it fired its bullets into the air or at one of its fellow Wounds, preferably at Fear, who Hate took delight in frightening. Fear reacted by flashing its machete back at Hate, whilst screaming a sound of terror.

'Ha, ha, ha! Are you frightened Fear? Delicious! The more you're scared, the stronger I become. Ha, ha, ha,' chided Hate, in such a vile way, as fear breeds hatred.

'Oh, and the more you hate, the stronger I become,' retorted Fear, in its frightened voice,
as hate only energises more fear.

The four other Wounds were Jealousy, Greed, Ignorance and Pride. Jealousy had such a vile tongue and couldn't help but knock its fellow Wounds, but this Wound knew that it only did this because it didn't feel good enough itself and lived under the Illusion that it would feel better if it continued to hurt others around it. Greed was an obese Wound, a manifestation of the archetypal fat cat. It was money it was after, not food. It held a bulbous purse within its hand filled with the money it was forever making from the souls it stole from in all types of greed, from extortion to robbery. All the crooked banks were present in this Wound. Ignorance, with its smug little face and folded arms, did not give a damn what it said or how it acted towards others. This Wound was perhaps the most hurt of all, as it was the cause of so much trouble in the world, and was the parent of all Wounds - Fear, Hate and Greed. Its "I'm alright Jack" attitude had caused poverty and war within so many cultures, yet there it hovered in its cycle in a state of arrogant bliss, not caring, never feeling. The final Wound that made up the cycle, Pride, had a similar pig-headed way about it with its nose held high in the air, as if it had detected the smell of excrement. It too had its arms folded and clung onto its aura of stubbornness, not wanting to sort or work anything out with anybody.

'Why should I sort it out, I'm not going to show my true feelings. I'm staying put. Why should I do anything else? Besides it's never my fault,' the Wound mumbled these words to itself.

This Wound fed off those who would never forgive. Each of the Wounds fed off the negativity of humanity, but also fed off each other.

'Ah Orwell, you have returned,' came the same voice that had spoken earlier. 'Come here, my pet, and show us what you have seen.' Obediently, the robotic drone made its way towards its master, who sat upon a Throne overlooking the entire control centre. His eyes were closed, or blinded, his whole form was shrouded in robes of deceit - the leader of all the magicians, Lord Asphodel. Orwell rested upon Lord Asphodel's palm as the head magician gently caressed the surface of its metallic back. 'Such an advancement in our great technology,' he said. 'Why love something that is of the flesh and has a heart to feel, when you can love a creature of circuitry with no heart? At least then it can never hurt you, it can only obey you.' Lord Asphodel's voice was hard and cold, reflecting the hurt that had long blocked his heart and kept it frozen, something the Wound of Hate revelled in. 'Gentlemen, let us first drink to the advancements of our technologies and to our twenty-six thousand year reign of control over the entire populace. One of our many achievements, long may it continue.' A lackey of Asphodel produced a bottle of the very best champagne, pouring each of the magicians a glass. Asphodel raised his hand, about to prepare his toast. 'Here's to being masters of the world, my dear brethren, and cheers to the taxpayers' money.' The room filled with laughter and cruel sniggering, as they gulped their drinks down. 'And now, Orwell, show us what we asked you to.' Lord Asphodel's face was serious again, as he turned his head to two of the magicians, standing nearby, as if by command, facing their leader. 'You, magicians 19 and 84, you were the ones who reported these people to me.'

'Yes, Lord Asphodel. As we observed, it all felt very strange to us. There was something so odd, yet familiar, about the writing upon the wall. This young man seemed different from his peers and elders.'

'Bah, fools, you speak of a mere child, a boy and his anxious looking mother. I believe that is how you described them to me,' snapped Asphodel impatiently.

'But sir, we thought it best that you should know. It did not seem normal to us.'

'I am losing patience with both of you. What can a youth possibly do that could ever pose a threat to us and our ways?' retorted the magician. 'If what Orwell has seen is nothing more than the everyday conforming of a tiny family, then I promise you it is your lives that shall pay the forfeit. Do you understand me 19 and 84?'

The two magicians quaked within their robes. They both knew of Lord Asphodel's temper and of the punishment that he could carry out when angered. 19 and 84 looked at their fellow magicians in the hope of finding some sympathy or some form of humanity, but their comrades just stared ahead, totally unmoved and impassive to their horror. The two magicians noticed a white substance forming around their comrades, closing their hearts and coating their entire forms. It was like frost, which seemed to get icier and icier, totally congealing their entire bodies. The magicians did this so that their hearts could never be reached, so that they could never feel pain or sorrow, not even for their own kind.

'No, please don't,' came their only words now as they looked upon their leader, who also seemed completely frozen in frost. Above them, the Wounds just laughed and jeered.

'Yes, kill them. Do it! They are better off dead, great wastes of space,' chanted the cycle, especially Hate, who liked nothing more than to soak up in a killing, no matter who it was.

Suddenly a weird sounding voice, that was music to 19 and 84's ears, called out to Lord Asphodel, breaking the silence.

'Sstop, Assphodel. Let 19 and 84 have their chance and allow Orwell to show you what he has seen. You need to see this, it is very important.'

The voice was strange in tone, like a whispering hiss from a serpent. The frost that had consumed the magicians, now thawed, returning them to their normal state, much to the relief of 19 and 84, who let out grovelled thanks to their dark master.

'Shut up, fools and listen to the voice of your true ruler.'

Looking up towards the cycle of Wounds, they saw two slanting eyes, yellow green in colour, appearing in the darkness, looking down upon the Wounds and the magicians, like some tyrannical king, observing his subjects from his mountainous fortress. It was the Illusion.

'Turn Orwell on, let us all see what he has seen before I lose my patience with you, Asphodel,' hissed the serpent like voice.

Like a frightened child jumping to attention to a dominating parent, Lord Asphodel obeyed.

'Yes, Great One,' he said, touching a switch upon Orwell's casing. A red beam shone out from its dalek lens, projecting the images of Suzanne and Jonathan in David's bedroom, next to the sleeping body of David. Elia's vessel could not be seen, as she lay cross-legged over the other side of the bed, away from the staring eye of Orwell. It was then that the glowing forms of Elia and David showed up. Their bodies seen but not their actual appearance, surrounded in their auric fields. 'Well done, Orwell. It would appear that there are two guests with these mortals, two spiritual guests. Thanks to our highly advanced Kirlian photography, we can now see the hidden world, or at least the spirits who are from the mortal world. And yet, the angels are still far too clever,' Lord Asphodel said, with a little anger. He now stood with his arms crossed, observing the entire scenario.

'Sound, Orwell. I need sound now.' Alas, the entire conversation was overheard by the magicians. Asphodel's face grimaced at what he was hearing, but as the first utterance of the Genesis Crystal came to their attention, the temperature of the control room changed from cold to extreme heat. The Illusion gave out a protesting hiss, as it heard the beautiful crystal's name mentioned and they could see the etheric glow that emanated from it via the Kirlian photography. It sent shivers throughout the chamber.

'The Genesis Crystal. They have the Genesis Crystal. That which we thought had been lost forever, now in possession of that young man!' There was a pause. 'and her,' Lord Asphodel's voice rose with frustration and a hint of terror. His cold features seemed to be even more drained of blood than usual.

'How could all this have come about? In twenty-six thousand years no one has ever been able to find it, so why now? No matter how far we sought to destroy it, no trace of it was ever found. It is as I have always feared, Asphodel,' came the Illusion's voice. 'The children of light are moving against us seeking to change the world and rob us of our control, taking away the one thing you hold dear my friend, absolute power.' There was such a tension in the room, you could have cut it with a chainsaw. Even the Wounds were silent. Ignorance and Pride didn't look so cocky, Jealousy looked perplexed, before knocking out an envious comment about David and Elia's light being too beautiful. Greed held on even more tightly to its huge purse of money, whilst Fear was even more frightened now than ever before, holding its machete up in defence to the forces that might threaten it. Hate clasped his disgusting weapon, clenching his teeth with anger. 'How dare these beings attempt to stop me. How dare they!'

'Great one, do you think that this boy, David, is a lightworker?' pondered Lord Asphodel.

'Yes, I do,' hissed the snake-like voice. 'He, like the woman Lotus, carries the golden energy of pure Atlantis within him and if that crystal plants its seeds within our world, the results will be disastrous for me and my children, the Wounds.' Lord Asphodel did not say anything about Elia, he seemed as if he deliberately wanted not to speak of her, one lightworker was enough. Suddenly the toast he had made earlier, seemed to be in vain. 'Be wary of this young man, Asphodel, the one known as Blue Robin. He is steeped in purity and his light represents that of an angel. Already his innocence is a constant thorn in my side.'

With a sharp intake of breath, Lord Asphodel whispered hoarsely,

'What should I do?'

'You must kill him in flesh, trap his soul and place the Genesis Crystal into suppression, for within his innocence, lies the universe's salvation, and my downfall. With his demise, the end of innocence, brings my ultimate victory. As for the woman Lotus, she carries such peace and wisdom, that it is close to unbearable for me.'

'May her bones rot,' came Lord Asphodel's bitter response. 'She will rue the day she ever dared interfere in any of this, with the Blue Robin. They are not the only ones, Great One. There are many more of their kind, those accursed do-gooding earth angels. They've been breeding for decades like rabbits, trying to break the cycle and bring back the light.'

'Yes, but it is he who has been summoned by the light for this particular assignment, to become the next keeper of the Genesis Crystal, to be the planter of the new......,' the Illusion's voice cut off. 'I cannot bear to even go on.'

'They will be stopped, Master. They will be stopped.' Putting Orwell aside and shutting down his camera systems, he snapped his orders to his minions. 'We must be careful how to do this.'

'Do not worry, my Lord,' came the sneaky voice of one of his magicians. 'Once you have secured their demise, I can spin a little tale about how they all disappeared. The world won't know they even existed.'

'Good, start making one up, Weaver.' Lord Asphodel sat back down upon his throne staring up at the nightmarish eyes that were looking down upon him.

'You have nothing to fear, Great One. I promise you our control will never be dissolved. We will not allow them to break the cycle. It shall go on forever.'

10

ATTACK

It was all quiet in David's household. His mum and dad were in a calm mood. Jonathan sat in deep contemplation on the sofa, the most relaxed he had ever been, his eyes gazing far out into space. It seemed that the whole world had stopped what it was doing and was waiting with baited breath for what the lightworkers were going to do next. Indeed, on a soul level, this was very true. David sat next to his father, stroking his arm reassuringly, his deep blue eyes gazing lovingly into his dads. Although he was invisible, Jonathan could now sense his son's gentle form and, as if in response, held out his own hand and placed it upon the seat directly where David's leg was. David longed to tell his dad how much he loved him. He could feel such forgiveness flowing within his soul, that he hadn't always been able to have in his physical body. He and Elia had tried to tell his parents about the wonderful realms they had seen and of archangel Michael, Shambhala, Nada, Sananda, Atlantis, not to mention Akash, that glorious keeper of the cosmos. Yet all his mum and dad could say was, "It sounds wonderful." It was so difficult to put into words the magnitude of such beauty and the glory of the truth.

Yet, already within their own hearts, Suzanne and Jonathan could feel something opening up - a warmth that they had been a stranger to since infancy. Suzanne had made a lovely lunch for everyone, chicken in white wine sauce with pasta, David's favourite. Good old mum, even in spirit form, she couldn't help but want to look after him by feeding him up. Although David had no need for food in his higher self, her invisible loved one still found it hard to resist his mum's cooking and, without any trouble at all, he had consumed the entire meal. The two parents watched with mouths open as invisible hands had lifted the knife and fork and the food disappeared completely from the plate. Although they had asked the invisible Elia whether she had wanted any, the earth angel had declined, preferring to stay upstairs where she would tend to the Genesis Crystal. David had decided to stay close to his mum and dad to help them acclimatise to this strange situation. He now deemed it wise to go upstairs and check on Elia, as she had been up there for some time. What must she be doing?

    David left his parents, silently chatting amongst themselves, as he floated up the stairway. Elia was sitting in the white room in the middle of the floor, cross-legged, as if in meditation. The Genesis Crystal, which was placed gently upon a soft cushion, shone and pulsated in front of her. This was the room in which David practised Reiki. Elia sensed the loving energy flowing through this room and considered it the perfect place to store the crystal. The wise healer held her hands out towards it, gently placing them over the shimmering sphere. The door to the white room was shut behind her, but David passed through it with ease, stopping briefly, halfway through the framework, as if checking to see what Elia was doing.

'Elia, what are you doing?'

Elia turned towards him with a serene smile. David smiled fondly back. This was such a profound moment that they should surely all be celebrating.

'Come in David, come and sit with me. Let us work together.'

The young man sat beside his Reiki master. Their angels floated around them in the form of golden orbs, soaking in the sheer abundance of the moment, for the joy coming from Elia and David's souls was spilling out from them like rays of sunlight. The only exception was Lady Nada, who dwelled within a sparkling rose-coloured ball of energy, serenely observing the happy moment.

'What are you doing, are you sending Reiki out to the Genesis Crystal?' Elia asked David.

'Yes, I am, but I'm also trying to communicate with it. Do you remember the final day when we created this beautiful object?'

'Yes, we were highly trained initiates back then. I was one of the high priests who could do this,' said David

'Yes, so was I, in fact I was High Priestess long before I became queen of Atlantis. During that time, the energy was so high no one needed to rule over them, for everyone was their own leader, their own master.'

'Those days were so long ago, and yet the time for them to return seems so near,' said Elia.

David nodded.

'Put your hands here and feel Atlantis in its purest state, reaching out to you.'

David felt the wonderful energy once again, flowing through them both. It seemed to be reacting to the Reiki, sending its powerful light back into the healers. If you send out love, you get love back and it was doing this threefold.

'Elia, you said you were trying to communicate with the Genesis Crystal. What are you asking it?'

David suddenly remembered what Akash had said, that it contained his consciousness, thereby allowing him to be near to them. Sure enough, there in the centre of the marvellous crystal, floated the form of Akash. It was like looking at a goldfish in a bowl.

'Greetings, beloved ones,' came the wise whale's voice. 'I see you successfully brought the Genesis Crystal, safely back to the mortal realm of earth. Many thanks for the beautiful Reiki. I felt it so strongly.'

'Hello, Akash,' they both called. 'We need you to help us.'

'How may I?'

'Well, it is true that we now have the Genesis Crystal upon the earth. You told us that within the crystal are the seeds of new earth, which we both saw.'

'Yes beloved, the seeds are the physical manifestation of my mind and soul, the gift for all humanity. They bear witness, and give the answer to, all prayers for the Illusion's nightmare to end.'

'But how can we release the seeds from the crystal in order to plant them?' David asked.

'The seeds cannot be released or taken from the Genesis Crystal. My consciousness is linked to the crystal, just as the crystal is to me. The Genesis knows the right time for the planting to occur. It is now finite, but the location for the rebirth is not here.'

'Then where should it be?' said Elia. Now they were both puzzled. 'The energy here is so pure, or perhaps it is at my house of white stone?'

'No, I'm afraid it is at neither location,' responded Akash, somewhat wistfully. 'You will know when it is time. What I will say is, don't be frightened of entering this dark place. You must heal what dwells within, you need to confront Illusion once and for all.'

'How can we do this?' asked the Blue Robin.

The angels answered in unison.

'Trace it, embrace it, and then release it.'

Akash seemed to smile in a way that only a whale could, through his beautiful eyes. 'Does that answer the question for you? When you do all this, then the love will truly return. Until then, there must be no fear or anxiety. Just go forward with all your beliefs and trust us, dear ones. We are not mistaken in mind. You can do it, David. Just know that you can.'

Akash then gave an encouraging wink with his wise eye before fading back into the golden light of the crystal.

Elia and David looked at each other. They would both have to trust, whatever the next days or hours might bring. They realised they would have to have faith that all would be well. Their thoughts were broken at that very moment, by a loud, terrifying scream from downstairs.

'Mum! That was mum. What's happening?' David flew through the door, closely followed by Elia, who grabbed, the glistening sphere to keep it safe.

The orbs of their angels hurried along beside them, as they glided downstairs to see what the problem was. Their eyes widened in horror at the scene. David's parents stood holding each other, as four magicians surrounded them.

'Don't move Suzanne, Jonathan, don't.....' but in their panic David's parents tried to make their way to the door behind them, only to be cut off by the four magicians, who were now standing in front of it.

The magicians walked towards them, forcing them back into the centre of the living room. How had this happened? How had they got in? His parent's guardian angels formed a protective circle around them, along with David and Elia, who rushed to help. The angels, led by Nada, enfolded the four souls, protecting them as much as they could from the dark energy of the magicians. Suzanne could not help but be horrified by the magicians' appearance.

'Elia, are these the magicians?' pondered David, trying to conceal his fear.

'Yes, David. Don't be afraid, we have our angels around us.'

Elia was beginning to regret that she'd ever brought the crystal downstairs. Within their shimmering light, they stood like lambs surrounded by wolves, holding onto each other, each one doing their utmost to protect the other, whilst their guardian angels kept the four of them and the Genesis Crystal firmly in their orb, like bodyguards in defiance against the intruders. 'What the heck are they?' Jonathan asked, trying to be strong.

'We are the magicians, your masters, the true controllers of your world, but please do not be afraid, we do not wish to hurt you,' was the calm response. 'We merely want something that you have, which belongs to us.' It didn't take long for either of them to realise what this was. Pointing to the Genesis Crystal, 'Hand it over and we promise no harm shall come to any of you.'

'Elia,' Suzanne spoke softly. 'They don't have any eyes, are they blind?'

'Yes - to the truth,' Elia answered frostily.

'Are they actually our rulers, then?'

'They would love to think so and I'm afraid they have had us under their thumb for far too long.'

'You speak disrespectfully of us, Lotus woman. Give us what we want and you shall at least be pardoned.'

'I would never dare obey you who work in the shadow. You call yourself rulers? True leaders don't hide like cowards in the dark, they walk in the sunshine and speak their truth.'

'ENOUGH! Now we tire of this, lightworker. Give us that crystal and your lives shall be spared.'

'If you're so powerful, magician, why don't you try taking it from us. Try getting past our wall of angels,' said David defiantly, empowered by divine justice.

'Davie, be careful,' said his mum.

'Don't you dare tempt us to destroy a mere boy. The little Blue Robin isn't it?' they retorted.

'David is the true keeper of the crystal,' spoke Elia, 'therefore you have no business with it and it has nothing to do with your machinations.'

'By whose authority do you speak like this?'

'By the light , the God of Creation, also Akash of Atlantis.'

This fuelled the heat of the magicians, who tried to reach out and take the Genesis Crystal by force, but despite their efforts they could not penetrate the circle of angels around them. The angels did not put up a fight, not even the slightest struggle. They looked on, knowing the magicians could not physically get through.

'Now,' said Elia 'why don't you just go and accept......Ahhhh,'

The wise woman let out a scream of pain, which brought her to her knees, almost dropping the crystal, but trying with all her might to hold onto it.

'Elia, are you alright?' they all exclaimed, as David knelt down to help her.

'Elia, what's wrong?' David said.

'Psychic attack. It's him, Jack Asphodel. He knows how to get to me!'

'That's correct Elia, now listen to me.' From the control room, Lord Asphodel had been watching the entire scene through the eyes of his psychic magicians, who lay kneeling in their own circle projecting their minds into astral images. This was how they had got into Davids house. 'Now that you have heard what my subjects have said, I want the crystal, Elia. I want it now.'

'You'll never have it. You won't be able to have it...,' Elia sought to control the burning pain from the vicious assault.

Asphodel's scathing image stung the lady like jabbing pins in her brain.

'Do not stand in my way, Elia, for your soul's sake,' came the reply. 'Nor the Blue Robin. I cannot, will not, allow your interference, and I hope for your soul's sake you are prepared for what's coming.'

'Leave her alone, do you hear me, leave her alone,' David shouted, enraged by the cruelty of Lord Asphodel. 'Angels, Nada, help her! This man, these magicians, they're hurting her.'

He was getting scared now.

'Quickly, your cape David, place it over Elia,' came Nada's reply.

'Of course, the cape, my psychic cloak. Get ready for a dose of your own medicine, Lord Asphodel.' Hurriedly, David placed the beautiful blue cloak, that archangel Michael had given him, around his Reiki master, remembering what Michael had said. 'Please, archangel Michael around me, archangel Michael above me, archangel Michael below me, archangel Michael to the left of me, archangel Michael to the right of me.'

In the control room, the circle of psychic attackers began to flounder.

'Something is wrong, Lord Asphodel, our psychic onslaught is being blocked.'

Lord Asphodel could feel it too, for he could no longer see Elia. Their horrid mistreatment of the third eye was useless against the earth angels, cloak.

'Our attack has been blocked by something that young man has done.'

'No, Asphodel, keep trying,' commanded the Illusion.

'I am trying, Great One, but the Blue Robin is blocking us. He wears the cloak of protection which can stop psychic attack.'

Lord Asphodel tried desperately to get through the blockage, to reach the mind of Elia, but to no avail.

'It's working David, it's working. Elia is no longer in pain!' cried Suzanne.

'Archangel Michael behind me, archangel Michael in front of me.'

And then it happened, a huge blaze of white gold light appeared directly ahead of them and in all his glorious might, there stood archangel Michael, his Sword of Truth now in his hand. Witnessed by everybody present, including Suzanne and Jonathan, the great archangel rushed like the wind towards the psychic attackers, scooping each of them in his arms, taking them into his custody. Then, just like a nightclub bouncer, he threw them out through the wall at super speed, their forms exploding and evaporating into nothingness. The mess that was left returned to Erratus Manor, back to the control room, into the bodies of those they had left, much to the boiling chagrin of Illusion.

'Asphodel, does this mean I have to scold you? Oh, how many more times is this?'

'No, my great Lord, nooo!'

Like a bully, Illusion seized Jack Asphodel, pumping more fear into him as the Wounds chuckled at the sight.

'Never fail me like that again, do you understand me, fool?

'Yes, Great One.'

David and the others helped Elia to her feet. She was a little shaken, her hands trembling slightly.

'Are you alright, Elia?' David asked, concerned.

'Yes, I am okay sweetheart, a little weak but I'll survive.'

The magnificent archangel came over to them, his stature towering above them and the other angels. Gently, his beautiful energy soon dispelled all traces of negative residue left over. Tapping David upon the back, as if to say "well done", the kind face winked at the boy, then enfolded the whole family within his wings, along with the other angels. Wrapped in Michael's loving embrace, Jonathan and David felt they were in the presence of a most loving father figure, whilst Elia and Suzanne almost swooned. The great being let them go, nodding his head as if to say "all is well" before flying towards the ceiling and disappearing in the same glorious blaze of light.

'Wow, what a guy, I mean angel,' said Suzanne. 'Talk about the strong silent type.'

'I can't believe it. Did you both actually see him?' asked David excitedly.

'Yes, I did Davie, he was gorgeous.'

'Yes, he certainly was,' added Jonathan.

'I beg your pardon?' replied Suzanne, bemused.

'I mean he was brilliant.' David's dad was now looking just a bit embarrassed. 'I mean he was just like Superman.'

'Ah, Dad, yes, that's it. Just like him only with blonde hair. Don't worry, Dad, the feeling is mutual I promise, for anyone who sees him for the first time.'

'David. I can see you. I can see you darling,' said Jonathan. 'I can see Elia too. How is this possible?'

'The psychic build-up of positive energy that grew stronger in this house once we brought the Genesis Crystal into this realm, must have caused a tear in the veil,' answered Elia. 'Coupled with David's affirmation when he placed the cloak around me. Hence, why you two also saw Archangel Michael. See, we are already doing some good,' smiled Elia triumphantly. 'Thank you, David, thank you so much, for your help.'

'You're welcome. Elia are you sure you're okay?'

'Fit as a fiddle, my child. I don't think the magicians will be trying that stunt on us anytime soon. The problem is, they now know about us and that we have the crystal. They won't rest, they'll be after us in full vengeance now.'

'You said they were watching us Elia' said Suzanne.

'Mum, that figure I saw outside Elia's house yesterday, and then on the way home and outside our house last night, I told you it was watching me. It must have been a magician. That person must have been one of them. What do you think Elia?'

'Possibly.'

Elia was already busy placing the Reiki symbols of protection around the walls of the house, drawing them with her index finger in the air.

'So those magicians we saw, they were projected thought forms, Elia?'

'Yes, Suzanne, the magicians send out thought forms of themselves, which creates astral projection.'

'Very clever,' pondered Jonathan.

Elia spun round.

'Yes, but also very dangerous.'

'Can anybody do that?' David asked.

'Yes, dear one, those who master it to perfection, like the magicians, can use it either for good or evil. You see, in Atlantis, our people could master so many things from projection, teleporting, telepathy and levitation, but the magicians used all these things for their own selfish gain, and this helped feed the darkness and so created Illusion. They have continued right up until now, working for this negativity, and so their cycle continues.'

'And this Lord Asphodel, the leader of them, you called him Jack, how did you know this?' queried Jonathan.

Elia's body language changed, as did her voice.

'It does not matter how I know him, and let's have no more questions please.'

Jonathan looked puzzled.

'Yes, Elia's right,' said Suzanne.

'Poor thing, grilling her like this. We need to move quickly. The magicians know we are here and they're bound to come back, but won't your symbols protect us?' said David.

'Yes, they will protect your house from further psychic invasion, but remember what I told you once. They are not a bulletproof shield. I'm going to take you somewhere much safer.'

Elia was right to do this, for the relentless magicians would soon be on the move. Walking over to a seat in the living room, Elia sat down and closed her eyes, as if she was trying to establish some form of contact.

'What now?' snapped Jonathan, impatiently.

'Dad, please have some patience. Elia is doing her best.'

'Hush, it's alright David. I am talking to the masters. They're coming through now. Can you feel them, David? They speak to you, just as they speak to me.'

'Yes, I can.'

Suzanne and Jonathan gazed in awe, as the crown chakras, right above the two earth angel's heads, opened up resembling a beautiful lily. In the centre, stood Sananda, Archangel Michael, Buddah, Lord Krishna, Ganesh, Mother Mary, Quan Yin and all the masters. Each sat perfectly within the lily, completely unrestricted by size, time or space, radiating perfection.

'Greetings to you, lightworkers,' said each of the masters, simultaneously.

'Dear masters,' said Elia, 'It was the magicians. They entered David's home, using astral projection.'

'Yes, dear Elia, we saw it all. The magicians have been spying on you since yesterday. They knew about the writing on the wall.'

'There we go,' thought David, quietly to himself. 'It was a magician that I saw. I knew that figure made me feel uneasy. That must have been it.'

David turned his attention back to the masters within his crown chakra, not wanting to lose this glorious sensation.

'We know it could have been dangerous to you all, but it is vital that you overcome all your fears as you stand on the cusp of the new dawn. It is important, David, for the sake of you, Elia and your family, that you keep the cloak of protection with you at all times. We cannot emphasise this enough.'

'Jesus? That's Jesus and the Buddah, isn't it?' Jonathan said in astonishment.

'Oh my goodness,' cried Suzanne, as a beautiful feeling washed over her.

'Yes, Mum and Dad, but in the inner realms, he is called Sananda, isn't it terrific?'

Elia continued.

'I have placed reiki symbols all over their house to protect us from further invasion, but I feel we need to be elsewhere.'

'Your instincts are indeed right, child. You need to take David and his family to your house of white stone. There are others who have gathered from your realms who are waiting patiently for you. They are looking forward to meeting you with all their hearts, David.'

'You mean I'm going to meet my soul family?'

'Yes, you already met some of them when you did Reiki with Elia. 'Like you they are Earth Angels'

'Just a minute, you called him a lightworker at first,
now you say he and Elia are earth angels. Which is it?'
said Jonathan, puzzled and with a hint of sceptism.

'David is of Shambhala, which means that he is a Rainbow child. His energy resonates with pure love. He is of the generation that has elected to usher in the new era of peace, which now lies within the palm of your hands,' responded Archangel Michael, pointing toward the Genesis Crystal on Elia's lap. 'You must go now Elia. Take everybody with you and protect the crystal by getting everyone to form a circle. Contact all earth angels on the planet and help to guide them.'

Elia nodded, understanding what she needed to do.

'Won't the magicians be able to get into Elia's house?' asked Suzanne.

'Yeah, what stops these people from doing the same thing they did , here' added Jonathan.

There was something within his voice that hurt Elia, a coldness, a sense of mistrust that she had never noticed with Suzanne, and certainly not within David.

'Please Jonathan, my house is protected by beautiful forces which, along with the crystal, will be amplified. It lives outside the Magicians comprehension, therefore their powers cannot get through it. We shall be quite safe, I am sure.'

'Just how sure are you?' Jonathan's manner seemed at times almost pompous, condescending.

'Quite sure. Only fear can weaken our protection and that only has power if you allow it to,' said Elia with a higher level of assertiveness.

Turning inwards once again, Elia and David thanked the masters.

'Oh Michael, Sananda, will the seeds of new earth then be planted?' asked David eagerly.

'You have heard Akash speak through the crystal, dear one,' smiled Sananda. 'The moment is being prepared for return, and that time will soon be here. Just remember not to be afraid, for the ultimate moment will soon occur.'

The masters then disappeared as the crown chakras of David and Elia closed its petals around them. Elia and David leapt up, feeling totally energised simply by being in contact with them again.

'Okay, no time like the present, let us go now. Take any belongings that are essential, as I don't know how long you will be with me.'

'Can't you give us an idea. Elia?' Suzanne said, half joking. She had never felt as out of control of her life as she did now. 'Are we talking weeks or months?'

'Darling, if I knew for sure I would tell you. It is likely to be until the seeds of new earth are planted. Now that the magicians know about us, it is not safe to be anywhere else. We must stick together. If you remain here or tell anyone about what has happened, the magicians will surely kill them.'

'Robert, next door, is a detective. I say we report this to them so they can handle this,' said Jonathan, matter-of-factly.

'By alerting another soul, you are simply putting them in grave danger, not to mention thousands of others,' came Elia's stern reply.

'Elia, I'm not sure what planet you're actually from. I don't know what you've done to our son, but in our world, we alert the authorities to these things. They can then sort out these criminals and give that crystal to the government, where it will be safe.'

'Safe!' The wise woman studied the man with an almost shocked expression upon her face. 'The magicians want that, they would love you to do something like that. Neither the police, nor the government have the power to stop them. They control everything behind the scenes and that is why it is up to us, the lightworkers and earth angels, to stop them. We can all do this by listening to Akash, Archangel Michael, Sananda, Buddah or any other master, for they speak the language of the heart.'

'The days of the old are dead, dad,' intervened David. 'Most of the systems that we have put our trust in for so long, are rotten to the core. That is why they are leaving our world. The Creator has said that it is time to do so. If we carry on holding on to what we thought we knew, we just continue giving power to the crooked. Something the Illusion wants us to do, meaning that the magicians will stay in control.'

David took his father's hands and held them to his heart.

'Come on, Dad. After all that you've seen today, me in this form, Elia in hers, the Genesis Crystal, the masters within our crown chakras, look you always said you wanted a revolution. Well it's happening Dad. It's a spiritual revolution that's happening in our world, and millions have started to wake up. This is the greatest awakening ever. Now is truly the time of the people, and it's all for us, it can be a reality if we allow it to be so.'

Elia smiled kindly at the boy, as she looked upon his shining soul, giving hope to his father's troubled one. Elia gently cut in.

'People have waited for so long, holding hands together in peace, waiting for this precise moment in time. Along with the angels, they have waited with infinite patience. Love has come to our world, Jonathan. We can either ignore it, pretend it doesn't exist, or we can open our hearts to accept and embrace it'

They were interrupted by Suzanne, coming down the stairs quickly, carrying a few belongings she thought they might need. She noticed the silence in the room and the single tear running down Jonathan's cheek. David had reached his dad, now if only he could try and trust.

'Elia, I've packed all we might need.'

'David and I will be fine Suzanne,' said Elia with a smile. 'Please excuse us, there have been one or two hearts opening in this room today.'

Dashing to the kitchen to get some food, crisps, chocolate and fruit, Suzanne suddenly exclaimed.

'What about you and David?'

'What of us? We are here, in the present with you.'

'No, I mean your actual bodies are still upstairs. What are you going to do with yourselves?'

'Do not worry. Our vessels are going to be fine,' said Elia confidently.

Jonathan had at that very second, come out of the thoughtful state he had been in. Shaking his head, as if to brush his true feelings aside, he once again looked doubtful.

'What are you going to do? Put some enchanted forest around the house, or perhaps the neighbourhood,' he said flippantly.

Ignoring his sarcasm, Elia spoke nonchalantly.

'I have placed the symbols of protection around this place, so David's vessel will be protected. As for myself....' she pointed with her finger as Elia's vessel hovered down the stairs, still in her lotus-like position. I shall come along with us.

'Holy, Moley,' uttered Jonathan, 'this day just gets stranger by the minute.'

'Come, let's get together. David, place your cape around us so that we will be protected from all outside forces.'

David did so, placing the flowing blue cloak around his loved ones and Elia. It felt warm and protective, shielding them from all hostility. Jonathan touched Suzanne's arm, whispering into her ear.

'I don't know what to do, Suzanne, do you trust her? Is she not like a magician, also?'

'Yes, I do trust her Jonathan, and I believe in what's happening. Take it from me, my whole life feels like it's been pulled inside out, but not in a bad way. We've just got to realise that we cannot control anything anymore. The angels want us to let go, and the magicians don't. They want us to think we all have control over our lives and we don't. The angels helped us when Elia was being hurt by that Jack Asphodel guy, whoever he is. The magicians threatened to kill us. I know who I prefer.'

'Yes, you're right. David said such lovely things to me. Perhaps, simply for his sake, I have got to trust. I must try.'

But in his mind, Jonathan still carried uncertainty, a frustration about being unable to be in charge, for control had always made him feel safe. He'd clashed with people at work who were stronger than he was, making him feel less of a person and causing him to feel out of control.

'Let us in Jonathan, let us in.' His angels had always said this. They loved him and always wanted to help him, to stop him from making the mistakes he had sometimes made in his life. Pride and fear had sometimes been so strong, that he just hadn't heard them, although he had always prayed every night before sleep. He was a good man, but had lacked the love growing up to show him the way. Perhaps now his prayers had been answered.

They all got into Elia's car, a strange and fascinating vehicle to be sure. Elia had found a way to power a car using Crystal Technology one of the many things the Angels and ETs had taught her. Very green, was Elia Lotus and she believed passionately in ecology. She started it up, its alien engine barely made a sound, and off they went down the road. In the back of the car, Suzanne looked back at the house she had left behind, her face broke into a grin as she saw two huge angels enfolding the entire property. These were the guardian angels of their house. No wonder that place had always had such a nice feeling. Knowing David's vessel would be looked after, made her very happy indeed. Looking about the neighbourhood, she saw huge angels enfolding every single house.

'I notice that you can see the principalities, my darling,' said Elia, looking in her rear view mirror. Suzanne felt like a child again. Amidst the danger, there was hope that love was around them all. 'Oh, and by the way, Jonathan, you mentioned putting up a magical forest. The Reiki symbols inspired the writers of fairy tales. That's why they used analogies to convey symbolism. The enchanted woods were based upon the protective forces of good, the Reiki signs.'

David, who sat next to his teacher in the front seat, looked with eyes of wonder. He had always loved fairy tales and enjoyed learning all the hidden meanings behind them. He had learnt to read only through being touched by the magic of Disney's Sleeping Beauty. Until that time, he had struggled to both read and write. How times had changed.

Without warning, a large laser beam, the colour of blood red, hit their car. The flash caused Elia to swerve dangerously, before regaining control.

'What the hell's going on now?' shouted Jonathan.

Turning around, he saw two magicians flying through the air about twenty feet behind them, but gaining rapidly. Another red blast of energy was fired. The energy blasts were coming out of the Magicians spears that they held.

'Oh no, Elia, it's them again! Screamed Suzanne. And I thought they'd seen sense and given in,' replied the wise woman.

'How annoying, and it's only thanks to David's cloak that we are not burnt to a crisp. We have the perfect force field.'

One of the magicians spoke via telepathy.

'We have a fix on them Lord Asphodel, they can't get away and we can see the crystal, but no matter how we try we cannot destroy them, our powers seem useless. Damn that cloak of protection, its shielding them from all our psychic weaponry.'

'Listen, I don't care how you do it, just get the Genesis Crystal. We need it now!'

Lord Asphodel's voice was fraught with desperation. His usual calm exterior now seemed upon the brink of madness. One of the magicians again fired his deadly laser beam, this time at the window, but still to no effect. Angrily, both the magicians made their way to either side of the car, their eyeless faces and blackened forms, sent chills through the hearts of all on board, even Elia.

'PULL OVER NOW. WE WANT WHAT YOU HAVE. IN THE NAME OF ASPHODEL, SURRENDER!'

Enraged by the nerve of these lost souls, Elia shouted at the top of her voice,

'NEVER, DO YOU HEAR, NEVER!'

The threatening duo let out an aggressive grunt before banging their spears against the windows. Usually, such actions would have smashed a glass window but the psychic cloak of protection stayed strong within its power, resulting in blue bolts of bio electricity flashing off the car, after each savage blow. Inside the car there was panic as Elia jammed her foot down on the accelerator. The speedometer was now up to a hundred miles per hour. Elia had never driven so fast. David was clinging onto the crystal for dear life. His mum and dad held each other, terrified that this could be the last day of their lives.

'Elia, what are we going to do, they are not giving up, and how come no pedestrian can see them?' asked Suzanne

'They are invisible. They work within the veil, so those who are not in touch with their clairvoyant side fail to see them. They are like the angels, only on the side of darkness.' 'They are the hidden people and that is just how they like it, except to us and all others who have the sight,' said Elia.

'Yes, at this moment unfortunately,' responded Jonathan.

Elia tried to quieten her mind, trying to stay focused. She, like David, started talking to their guardian angels, asking them for help.

'We're trying to get through to you beloved ones, but the anxiety within you is keeping us out. Try to stay calm. We know this is difficult, but you must ignore the magicians who try to distract you.'

'Archangel Michael, can you get him to come through?'

'Yes, but keep calm. You are not far from your destination.'

Both David and Elia tried to focus on the light that was around them, not these terrifying attackers.

'Focus, Michael is trying to get through,' Nada kept saying.

David began saying the prayer to Archangel Michael whilst his parents started to recite the beautiful Lord's Prayer to each other.

The magicians, who were at this point so frustrated by their pointless efforts, suddenly had a cruel and ruthless idea. If they could not kill them, then they would make them kill others. Oh, wait and see what the Law would do if they killed an innocent victim through dangerous driving. Seeking out their prey, the two magicians craftily nodded to one another as, not too far ahead, a man with his son and daughter was just about to cross the road. Upon seeing the speeding vehicle hurtling towards them, the trio tried to make a run for it , but upon reaching the middle found themselves unable to move, as if they were frozen in time. No matter how they tried, they could not move anything. Their faces looked terrified as Elia's car raced towards them.

'No,' shouted David, 'It's Rob and his children, please no! They're innocent, they've done nothing to you, please don't do this!'

'Well, Blue Robin, give us that sacred crystal you hold and they shall be set free. Otherwise, we keep them immobilised to become street pizza. Would you like that on your conscience?' Elia courageously swerved, narrowly avoiding their neighbours, but the sudden force of the swerve flung the car into the air, straight into the direction of a house, whose residents screamed at the car coming straight towards their window. David shut his eyes, making one final cry for help. Elia clasped his hand tight waiting for the dreadful crash to occur.

11

SANCTUARY

Suddenly a huge flash of golden light surrounded the hurtling car, as archangel Michael appeared between the vehicle and the house. It was a scene that would have made Superman proud, as the miraculous being held Elia's car in his bare hands, taking it away from danger, sparing every life involved from certain death. The souls inside the house let out huge sighs of relief. As they watched in amazement, the car floated away from them, held by some invisible force, for they could not see the archangel, whose powers were limitless. His strength knew no bounds. What was the weight of a mere car to him? David and Elia held up their hands in praise of their saviour, whilst Suzanne hugged Jonathan.

'Oh, thank God, we're all okay. Thank you, Archangel Michael, thank you so much! I thought that could have been the end.'

Elia turned, letting out a deep breath.

'Never, whilst there is light, darlings, never whilst there is light,' she said.

Archangel Michael put the car down safely at the side of the road and passed into the car without even opening a door, to check on them all. They were all just a bit shaken, but Michael's presence had a calm and supportive effect, as his energy passed through them.

'David, Elia, I shall take you all to your destination. It will be safer this way.'

Elia and David nodded, still getting over the ordeal, as were Jonathan and Suzanne, who sat like little children in the back, in awe of this mighty being who had just saved them.

'Yes, Sir,' they all said in unison.

Archangel Michael stepped outside to face the two magicians, who were standing like lemons in the road their faces aghast, yet infused with anger at their defeat.

'How much longer does this madness have to go on?' said the Archangel in a voice booming like thunder. 'How long will it take for you to see the light?'

The pair were wary of Michael's presence.

'Never,' came the defiant reply of the magicians, who were trembling at the sound of Michael's voice. 'Our master's darkness shall last all eternity, archangel. You only have to look at the state of this world to know that.'

'I doubt that very much,' came Michael's response. 'You are just slaves chained within a dark cave and it's time for you all to leave it.'

Archangel Michael raised his arm, as if trying to reach these lost souls. They could feel his glowing light, like fire trying to melt the frost from their hearts. They could sense his love, so beautiful, yet so alien, trying to reach them.

'Come back, come back you fools, now,' screamed Lord Asphodel, via telepathy. 'Quick, before it affects you.'

The deadly duo raised their hands up to their faces, in an effort to shield themselves from the great sunlight.

'Don't be afraid. Please don't go, don't go back there,' said Michael with the voice of a loving parent. But the fear within them both overwhelmed them and they exploded in a ball of red fire, teleporting themselves back to Erratus Manor. Archangel Michael looked at the clearing smoke sadly. 'Too afraid. They were just too afraid,' he muttered to himself.

In the car, all eyes gazed at the glowing figure of white and gold.

'What was Michael trying to do, reason with them?' asked Jonathan.

Looking at the archangel and picking up on his sadness. Elia spoke gloomily.

'He was trying to help them but they were too afraid to let him in.'

By now, many people, having witnessed the miraculous event, came running out of their houses to see if these people in the car were alright, including Rob and his children, who were now completely free from the magicians' power. But before they could do so, the car once again took to the skies, carried, invisible to them all, by the great archangel. At this point, all mouths fell open, followed by cheers and loud hurrahs, as if they knew that something truly wonderful and full of goodness had taken place. Most people are good, and can still feel love within, and marvel at the wonders of life, from the simple to the profound. As for Rob, his face broke into a smile, detecting a joy he hadn't always felt.

'Go for it, David, just go for it,' he said.

Archangel Michael had now carried the car high above the clouds, as they set course for Elia's home. Jonathan, who had always loved flying, found himself enjoying this experience even more.

'This beats flying by plane, right David?'

David turned, still holding the crystal.

'Well they do say flying is the safest way to travel.' Usually David was quite afraid of flying, as was Suzanne. Elia didn't mind it too much but due to being enfolded by Michael, and supported by their angels, their fear had completely gone. They found they could even look out upon the fluffy white clouds. There was no place for fear anymore. 'Elia, will Robert and his family be safe?' David asked.

'Yes, they will be fine, they were simply used to threaten us. The magicians have no need to worry about them, as they do not possess what we do.'

Nada then spoke in her usual gentle way.

'They are protected, beloved one. Their guardian angels told us they are protected, as are all the souls who saw what they did. Robert and his family were affected by the magicians' control because they are not in touch with us, they do not ask us for help, and, as you know, we can only come in if we are invited. But keep sending them love and this will invoke us to be near to them. Simply say their names and ask for their angels to be with them and it will be so. It is that simple.'

David's dad looked perplexed again.

'Suzanne, who is David speaking to?'

'His angels, Jonathan. They speak to him and Elia just like you would to other people.'

Jonathan sceptically raised his eyebrows. Despite all he had seen, he still sought proof in everything.

They had now reached their destination. Elia's house of white stone seemed to glow like an opulent pearl, getting brighter and brighter as the car began its descent back down to land. Archangel Michael placed the crystal powered car directly upon the driveway.

'Oh, sanctuary. It's good to be home,' said Elia, in a very satisfied tone, looking out of her window.

'Elia, who are they?'

A group of shining souls stood waiting for them. Several of them were standing, one was hovering around the building. They waved excitedly as Elia and David, got out of the vehicle.

'It's alright, they are all friends,' the wise healer said. 'Come, everyone, let me introduce them to you.'

David, Suzanne and Jonathan followed cautiously. These souls were not unlike the forms that Elia and David were in. Their bodies glowed with radiant light, their chakras were also visible from their crown down to the sacral and their heart centres glowed with warmth and openness. Any form of defence had, long since, vanished. David looked upon them all with interest as he observed their appearance. Two of them seemed to sparkle with starlight, so David thought they were part of Commander Ashtar's intergalactic federation. It was then that David realised that he had known them from a past life. Ah, yes, somewhere in the Pleadies Star system wasn't it?

'This is Lorian and Casper,' smiled Elia, as she pointed to them. 'They are incarnated star people, and two of my other Reiki students.'

The two star people gave a friendly smile, yet held back in a reserved fashion, as was a star persons trait. It didn't matter, for they were so beautiful on the inside. The other lightworkers walked towards David. He was greeted with hugs and he knew them all. There was Lynda, a dear sweet lady whose warmth poured literally from her heart, her face looked sweet and cherubic, for she too was an incarnated angel. Her heart centre and entire aura glowed in a sparkling pink energy. Then, there was Nina, an incarnated wise woman who smiled serenely. She was a Janus Hindu in physical life who believed strongly in peace, her energy seemed near Buddah-like. She wore a sari of deep orange. Nina had such a calm demeanour. Crystal was the next to be introduced, she was known as a Crystal Child and her energy sparkled literally like a huge crystal. She had first come onto the planet back in the late seventies and it was up to her generation to teach the young crystal children here how to get by on earth. Lastly, there were Brian, Catherine and Tony, two other incarnated angels and an incarnated elemental. Tony possessed a cheeky chappie type of persona. He had long curly hair, a rich Irish accent,and his energy was of deep green, reflecting his love of the earth's natural world. He, like the incarnated angels, possessed wings, not like his friends, but shaped more like beautiful dragonfly wings. Each of the lightworkers smiled lovingly when they saw the Genesis Crystal.

'Elia, it has been returned to us,' said Lynda.

'After all this time,' continued Nina.

'Yes,' Elia said 'at long last'. 'The time of the new dawn is upon us. Come, let's all go inside and start our Circle to contact the other lightworkers all over our planet. We have all dreamt of this moment, so let us begin. Sananda and Michael told me and David that we are to contact all our soul pod and then to work with the seeds within to await the time of rebirth.'

They all turned at that moment to see the glorious sight of Archangel Michael veer upwards above the road.

'Take care, beloved ones, and remember, David, if you need to invoke me just use my cloak and I shall be there.'

He was then gone again in a blaze of great light.

'He saved us all,' smiled David. 'If it hadn't been for his blue cloak of protection, we'd have been destroyed by the magicians.'

'The magicians attacked you?' came Brian's concerned tone. 'Elia, do the magicians know about the crystal?'

'I'm afraid they do, but fear not, we will be safe for now. My house, due to the spiritual energy around it, remains safe from the Magicians. They can never attack us here. David's cape can amplify this.'

As they entered the house of white stone, Suzanne couldn't help but ask,

'Elia, these lightworkers, they are earth angels like you, I take it?'

'They are' just like David.' They are all part of our soul pod. They are in their truest state. It is better like this, as we are all operating outside the status quo. The magicians' craftiness knows no bounds, but we will remain undetected here.'

'Can this protective bubble we are in be broken?' asked Jonathan.

'Only by giving in to the urge of fear, but that can only happen if one of us were to betray us to the magicians. I do not see that happening, do you?'

All of them agreed with Elia, all of them except for Jonathan.

12

THE PLAN AND THE TRICK

At Erratus Manor all was silent. Not one magician had uttered a single sound in fear of Lord Asphodel, who sat slumped upon his throne, his face staring down at the floor, as if lost in a dark chasm of thought. The look upon his face said it all, as it twitched now and again with an anger that he could only just contain, whilst mulling over his failure and of being thwarted by the lightworkers. He felt the Illusion's chilling eyes looking down at him, chiding him due to his defeat, which the Wounds joined in with. Oh, how they loved to torment him, never allowing him any form of peace. Lord Asphodel puffed away on a cannabis cigarette. He felt it running down his throat as he inhaled the substance, relaxing him, or so he thought. He liked it, as it numbed the pain within him. He saw it as a substitute for the love he had never felt. But still, his pain had taught him how to survive and how to win at all costs, and through that ruthlessness, he had built his empire, preying upon the idleness of others, making billions out of the people of earth, so at least some good had come out of it. Yet, why was he never at peace within? Why was he never happy? The lost soul reached into his pocket, concealed within his long black robe, fishing out a photo of someone he had loved very much, the identity of whom he kept away from his fellow magicians who knew when not to disturb him. Lost within this moment of reflection, Lord Asphodel stared intensely at the tiny picture.

'You were the one I loved. I thought you were the Saviour, my only hope and yet even you betrayed me. You, like everyone, rejected me. Why do I still care about you? Why? Bah! enough of this mush, no one makes me weak anymore.' Suddenly, looking up at his subjects, he fixed his gaze upon the two magicians, who had failed to capture the Genesis Crystal. They both stood like two nervous schoolchildren before their dark master, aware and embarrassed by, their failure. Continuing to inhale his cannabis, Lord Asphodel looked with his eyeless face into theirs, disturbing the very marrow of their bones.

'Tell me both of you,' he said in a calm but menacing way, 'Why do you not have the crystal?'

'Lord Asphodel, you saw what happened.'

'Well, I saw that you failed. So, tell me, why did you fail? We are the rulers of the world. Few on this mortal coil possess what we do, so answer me, I repeat, why did you fail me?'

The two magicians spoke with quaking voices trying to reach the icy barrier of their master.

'Lord Asphodel, you saw what happened, it was the cloak. The Blue Robin wears it. It has the power to protect all who wear it from psychic attack. We tried, believe us, we tried so hard to get into the vehicle they were travelling in. It was like trying to get into a force field. But then we tried to make the car hit those people, we immobilised them with our magic, but they swerved and just when we thought they would be killed, Archangel Michael appeared.'

'They must have invoked him. Michael, how dare he interfere,' interrupted the Illusion. 'Asphodel, you know what this means. The veil is weakening due to the light these earth angels have been sending out. If they continue to do so, my veil will be damaged beyond repair.'

Lord Asphodel put his hand upon his forehead, overwhelmed by the problems they were all facing, as if unable to cope any longer.

'And then, our Lord, the archangel confronted us, his light was too powerful. We could not get to the others, as he was guarding them and ..... '

'ENOUGH!' shouted the voice of Asphodel, unable to take another moment of this story. 'You have told me enough already. I tire of this pathetic excuse for an explanation.' He became menacingly calm, touching the two magicians' deepest fears. 'And yet, you two miserable wretches both liked it didn't you? You nearly succumbed to the archangel's power of love. I could feel it stirring within you both. Had it not been for me summoning you back to Erratus, I am almost certain you would have turned your backs on our darkness, to your true master, and embraced the sunlight.'

'Yes, you are right Asphodel, they would have betrayed us all. These two fools cannot be trusted,' hissed the Illusion. 'They would have been the downfall of you all.'

'Oh, no, my Lord, please, no. You cannot think this of us, we have served you humbly for aeons.'

'No matter how long a time, traitors are born within a day,' replied Lord Asphodel. 'The fact is, you both nearly succumbed to love and that is a sign of weakness. You know the penalty for weakness, don't you?'

Dread flooded through the two magicians' vessels. Their hearts, what was left of them, now beat in resounding booms like a clock out of control.

'Please, Lord Asphodel, give us one last chance. I know we can succeed,' begged the desperate duo.

Their countenance sank to its lowest depths, upon hearing what Lord Asphodel said next.

'I am not in a giving mind this day. You will both wish you had stayed with the archangel.'

'No!' the petrified magicians screamed, as a red laser shot from Lord Asphodel's hand.

The two magicians let out a last cry of horrendous pain, glowed cherry red before dissolving into a pile of smoking dust, leaving behind only the melted remains of their robes. The rest of the magicians looked on in mild surprise at what had happened. Their hearts were so cold, and had frosted over whilst the execution had taken place, so they could not feel for their unfortunate colleagues. If only they had trusted the light. Gesturing to one of his magicians, before pointing down at the evaporated remains of the tragic pair, Lord Asphodel spoke in a nonchalant way, despite what he had done.

'Once the ash has cooled down, clear up the debris.'

'Yes, Lord Asphodel, immediately.'

The lost lord paced around the control room observing his subjects, who were working upon their computers. Their dark crystalline surfaces sparked and eerily hummed. He approached one of the magicians who was operating a large black console, along with Orwell who was projecting an image of David's house. Both their faces showed a mutual look of dislike and fear, as if terrified of the pure energies that existed there.

'Is there nothing you can do to penetrate the protection the vessel of the Blue Robin is under?'

'Nothing, my Lord,' came the sombre reply. 'The Reiki symbols that have been placed around and within the abode are too powerful for the psychic keys to unlock. There is no chance of us being able to invade the dwelling.'

'Reiki. It should have been banned when we were still in Atlantis. Now it has been brought back to the modern world and shared by earth angels everywhere, reaching into people's hearts, trying to help them to be free and to live their lives without control. Heaven knows what the world is coming to,' Lord Asphodel said resentfully. By now, the whole control room reeked with the smell of cannabis. 'Enough, Orwell. You have done well today.'

The robotic drone obeyed its master, turning off its projection ray to join Lord Asphodel, who had returned to his throne. The Illusion's eyes seared into his brain.

'We musst get to them. You musst find a way of trapping the Blue Robin and the woman, Lotus. If they plant the seeds you know what will happen.'

'There is no way to do this my master,' said Lord Asphodel, once again inhaling his drug to try to relieve him of all the pressure. 'You heard what my minions have said. The Blue Robin's house is protected by the symbols of Reiki. Its power is equal to all our magic and more. At this moment, we are truly lost.'

'Fool,' chided the Illusion harshly. 'There's always a way. Have you not studied the minds around the Blue Robin, those who are nearest and dearest to him?'

Lord Asphodel suddenly snapped with impatience.

'Do you think me a fool, master? Have I not learnt what you have taught me? Yes, I have studied their minds. I made a study of them before I did anything else. Elia's mind shines like her soul, with the brightest truth. Whilst the Blue Robin's mother's strength is the love and trust she has in her son. So, yes, we are dealing with pure love and innocence here, the infamous enemies of all of us.'

'True,' hissed the Illusion's response, 'We are dealing with light in its highest level. But you are forgetting someone. The father of the earth angel. I have studied his mind, Asphodel. He is not as strong as the others, for I have sensed both fear and doubt enter into his head, Something my Wounds gave him a long time ago. You see, he doubts the woman Lotus, he questions her wisdom, even though his heart tells him it is true. He fears what is happening, internally.' He does not trust,

'Oh, my dear Wounds, you have done so well, Lord Asphodel said sarcasticly. But even if that is true, my master, the house of white stone is protected by spiritual energy. Not even with our abilities of mind power, have we ever been able to penetrate it, and now the psychic cape of protection has blighted our chances even more.'

Lord Asphodel was always a pessimist when he felt defeated.

'That is true, Asphodel. We can destroy many people from within. We can cause death, set brother against brother, sister against sister, time and time again. Such is the power of my Wounds.' Hearing this, the Wounds chuckled viciously. 'But these souls are in touch with their higher power, as are many lightworkers. Our powers would have no effect on them.'

'Then once again, we are lost,' said Asphodel.

'No, my friend. I feel that we are not lost.' hissed the Illusion. 'The doubt within the boy's father is just strong enough for me to reach his mind. With enough effort from my Wound of Fear, I can start playing some games. Even the tiniest hint of doubt is enough for me to pour my poison. We need to lure him out of the house, where he will be at our mercy. His mind is not clear enough to hear his higher self, or his angels' warnings.'

Lord Asphodel now stood up with a cunning grin upon his face.

'Of course, you are right, Great One. To use fear to your advantage, just add more fear. He already has enough that you can play with. Using his own weakness against him. Ha, ha, ha! Yes, this is what we shall do. Everybody, gather round. We have work to do.'

'That's my boy, that's the way to go,' hissed the Illusion. 'Oh, and Asphodel, just to let you know, about what you said earlier, yes I do see you as a fool, just like all human beings. You are but ants, so easily squashed beneath me.'

Lord Asphodel didn't react badly to the Illusion's comments, it only goaded him to not fail this time, for there could be no mistake. Beckoning the two magicians 19 and 84, Lord Asphodel recklessly stamped his cigarette out on both their faces, causing them to yelp in pain.

'Now you two, go and fetch me the Box. I feel it may prove useful against our friend, the Blue Robin.'

'The Box. Yes Sir, right away.'

19 and 84 hurried to the far side of the control room before operating a switch. This opened, what looked like, a type of fridge, revealing a large box made of dark crystal and big enough to contain one person. Upon seeing this, Lord Asphodel rubbed his hands together in glee.

'Do not worry, Great One. Our problems are at an end now. We have the key to their undoing.'

The house of white stone was lit by candles throughout its rooms. The aroma of incense flooded the entire house and there was such a feeling of joy, so infectious, it would have brought a smile to even the hardest of hearts, perhaps even Lord Asphodel. At least we can live in hope. Elia, always a wonderful cook, had prepared a sumptuous meal of Goats Cheese , Sweet Potato and cous cous, which everyone enjoyed. Even Suzanne, though not an actual vegetarian, had found it incredibly appetising. The herbs, which Elia had used to flavour the meal, certainly added to the flavour. They were now seated upon soft chairs, in a large circle around the Genesis Crystal, which continued to glow and pulsate. The seeds of New Earth danced happily within, as they could feel the love and joy within the entire house and they clearly loved responding to it. Everyone sat in silence with David sitting next to Elia. Every lightworker in the room glowed with the intention of pure love. Their eyes were closed as they reached out to the others, to every lightworker, earth angel, indigo, crystal and rainbow child on Mother Earth and on every other world beyond, telling them about the return of the Genesis Crystal, and to prepare for the coming New golden age. It was so exciting that some, like David, found it hard to maintain the spiritual contact, but maintain it they did. David smiled as he saw the excited faces of the crystal and rainbow children across the universe, who were all so happy about this great event, which was finally occurring after all this time. Now there truly would be peace. David loved this experience as he shared a very special bond with all these souls. Star people Lorian and Casper loved working with the star people upon other worlds. The planet they were connecting with was where they had once grown up and lived, so it was lovely to tell their soul group all the wonderful news. Linda, Brian, Tony, Catherine, Crystal and Nina loved working and telling all their fellow incarnated angels and wise ones, about what was going to happen, whilst Elia spoke directly to the council of light on Shambhala, who were imparting powerful instructions on what she needed to do and what she must tell all the others out there. Afterwards, when the meditation session had ended, Elia put on some music, a beautiful piece recorded by some renowned spiritual artiste, with harps and flutes, intermingled with exotic drumbeats, that could have enticed even the shyest person up onto the dance floor. This was truly a time for celebration, and what a party it was.

Jonathan remained somewhat distant and detached. There was something wrong, but what? He had, in fact, pretended to meditate, as he found this hard to do. He hoped no one had noticed, but he suspected that Elia knew. His angels longed to get closer to him, but he was a tough customer. He wished, deep down, that he could join in with the festivities but was plagued by this brooding doubt. Was it a distrust of Elia? Somehow this once mild form of distrust was getting stronger within him, to the point where he heard a voice telling him,

'Be mindful of this woman, is she truly wise? Is she who she says she is? Are any of them to be trusted? You and Suzanne are being hoodwinked, and poor David, what about poor David? He is so innocent, so trusting, do you know that he truly is in danger?' it was Illusion beginning to get to him.

Trying to switch off this constant worry from his mind, Jonathan went out to the kitchen. Perhaps Elia wouldn't mind if he made himself a cup of tea. Taking his I-phone from his pocket, he scrolled through all the local news to see what was happening, whilst waiting for the kettle to boil. He very nearly dropped his phone in sheer horror. On the screen the headline, "WOMAN WANTED IN CONNECTION WITH MURDER IN STRANGE SACRIFICIAL RITUAL." Under the headline was the picture of the suspect, none other than Elia Lotus herself. Jonathan's legs shook and he had to put the phone down for fear of dropping it again. What the hell was going on? This woman, who he had never truly trusted, was a murderer, a member of some dark cult. Reading the article, everything seemed to fit the fear he felt.

'So, this was why I felt the way I did, why I always had my doubts about her. She's nothing but a sick and twisted woman. What can I do? I've got to tell David and Suzanne. I must try to get them away from her, but how?'

Suddenly his phone rang. Picking it up with some trepidation, he answered coyly.

'Hello, who is this?'

'Hello Sir, we are from MI5. We have reason to believe

you and your family are in great danger. It concerns a woman by the name of Lotus. She is wanted in connection with an appalling crime committed earlier this year. We believe you and your family are staying with her and her associates, who are just as dangerous.'

'Yes, I know, we are in her house right now.'

He tried to remain quiet so that no one would hear him as he closed the kitchen door with a violently trembling hand.

'Sir, are you there? It's okay, just try and stay relaxed.' The voice sounded so calm it almost sounded hypnotic.

'Listen, what is your name Sir?'

'My name is Jonathan, Jonathan Joseph.'

'Thank you, Jonathan. We want to help you and your family, but in order for us to do this, you need to help us.'

'What can I do? These people are strange, they glow as if they are lit from the inside, and so does my son. He's not even like my son anymore, he's left his body, and so have all the others.'

'What about anyone else, Sir? Is everybody affected?'

'No, my ex wifes unaffected, like me. It's my son, David, she's done something to him. I've got to do something to help him.'

Jonathan's voice was now desperate.

'We understand, Jonathan. Please, you have to remain calm. It's imperative that you do so, do you understand?'

'I do.'

'You need to leave the house, but do not alert David or his mother. We understand your desire to protect them both, but if you do this it will alert the suspects. Just come out quietly.'

'But where do I go?' queried the distraught man.

'Walk calmly around the corner. We are there right now, waiting for you. You will see a dark coloured van parked there. We will give you a signal, but you must not say anything to anyone. Just come on your own, your son's life depends on it.'

The phone then went quiet and, steadying his nerves, Jonathan made his way into the hall. The lightworkers were still busy partying, listening to the wonderful music. None of them noticed him, not even David or Suzanne, as he slipped out of the front door. He longed to grab both of them and take them to safety. He felt so helpless that he wanted to throttle Elia and call her all the names under the sun, but at least MI5 knew about it. At least they could straighten out the situation. If only Jonathan knew, for just as he was thinking this to himself, the man who he thought was part of MI5 sat next to his partner inside the van. They were cackling to themselves wickedly.

'I can't stand it 19, that was just too easy, what say you?'

'I couldn't agree more 84, the pitiful fool.'

Touching a button on their dashboard, the face of Lord Asphodel appeared on their scanner.

'It is done, my Lord Asphodel, he took the bait. The Great One was right, his fear is so strong.'

'Of course, what else do you expect from these primitives? Once he has come to you, tell him all that we have planned and give him the Black Candle.'

The two magicians nodded in agreement. As Jonathan turned hurriedly around the corner, he saw the dark van, flashing its headlights just as promised. Jonathan approached the vehicle cautiously, for it seemed to emit a sinister energy. Inside his head, Jonathan heard the voices of his angels trying desperately to stop him.

'No, dear one, don't do it. Don't approach them, what are you doing?'

But he preferred to think of them as just his imagination, dismissing them as remnants of his guilt, thinking foolishly that it was he who was betraying David. It was too late. As the blackened window wound down, he saw two smartly dressed, clean shaven men in dark suits and sunglasses.

'Hello, Jonathan. Come close, there isn't much time.'

The voice was so calm and reassuring, it put Jonathan at ease immediately.

'Guys, I can't thank you enough, I just feel so ashamed that I was taken in by this person. I put those I loved in danger.'

'Jonathan, it is an easy mistake to make. She has fooled shrewder men than you, believe me,' said one of the men. 'At least now she and her cohorts can be stopped. This woman is a member of a highly powerful cult that operates underground. Very few people know about it.' The liars continued, 'This cult practises black magic. It has infected her and those she is close to. Now this very magic is affecting your son, causing him to be in the state that you found him in.'

'It's odd you know, because if I didn't know better, I'd say it all looked so lovely, how she looks, how David and the others look. It's like the embodiment of all that is pure,' said Jonathan.

There was a brief pause before one of the men replied,

'Ah, yes that is because this magic makes what is bad appear and seem good. It tricks your senses, not to mention your eyes.'

The two men glanced at each other, as if unsure their story would be bought. Unfortunately, it was, as Jonathan gave them the answer they'd been waiting for.

'Just get my son and his mother away from her. Go in and do your worst.'

Smiling, the driver reached for the dashboard, pulling out a long object.

'This is called the Black Candle, he said, handing it to Jonathan. 'We want you to take this into the house with you. It's the only thing that can save your family now.'

'What does it do?'

'It has the power to reverse the spell that is upon your child, freeing him from danger. It will also protect his mother. As for Lotus and her fellow criminals, it will remove their powers forever and they will no longer be a danger to our society. We can put these murderers behind bars, where they belong.'

'This Black Candle, how does it work and how do you know how to use magic?'

'All you have to do is light the wick, just as you would any candle,' came the reply. 'That's all you have to do to save your loved ones from the evil that woman has become. As for our knowledge of magic, let us just say that we of the MI5, know everything necessary to enable us to fight back against the darkness that grips your world. Now hurry, you are wasting time. We've done all we can. Now it is up to you.'

Jonathan started to turn back to the house of white stone, yet he hesitated. Surely these two men knew what they were talking about? Surely, they meant well? Yet he had felt strangely uneasy the moment they had placed the Black Candle into the palm of his hand. The voices of his angels still persisted in the core of his gut, but Jonathan had shut them out. As fear got the better of him, he saw them as just a nuisance. He continued to run back around the corner. The window of the van wound back up as the two men complimented each other on their deception and waited to be praised by Lord Asphodel, who had re-appeared on the scanner.

'Well done 19 and 84, you shall be rewarded for this quite handsomely.'

'Thank you, our Lord, thank you.'

'Just remember to take the Box with you, as our young lightworker will need a new place to live ha ha ha'.

Inside the house, the joyous party was quietening down. Elia had taught David and Suzanne a new dance, which she had learnt many years ago when she had visited the rural community of Findhorn in Scotland.

'Elia, I've had such fun,' laughed David.

'Me too,' added Suzanne. I don't think I've danced like that in a long time. I shan't be doing that for a while now. I don't think it's done my hips any good.'

'So glad you enjoyed it, dear ones. That dance was one of the highlights of my time at Findhorn. We all had such fun. Linda and Crystal were both there, they called it the Fairy dance.

'I remember, I saw so many fairies come out of the flowers and dance with us,' smiled Linda.

'Yes, there were many nature angels present that day,' laughed Tony. 'It was a weekend not to be forgotten.' Their happy mood was interrupted as Jonathan entered the room, his eyes looking downward, avoiding all eye contact, so that nobody could see into his soul.

'Dad, where were you? We've all been having the most wonderful time.'

'Hmmph, have you now?'

Elia knew something wasn't right, as she already sensed something dark within his energy.

'Jonathan, where have you been? You've missed so much,' smiled Suzanne.

Turning away from them all, keeping his back to them, Jonathan placed the Black Candle on the table in front of him.

'I have been somewhere where I have been shown sense, where I've been made to realise what's truly going on,' came his cold reply.

'Jonathan, I'm afraid I don't know what you mean.'

'Don't you, Elia? Well, all I can say is thank goodness I've found out about you just in time. I'd like you to step away from my son and his mother. David, Suzanne, come and stand beside me, please.'

'Dad, what do you mean? I won't have you talk about my friends like that,' snapped David, feeling confused inside.

'They're not your friends, David. These people, whatever they are, are monsters and she, (pointing to Elia) is a murderer.'

'I beg your pardon. I have never harmed a creature in all my life.'

'You're so good aren't you, lady. I'll give you that, but MI5 have told me that's all about to change.'

Stepping to one side, Elia gazed in total shock at the Black Candle on the table.

Where did you get that?' she screamed. Remove it now!'

'What's the matter, Lotus, frightened of a candle? Scared that it might take away your power? I wonder what would happen if I lit it?'

'Remove it now, you don't know how dangerous it is, to all of us.'

'Dad, no don't!'

It was too late. Jonathan had struck one of the matches and lit the black candle. At first the flame looked the hue of blue, but then it turned into a deep dark black, as an invisible force gripped each of the lightworkers and held them like some huge demonic hand, pulling them high into the air, including Suzanne and Jonathan. It was as if some horrendous black magic, which should have remained locked away, had been unleashed to roam, rampant upon them. David struggled with all his might to break free of this vile force that now threatened them, but to no avail. He tried calling upon Archangel Michael, repeating the mantra to invoke him as he had done before, but nothing happened. All the candles in the house suddenly went out.

'Archangel Michael, help me, help us, why don't you answer me?'

David tried to then call Lady Nada for help, as did all his friends. They had been aware, just five minutes ago, of the angels who had danced with them, enjoying the party. Now they were nowhere to be seen.

'Oh dear, it seems your pretty angels have eluded you,' said a mocking voice, as the two men smugly entered the room. 'I'd save your breath, Blue Robin, and that goes for all of you. Your guardians cannot help you now. The Black Candle is lit, its magic blocks them like an astral brick wall, just as it blocks your ability to communicate with them.'

The forms of the two smartly dressed men began to flicker, like lights going on and off, before revealing their true magician forms of 19 and 84.

'How good it is to be back in our true appearance. All that sincerity was beginning to do my head in.'

'Mine too.'

'You lied to me,' Jonathan squawked, as they were all gripped by the throat.

'Yes, indeed we did. You were so easy to frighten, so predictable mortal. The Black Candle does indeed take away your power. It also robs you of the spiritual protection around your house of white stone. It's the only thing that could.' All it took was you to betray them all.

'It was used during the dark times of Atlantis, just before the fall, and helped create the dark arts and brought into fruition the ability to curse another and promote damnation,' gasped Elia, struggling to speak.

'Quite right, woman of Lotus. My, hasn't she got a good memory? Not even Archangel Michael's psychic cape can withstand it. From now on, all communication with the beings of light is impossible.'

Looking about the room, with their eyeless features, the two magicians set their sights upon the Genesis Crystal, which glowed in the centre, still radiating a purity, that the Black Candle could not extinguish. Tuning inwards through their telepathy, 19 and 84 contacted their feared leader.

'Lord Asphodel, the lightworkers are under the Black Candle's power and we have found the Genesis Crystal.'

'Excellent. Take possession of that crystal immediately and bring it to me, Oh, how I have waited for this moment for centuries.'

'Indeed, our Lord.'

The two magicians cautiously approached the glistening object, like two wolves, strategically planning to move in for the kill.

'No, please don't touch it,' Elia tried to shout.

Frustration, mixed with anger crossed her face as all the lightworkers looked on in horror. They were like helpless parents who could not protect their defenceless infant from the predators. 19 picked up the crystal before handing it to 84.

'We have it, Lord Asphodel. We are about to return to Erratus Manor, but what should we do with the lightworkers, kill them?'

'No, I want them alive, especially the woman, Lotus. I want my once fair queen to join me. Bring them all back. They shall make such model prisoners, except the Blue Robin. You know what to do.'

'Yes, Lord Asphodel. What about the boy's parents. Should they join him?'

'No, I think they'd be better off coming to Erratus. They've seen too much to possibly be allowed freedom now.'

The two magicians turned to face their prisoners.

'You are all invited to be Lord Asphodel's guests at Erratus Manor.'

'Guests or prisoners?' said Elia.

Even at her most powerless, she would not show any sign of weakness to the magicians. But the mere mention of Jack Asphodel sent such conflicting feelings coursing through her, for the wounds had never gone away.

'I'm afraid, your Majesty, that how Lord Asphodel conducts his business is up to him and no-one else. Unfortunately, you are not invited, Blue Robin. Instead, Lord Asphodel has decided you shall have a new home in which to spend the rest of your life.'

Pointing to the Black Box, which had followed 19 and 84 into the room. The magicians uttered a spell.

'Ish, nor, vie, sah, sac ne vor hye' as a hurricane noise was heard coming from the Box.

David started to be pulled nearer and nearer to the object, much to the horror of those around him. Poor Suzanne screamed.

'Davie, no, oh no.' She fought like a helpless rag doll, kicking and punching at the air around her. 'Elia, please tell them to stop.'

Jonathan was beside himself, but all he could say was,

'I'm sorry, truly I am so sorry,' before he too punched and kicked, trying to reach his son, but to no avail.

'Please, you can't do this to him. Let him go, I, once your queen of Atlantis, command you!'

'We are sorry, oh queen, but you see we only take orders from our king Lord Asphodel now.'

It was no good, David was powerless against the force of the wind, as it sucked him nearer and nearer. The two doors at the front of the Box flew open, lightening and roaring grey vortexes could be seen inside.

'David, try and hang on to something and don't let go, don't let go!' screamed his dad.

It was no good, there was nothing to hang on to. Looking up one last time at his parents and all the others, he tried to remember their faces, accepting the possibility that this could be the last time he would see them. He shouted with all his strength,

'I LOVE YOU.'

Then he was gone, his body swept into the black crystal Box. His loved ones stared in shock, as they watched David's body being swept away into the great currents of the vortex. Lit by lightning, his tiny frame became smaller and smaller, until they could see him no longer. The entrance suddenly slammed shut, and all was quiet again. The only sound was the sobbing of Suzanne and Jonathan, as their only child had been taken from them. The magicians picked up the Black Candle and the Genesis Crystal and departed with the Lightworkers, who were being pulled like dogs on a leash towards Erratus Manor.

13

LIVING IN A BOX

When David opened his eyes, (he had kept them shut whilst he had spun further and further down the vortex, afraid his entire soul would be ripped apart), he found himself in his bedroom. It was his room, no doubt about it. The walls were the same, the bed, his curtains, wardrobe, all seemed just as it should be. Everything seemed intact. Each of his chakras had stopped glowing, as if turned off, and he now wore normal everyday pyjamas, instead of his wonderful purple, tunic and blue cape. Sitting up to gather his thoughts, he tried to remember what had happened. Had he really slept for such a long time? It certainly seemed like it, for he could not remember anything, except saying goodnight to his mum, the night before, and her telling him not to worry. Suddenly his door opened. Suzanne walked in with a steaming cup of tea.

'Hi Davie, how are you my darling?'

'Mum, uh good morning. How long have I been asleep?'

'Well, I think it's been about ten hours. Let's see,' she replied, reaching for the clock on David's windowsill. It was 8.30am. 'It's still early David, I always love it when you give yourself an early night. Anyway, I've made you your tea. Try and drink it while it's still hot.'

David took the cup and began sipping the hot drink. It was very nice, just how his mum always made it, always putting a little sugar in his tea and coffee, which Suzanne always insisted was needed to give him energy. David's mum opened the curtains, revealing the early morning sun. There was not a cloud in the sky, and already the garden was coming alive with the beautiful sight of summer flowers. Suzanne gave her son a loving smile, as if she was surprised by her son's puzzled demeanour. David smiled back at her. Somehow, everything seemed so perfect, felt so right. What had happened the day before? He tried hard to think but he simply could not remember. Yet it didn't seem important. Who cares what happened yesterday? It was a gorgeous day, everything was great. A familiar voice was heard calling from downstairs.

'Hello, my little family.' He always said that whenever he greeted them. 'You alright David, son?' The young man shot from his bed and ran to the landing to see the familiar face of his father smiling up at him. 'You alright, youngster? Hey, do you know we might be going out for a picnic later, as I've got the day off. What do you think?'

'A picnic? What, you and me?'

That's a bit different from going swimming like we usually do, thought the young man.

'No silly, I meant all of us together. We always go everywhere together, you, your mum and me. We're the Three Musketeers, remember?'

The Three Musketeers? It had seemed such a long time ago that his dad had said that. Taking Davie in her arms, Suzanne lovingly kissed him on his cheek.

'Davie, you are so silly, what are we going to do with you?'

'But mum, you and dad, you split up, didn't you?'

Even that now seemed difficult to remember.

'No, David, we have never separated,' said Suzanne.

'Why on earth would you even say that? I'd never leave either of you, not now, not ever,' came Jonathan. 'You and your mum are the best thing that ever happened to me, the only things in my life that I've ever been proud of.' David appeared to react to this, it was like he was hearing what he had always wanted to hear. Somehow, he knew it, without knowing how. He flung his arms around his dad and embraced him tightly, for he did not want to let him go, nor his mum. 'How about we all go out for that picnic now?' smiled Johnathan.

David looked up, smiling at his dad.

'Sounds good to me.'

'Great, then get up and get washed, darling, and we can all go out and enjoy ourselves.'

Hurrying into the bathroom and feeling like a kid again, David quickly washed. He was excited, no doubt about it. It felt as if he was living in a dream, it was just brilliant, yet everything felt real. To hell with it, his mum and dad were together, they were still a family. What had he been thinking of earlier? Had it all been just some sort of nightmare? He went into his bedroom to dress, looking at the walls around him. Something didn't seem right, but what was it? Everything seemed normal enough, but wait, didn't he used to have something on them? Oh yes, pictures, that's what it was. What were they? What did they look like? Images of what he thought they were, tried desperately to flash across his mind, but the pictures were hazy. It was most annoying, almost as if they were trying to spoil his new-found happiness.

'No, go away!' David found himself beginning to shout at the very air around him.

'David, are you alright?' called Suzanne, with concern in her voice.

He rushed out of the bedroom, relieved to hear his mum's voice.

'Mum, can I ask you something?'

'Yes, of course darling, what is it?'

'Do I, did I have any pictures up in my bedroom?'

Suzanne's reply was simple.

'No.'

'What never? Not any at all?'

'Well, I think you used to have posters up when you were little, you know ones of Superman, Batman, Batgirl, Wonder Woman.'

'Yes, those I remember, but none after that? None of, oh what were they called?'

His mother's voice was adamant.

'No, I'm afraid you've never had any pictures up since those superhero posters. You complained about all the blue-tack which messed up your wallpaper. We decorated your room that lovely off white that you loved so much.

After that, you never wanted another picture up ever again.'

'Oh, I see. I could have sworn I'd had something else up.'

'No, never. Come on, it's time for the picnic. Your father's just putting some oil into the car, then we can all go off and have an absolutely wonderful time.'

Outside, the weather was so warm, so delightful. Birds chirruped in the lush green trees, and the air smelled of fresh cut grass, as they got into his dad's car. David felt it seemed almost too good to be true. Why did he have this strange, almost distrustful feeling? Oh, what was he saying? How could he doubt the love he had for his mum and dad? They were happy, he was happy. Surely this doubtful feeling would go away soon. What was all the worry about pictures for anyway, they were only angel pictures. Angel pictures. That sounded somehow familiar.

'Mum, Dad, what are angels?' said David, inquisitively.

'Angels? They are mythical beings invented by some religious folk to make you feel better. A nice metaphor,' said his dad, 'but not at all practical, and you have never believed in them, you just believe in what you see. That's the best way.'

David sank back into his seat. Despite all the glorious weather, he found himself feeling depressed, for he knew he did not like what he had been told, almost like he knew they were wrong. Something wasn't right, but what? He closed his eyes, as if to shut out all that was around him. He would only open them once they had arrived at their destination. Perhaps the picnic would help take his mind off it all.

Watching the scene from a miniaturised version of the Box that he held within his hand, Lord Asphodel smiled, satisfied with what he had witnessed. He shut the lid and looked upwards at the Illusion, who also seemed to show great satisfaction through his yellow green pupils.

'We've done it, master. The Blue Robin has been taken care of, no longer shall he pose a threat to you.'

'Yes, you have done well, my son. He will never be able to leave his prison. He is completely baffled,' came the Illusion's spine tingling voice.

They were interrupted by 19 and 84, who had returned, holding the Genesis Crystal, with what looked like two black tongs, for they had found the crystals energy of love so overwhelming that they decided not to touch it. They thought this was the best way to handle it. Warily, looking upon the beautiful ball of light, each of the magicians gingerly crept around it. Just like 19 and 84 had done, forming a crowd around it, each one whispering to another a word of fear and distrust about the crystal. It was easy to see just how frightened they were of it. Lord Asphodel remained upon his Throne as if frozen. He, too, possessed an uneasiness at the sight of the Genesis Crystal, as it glowed undeterred by the engulfing darkness.

'At last, the Genesis Crystal is at our mercy. How long we have all waited for this moment, but then everything comes to he who waits.' Raising his hand, Lord Asphodel ordered the prisoners to be brought in. The Black Candle floated into the room, followed by Elia, Jonathan,

Suzanne and all the other lightworkers, still held captive by its power as they hung within the air. 'My dear, how lovely to see you again,' Lord Asphodel said to Elia, who said nothing but looked upon him coldly. She tried to evade the sight of him by turning her head away, but the grip around her throat prevented her from doing so. Looking around at the captive lightworkers, Asphodel gently nodded as if satisfied with the number they had caught. 'You will make such pretty decorations for my master' he said, pointing upwards to the Illusion and its Wounds. Their ugly, distorted faces glared down at Elia and her friends, which made the lightworkers wince in disgust. Suzanne and Jonathan looked in horror at the hideous Wounds.

'What are they, Elia?'

'They are the Wounds, Suzanne, those who exist within the cycle which keeps much of humanity in duality. It's due to these Wounds not being healed that there are still wars, hatred and conflict going on, thus the cycle remains intact, causing history to repeat itself.'

'I apologise for the way I brought you and your friends here, Elia, but I knew you might never accept such a formal invitation.' said Lord Asphodel, coldly.

'Why are you doing this, Jack? You have me, I am here. Why don't you let the others go? They can't harm you.'

'I'm sorry, Elia, but goodness is such a dangerous thing. To release such lightworkers after they have seen so much, would be quite wrong. This is the penalty you all pay for going against your true rulers. But now we have the Genesis Crystal, which we can't thank the Blue Robin's father for enough.'

Jonathan looked ashamed at the fact that he'd betrayed all these people, and his own son.

'Elia, please forgive me. I am so sorry for what I have done' he said apologetically.

'You were a complete, idiot,' said Suzanne sharply. 'Have you any idea of the mess you have got us into?'

Elia's soft voice cut in.

'No, Suzanne, don't blame Jonathan. It's alright, dear one. You simply reacted through fear. The Illusion saw this and realised it could be used as a weapon against us all. By sensing doubt in you, they amplified this, making lies up about me.'

'But I saw a headline about you saying that you were wanted for murder and involved within a cult that carried out sacrificial rituals. How did they manage to do that? How did they put it on my I-phone?'

'Oh, it wasn't difficult really,' said a creepy voice. It was the weaver. 'You see, I was simply able to weave a little lie. It isn't much bother, I've done it at least a million times before. You just tell a juicy tale about the person you are trying to tarnish. This induces fear within the reader, which results in paranoia, allowing you to control whoever it is you are trying to manipulate. As for being on your I-phone, we just planted an optical illusion upon your screen. You humans are so gullible, you believe everything you read. Few of you bother to question anything. The rest was carried out by 19 and 84, whom you met earlier.'

'You sick, twisted person,' snapped Jonathan, 'You must be the ultimate spin doctor.'

'Thank you,' replied the weaver, taking it as a compliment.

'You, who have tricked humanity for centuries, trying to keep us in thrall, keeping the veil of corruption and the threat of war alive, through the Wounds, it is beyond diabolical.' shouted Incarnated Angel Linda.

'ENOUGH, lightworker,' screeched Lord Asphodel, 'Now that you are in our power, you have no right to speak. Freedom of speech no longer exists here, not that it ever did. We just wanted you all to believe that was so.'

'And what about my son?' Suzanne spoke defiantly to Lord Asphodel. 'What have you done to my son?'

'Uh, you mean the Blue Robin? You must be his mother. How sweet your concern is, if only I had someone like you to love and guide me.'

'David, his name is David,' cried Suzanne. 'Your men put him in that thing, that box. Where has he gone? I want to know.'

'Your son is alive and well, just out of my way. In fact, he's in the safest place possible.'

'I want him released. You must have the means to bring him back to me'

'You seem to think that what I have done is some sort of punishment. Why? I've actually done him a favour.'

'A favour? Elia, what does he mean?'

'I'll let the noble Elia explain.'

Lord Asphodel spoke with a tongue dipped in venom, which struck the heart of Elia like a plethora of tiny daggers.

'That box traps the soul into a fake reality. It is the magicians' matrix. Once inside, David would have developed spiritual amnesia. He has no recollection of what he has experienced with me, no memory of who he truly is. He doesn't know that the angels exist. He would have forgotten completely about the Genesis Crystal. He is as cut off from his higher self as we are to our angels, due to the Black Candle.'

'Very good, Elia,' clapped Lord Asphodel. 'Yes, I suppose that's it in a nutshell, although you haven't told them about the positive side. Such negativity, indeed.'

'I'd rather not,' returned Elia.

'What positive? Is he alone, all by himself?'

'Suzanne, please don't force me to....'

'Oh, very well, Elia, if you won't tell them the good news, then I certainly shall,' cried Lord Asphodel, buoyantly. 'Your son is not alone. You, mummy and daddy, are both with him.'

'With him? How can we be?' queried Suzanne.

'What are you talking about, you swine?' Jonathan demanded.

'Well, I say you are both with him, that is your digital duplicates, downloaded from David's brain. And what's more, you never ever parted, you are still a couple.' Lord Asphodel seemed to sadistically be enjoying telling them this.

'How can any being stoop so low?' thought Elia to herself.

'The Box reads into the wants, needs and desires of the person. It then projects these wants into a physical form, such as the two of you. Your digital copies act and behave the way he wants them to. They will continue to cloud his mind of any scintilla of spiritual belief and, due to his love for you both, I doubt he will cause much of a problem. So, you see, I have given him the best. The Box has given him the thing he never had, stability, and a father who never left him.'

Jonathan's eyes welled up with tears, as did Suzanne's.

'But it's not the truth. You are sick, Jack,' said Elia.

'You were quite a fool to open your heart to me, Elia back in Atlantis and I was an even bigger fool for allowing my heart to open up to you!'

'You mean that you and he were once an item?' exclaimed Suzanne.

'Yes, but it's ancient history now,' sobbed Elia.

Jonathan glared harshly at Asphodel.

'You don't know our son. He loves us both the world and over, but I know him, he will see through the ruse you've put him in. He's an argumentative little wotsit, he's not going to just sit back and take this reality you've cooked up for him. Whatever it is you've put him under, he will work out that it is all a hoax.'

Lord Asphodel gazed upon Jonathan.

'Be that as it may, he shall not survive the storm.'

'What's the storm?'

'Our Box comes with a self-destruct system. If your precious son shows any form of resistance, the virtual world he is in will collapse around him, sweeping his soul into a singularity beyond imaginings. It will destroy him.'

Suzanne could take no more. All her emotions rushed to the surface, as she started to weep bitterly. All the lightworkers, especially Elia, tried desperately to comfort her, but they were all held firmly in place by the magic of the Black Candle, which had perched itself near to Lord Asphodel, sitting impassively on his throne. Realising they could not help her physically, each of the lightworkers sent out rays of love from their hearts to Suzanne. It would have been more powerful if they had not been suppressed by the Illusion's magic. Jonathan felt his hands shaking violently with anger. He longed to strike this evil man down. He was almost frothing at the mouth.

'Listen to me, you damn, malicious fruitcake. If you harm our son in any way, I'll kill you. I'll tear you limb from limb, do you hear me? I'll hunt you down, I'll go to the police, or the government. I'll tell them all about you and your cronies. You're just a bunch of cowards, hiding in the shadows. Threatening, bullying cowards, who try and make people, who stand up to you, disappear!'

Asphodel paused for a moment, as if shocked by the stupidity of this man who dared argue with him. Raising his hand towards Jonathan, he pulled him straight towards him, until they were almost touching face to face.

'You poor, pathetic tiny human. Do you really think I am frightened by your churlish insults? Your threats don't bother me. I could just snap my fingers and all of you would be gone. You are like clay within my grasp. I can mould and twist your entire lives within my hands and I have already made you disappear from this world. Believe me, you're never again going to see your world, never. Do you understand? For we are soon going to be taking steps to ensure your footprints are washed away forever. That's how malleable we, the magicians, are. Nothing can change that now that we have the crystal. As for the government that you intend to alert, well there may be a problem with that. You see, I run the government. I tell your Prime Minister what to do next. I am the secret voice that controls all the leaders of your world. So, you see, one way or another, it all works out to mine, and my master's, advantage. You have no freedom, it's all a trick.'

With that, Asphodel raised his hand again, controlling the magic which pushed Jonathan backwards so fast, that he hit his head on the wall, leaving him stunned for a good few minutes. What a waste of Creation muttered Lord Asphodel to himself.

'Jonathan,' screamed Suzanne. 'No, I beg you, please don't hurt him.'

'Never beg to a bully, dear one,' said Elia softly. 'You are stronger than him, always know that.'

'Shut up, Elia!' retorted Lord Asphodel. 'As for you, you mewling quim, any more of your whimpering, and you'll be next.'

'Come, it's okay, be strong,' said Elia. 'Let him do his worst, for he won't be able to hide forever.'

Rising from his throne, Lord Asphodel walked towards the Genesis Crystal, which still pulsated, held by the black tongs.

'The time has come, my friends. The crystal must be placed into The Well of Suppression so that it can no longer be a threat to our control.'

One of the magicians activated a control on their console, as the centre of the floor opened, revealing a huge, deep dark well. 19 and 84 held the Genesis Crystal with the tongs, over the black hole.

'No Jack, don't do it. Don't put the crystal in there. It is a gift from the Creator to all of us. It can allow light to come in and free us all. It carries within the seeds of new earth!'

'The new earth, Elia?

'Yes, one where we would become mere nothings. We, who have ruled this world for millennia, would be reduced to being like insects upon a leaf, just like all of you.'

'The cycle of my master has spun for centuries, why should it suddenly stop now?'

'For love, Jack, love is coming to this earth, stronger than ever before. You must let go of control, before it is too late.'

A loud rumble came from down below, as astral vapour rose from the well. The crystal shuddered as if trying to break free from this grip of darkness.

'Listen to her Jack, you have no choice.' It was Akash, speaking through the crystal. 'You think that by burying the Genesis Crystal, you can stop the Creator's love and light from returning. Well, you can't, for no matter how much you try to hide or bury the truth, to try to suppress it, it will always be there, waiting to return, like the earth's great star. It is always there, even when tucked away by the darkest of clouds. No matter how the darkness tries to engulf it, the light will never be eclipsed.'

'You know, frankly I'm a little disappointed in you, Akash, placing all your trust in a weak and feeble boy, one so easily taken in,' chided Lord Asphodel.

'All shall not be lost. This madness can still be undone,' came the hopeful voice of Akash. 'The Blue Robin just needs to learn how to fly.'

'Don't listen to Akash's piffle, Asphodel. You know what needs to be done,' hissed the Illusion. 'Have I not been like a parent to you?'

'Let the lightworkers go, Jack Asphodel,' came Akash.
'Let them be free. The time of control is finite. You are holding on to the ideals of an outdated nightmare. Jack, please. You know it is the truth. Take the crystal away from the hole.'

'NO, DROP IT IN, ASSPHODEL, DROP IT IN NOW! DROP IT IN, NOW, I COMMAND YOU!'

The tongs holding the crystal were now glowing molten red and getting hotter.

'Lord Asphodel, we cannot contain it much longer, what must we do?'

Lord Asphodel hesitated for a moment, for even in his jaded mind, ridden with darkness, cracks of light had started to appear. What should he do? Should he finally let go, every word of Akash, words which had begun to seep through, trying to cleanse the smog that had clouded his heart for far too long? But his master, was the one he always listened to, he must not allow love to make him weak, for when he had once allowed it in, it had hurt him. He couldn't have that, not again. No, he must be strong, surely that was the right way?

'Let it go, drop it, drop it now!'

19 and 84 finally released the tongs from the crystal. For a few moments the Genesis Crystal remained hanging above the hole, as if trying to cling on, but eventually the astral mists engulfed it, weaving around it as if tying it in a net, before taking it down into the deep, dark abyss, where its light and the seeds would be suppressed, robbing the world of the great hope that it promised. The lightworkers' hearts fell so low at this point, even the magicians seemed to be highly fazed, exhausted and

relieved that the ordeal was finally over. Lord Asphodel sweated with exhaustion.

'Close it, close it quick. I do not wish to see it.'

He took one last glance, as the floor closed up again. Lord Asphodel was somehow affected deep within by a faint sense of remorse.

'What shall we do now, Elia? With the crystal suppressed, there is no hope, surely,' said the lightworkers.

'There is always hope, my friends. We cannot help David anymore but Prayer can, for in Shambhala, all the angels and masters are watching this. They wouldn't want us to give up so easily. Remember Akash's words. The Creator's light is like our sun, its light shall never go out, even in the darkest of situations.'

Turning their hearts inwards to pray, each of the lightworkers reached out to Shambhala for help, something the magicians' magic could not stop. Elia prayed for the freedom of the Blue Robin, as did Suzanne, for Elia knew that all hope lay with David. The lightworkers' prayers passed through the barren threshold of Erratus Manor, escaping the dark dimension up into the clouds and into the universe, as every lightworker throughout the cosmos, was now informed of what had happened. In distant worlds the children heard them and joined in the Prayers thus increasing their strength and echoing throughout the Cosmos like a powerful, resounding drum. Every single one prayed to the God of all gods and goddesses.

The beautiful, humble prayers passed into the light, turning into tiny shining bubbles, each one carrying the wishes and best intentions of the lightworkers from all over the galaxy, before making their way into the glorious realm of Shambhala. The plethora of bubbles were received by the two glowing wise ones at the entrance of the Temple of Truth, who took the menagerie of prayers into the great hall. The ascended masters stood around the ball of Mother Earth, whilst all the archangels led by Michael, hovered directly above. Extreme concern showed on their faces, as the eyes of the earth mother, Gaia wept tears of azure blue, for they indeed knew about what had happened. Mother Mary caressed the earth mother tenderly, trying to comfort our beautiful world, as tears from her eyes dropped into the oceans of Earth.

'She weeps, dear ones, due to feeling the darkness of her children and their inhumanity to the lightworkers.'

'Indeed, Mother. Their negativity is strong, no question, and is hurtful to witness,' said Sananda. 'However, we must all hold onto hope and trust the word of The One.'

Each of the masters nodded in agreement.

'The One would not have guided the Blue Robin and Elia, nor all their friends, to come so far, to then be defeated,' said the Buddah, 'for there must be a higher plan behind all of this. We must trust in the Creator's wisdom, as much as in his word.'

'Here, here,' they all said in unison.

'Dear sweet masters, we bring you the prayers of all lightworkers,' said the shining wise ones as they came into the vast room.

'Thank you, sweet ones,' came Archangel Michael's upbeat voice.

The prayers floated in the air before coming to rest upon the hands of every master, archangel and angel, gazing lovingly at the prayer bubbles, hearing the voices of many, energising the love vibration.

'Help David to escape from the prison he is in, please, dear God, masters and angels. Let the Blue Robin fulfil his divine mission. Let the magicians see the error of their ways. Help them to heal the darkness within themselves. Please, please great teachers. May Elia be safe. Let them be released, change the magicians' minds. Help them find their hearts. Please help our friends. Let David's mum and dad be alright. Help send David hope so that he shall, once again, see the light and get out of the Box.'

So many beautiful voices, each one united in one great prayer of love, an ultimate prayer for the divine plan to succeed, and for God's will to be done. No judgement, no blame, just cosmic pure love.

'This is how we can help the Blue Robin,' smiled Sananda.

He was about to say more when a huge thundering sound of erupting water was heard. It was Akash. He had left Atlantis to join the others within the Temple. Akash moved just as easily as he had done within the Akashic, floating or flying upon the air of Heaven, entering the Temple of Truth without any effort.

'Greetings, Akash,' they all called, bowing their heads, to which the mighty whale humbly greeted them, so powerful and yet so gentle.

Archangel Michael kissed the great being just below Akash's blowhole.

'Greetings to you all, my dear friends,' came the peaceful voice. 'I have seen all that has happened. My consciousness has been blocked from getting through to

Elia and the other lightworkers, as the magicians have suppressed the Genesis Crystal. I tried to reach Jack Asphodel and I could sense his redundant light flickering within him, trying to awaken, but he's afraid and continues to hide behind Illusion, still seeing it as his master. And David, I believe they succeeded in apprehending him?'

'Yes, Akash, he is trapped in the Box, within the magicians' matrix, blinded by the fake reality,' said Lady Nada, sadly. 'I have tried to reach him but can only do so faintly, for within their matrix our power fades.'

'And Elia, she and the others have all been captured?' enquired Akash.

'Yes, the magicians' used the Black Candle against them, which has blocked us from being able to reach them,' said Christia, Elia's guardian angel.

'The One has consulted with me, Akash responded. 'Azna/Om says the final pieces are in place and that there is a way we can stop this, that we can save the Blue Robin from the Box.'

'Yes, Akash, we have felt it within these prayers,' Sananda said, holding up the beautiful bubbles within his hand, as did every being of light. 'For within these, lies the answer to our own prayer. Each one of these generates enough love for us to transcend all barriers, even the ones fashioned by darkness, like the Box.'

'Dear Sananda, great Lord Michael, dear masters, look!' cried the excited voices of the shining beings. 'There are more prayers coming.'

At that moment the light within the Temple became even brighter. Hundreds more prayer bubbles floated through into the Great Hall. No, not hundreds but thousands upon thousands, all sent with pure intention from hearts across the cosmos.

'Ah-ha,' laughed Sananda, 'Will you look at these.'

'Yes, my brother, the hearts of the universe, so bright around us. This is perfect,' exclaimed Archangel Michael. 'If we focus together, we can use these prayers to open a bridge of light, which will enable us to penetrate the Box and locate David.'

'But our rainbow bridges have never ventured this far into darkness, and the storm within is merciless to any being,' sighed Krishna.

'Indeed, it will be difficult, but with enough focused intention, our light will be able to get in just enough, so that we can generate a small strong beacon of hope, that David can get to,' beamed Michael.

Sananda, once again cradled the lamb that never left his master's side, staying, at all times, by his feet or close to his heart.

'We must do this, whatever the dangers involved. It's the only way. Half of it has already been achieved by the lightworkers prayers. Thanks to them, we can get through.'

'And I shall do my best to make the obstacle as small as can be,' said the ascended master Ganesh.

'Yes, Ganesh, please do. That's all we can do at this moment.'

Akash then spoke.

'Come, my dear ones, it is time to form our circle.' Great Archangels come all of you.

Each of the ascended masters and Archangels came together in one absolutely vast circle.

'Sananda, Buddah, Krishna, Ganesh, Quan Yin, Lady Nada, Mother Mary, Mohammed, Moses, Sita, Tara, in all your forms green, white and red. Yogonanda, Babaji, White Eagle, Pavarti, Gandhi, Mother Teresa, Athena, with your owl, Zeus, Aphrodite, Apollo, Venus, Lord Kuthami, Lord Mattreya, Horus, Maat, Osiris, Artemis, Diana, Jupiter, Paul the Venetian, Solomon, Sanat Kunara, Serapis Bey, St. Germain, Spirit of Christmas, Pan, Green Man, Saints of all paths, Ashtar within the mothership, Lady Liberty and Lady of Justice, Portia, Iris, goddess-maker of all rainbows, Aurora of the Dawn, every being of the light present, let us focus upon these prayers, especially the ones that are focused upon the Blue Robin. Let us concentrate. Our true love must reach all dimensions, especially those where the energies are so low, for these places are where our light is needed most. Melcheizedeck, my ancient brother, Lord Lanto, our light must give hope to all in the dark. The great whale swam within the air, circling calmly in the masters' circle. Holding the prayer bubbles up to the great light, each of the beings felt the great love of God fill the entire Temple of Truth. The One's love was always present here but in this moment, the One's presence was felt like never before. Beautiful rainbow coloured rays called the Chohan, flowed from the masters' third eyes and heart centres, going into the prayer bubbles.

'Creator of all, help us send your light into the darkness, known as the Box. Help us to reach Blue Robin. Help us to let him see the truth. Help him find a way out. Help him to remember,' the masters chanted together.

The rainbow rays came together, creating a kind of wormhole entrance.

'It's working,' cried Michael. 'Dear Creator, thank you, thank you!'

A square shape began to appear, it's image blurry at first, but finally it became clear. It was the Box.

'Okay, Nada, it is up to you, as David's guardian, to go and reach inwards. We can hold the Box for a while, as the prayer energy is so strong, but even so, it will not be long before your presence is detected. You must hurry,' said Sananda.

'Do not fret, my sweet Sananda. I shall return. Take the lifeline with you. It will enable you to breach the matrix and talk to David,' said Akash.

Lady Nada reached into the dark prison after throwing a long silver cord into it. This was the only thing that would connect the angel to her own reality.

'I must go, also,' said Archangel Michael. 'Akash, I have always been a source of strength for David. He will benefit from my presence.' I am very powerful with him.

'True, then go, Michael. Our love goes with you. The masters and your fellow Archangels will use the prayers of light to create a beacon of hope. Once David denies the existence of the matrix, you know it will self-destruct, revealing the Box's deathtrap?'

'Yes, I do.'

'Very well, warrior of light. You know what to look for.' The masters looked on, with calm concern, as the great archangel went into the Box. 'Now we must wait and hold on to these beautiful prayers.'

David had, by this point, returned home from the picnic. It had been a pleasant enough time, a great beauty spot. The hamper that Suzanne had brought with them had contained the most delicious delicacies. All of David's favourite food and drink had been packed especially for him. Throughout the day, David had been terribly spoilt. He felt like a king. Yet, despite looking up into the deep blue sky, whilst laying upon the fresh grass, not seeing a cloud in sight, this just didn't feel real. The food and drink, although very nice, seemed somehow artificial, as if he was eating and drinking what it was supposed to be, rather than what it truly was. This was such a strange feeling. Why did he feel like this? Surely this was not how it should be? This was, arguably, the happiest day of his life, yet why did a voice inside him keep telling him it was wrong? David didn't dare utter a word of this to his parents, for they seemed so happy. He hadn't seen them like this in a long time and they were together. Why spoil such a moment in time? He wished he could have taken a picture of them , but at least he would remember this day in his memory. It was odd that neither Suzanne nor Jonathan felt like he did. They seemed perfectly content, and acted so laid back, almost too laid back. For that matter everyone did. People went around mowing their lawns with an almost robotic look upon their faces, they for some reason just did not look natural.

Returning to the house during early evening, it was still light outside. Jonathan and Suzanne sat down to watch the television. It was news time and David had decided to watch it with them. All the headlines had been so positive. How nice it was to see news involving good things, it was about time. Yet it just somehow wasn't right the way the newsreaders announced events, the way they behaved, as if they were well robots. The way they mimicked the others actions, made them look like clones at best. Everything seemed a bit synthetic, with no real substance. As David continued to watch the endless parade of artificial, sugar-coated headlines, he felt almost as if he were a clone too, as though he was conforming to some huge untruth. He looked at his mum and dad, who continued to stare at the TV as if they were hypnotised zombies. What was going on? A voice suddenly interrupted David's thoughts.

'David, please leave the room and come upstairs.'

Who was this? No one else could have got into the house, it was impossible. The voices continued, yet somehow, David didn't feel afraid. He seemed happy to hear them. It felt as if they were genuine old friends whom he'd not seen for ages. He felt relieved, in fact. Leaving his mum and dad on the sofa, he climbed the stairs, following the direction of the voices. As he walked into his bedroom, he called out to them,

'Who are you? What do you want?'

'David,' responded the voices, 'It is us. It's me, Nada, and Archangel Michael.'

'Nada, Michael? I don't know you. Why can't I see you?' Suddenly he saw, to his astonishment, the forms of Nada and Michael, very faintly. Their powers were too limited, inside the Box, for him to see them properly. 'Nada, of course, Lady Nada and you Archangel Michael. I remember, you're my friends. But I don't know how I know this?'

'David, thank goodness you remember us. Had it not been for all the lightworkers across the universe praying for you, we would never have been able to see you again.'

Michael and Nada reached out to David, wrapping him in a loving embrace. It felt lovely, and despite the cuddles he'd shared with both his mum and dad, this felt real.

'David, you must come with us. We've come to take you home.'

'Home? I am home, this is my house. What do you mean?'

This was all very puzzling.

'You think this is your home because you've been made to think that it is so,' said Nada, softly.

'David, do you remember anything before you found yourself here?' asked Michael.

'Well, come to think of it, I've not really thought about it much, but no, no I don't.'

'This is because, dear one, you have spiritual amnesia. This happened the moment you were put into the Box.'

'The Box? Do you mean my home?'

The archangel gently shook his head.

'The Box is the reality you are in now. This looks like your home, but it is all part of the Illusion. Everything around you appears to be the same, but it isn't. You are existing in a virtual world. You're basically living a lie.'

David drew in a very deep breath, struggling to process what he had just been told. He walked over to sit on his bed, his hands clenched at the covers as he could not bear to think that all this was not real. Nada sat down next to him, taking his hand, releasing it from the covers, holding it in hers.

'It can't be fake. I know it can't be! If it was virtual, I'd be able to put my hands through the walls and walk through them like a spirit.'

'We are sorry, David, but we do not lie to you. This place isn't even a house, it's a digitally enhanced projection, downloaded from your mindset.'

'But I went to Southend seafront today for a picnic. I sat on grass, I ate food and had drink,' the boy argued.

'The magicians' technology feeds off all your wants, needs and desires, David, creating a reality that has always been familiar to you, a reality that also sells you what you may have always wanted, but never had in your actual life.'

'Even you, deep down on a very obscure level, know this to be true,' added Lady Nada, 'for have you not felt there was a superficiality to the day that you have had?'

Thinking about what he'd been told, David was quiet for a few moments.

'Yes, nothing has seemed authentic.'

'On a soul level, you are picking up upon the fraudulence of this environment,' said the archangel.

'But what about my mum and dad? They're real, they're both here with me. If I was trapped, how come they both seem fine? Surely they would know?'

Somehow, David knew in his heart, that he wasn't going to like the answer. Both Michael and Nada looked deeply, lovingly at the Blue Robin. This was going to be difficult, even for an angel, to explain.

'They are not real David, they are downloaded from your mind by the matrix, just like everything else.'

'But they're together, they're together all the time, just like they used to be.'

Kneeling down next to the boy, Michael placed his hand upon David's shoulder.

'This Box you are in feeds off your deepest desires. Somewhere deep inside, you never wanted dad to leave, so you've been given a mum and dad who are inseparable, a dad who was always faithful. But none of it is real and remember, your real dad loves you a hundred times more than the digital copy you have been given. Your real mum and dad, though not together, know truly what love is.'

David felt like his world had fallen in on him, just like when he was a young child, knowing his dad was going to leave. He felt the tears come quickly, as his body shook with emotion. Nada placed one of her hands on his back, the other upon the centre of his chest, sandwiching his heart chakra, as this is a very comforting position whenever you feel like crying. That was why everything had seemed too good to be true. Poor David, the dear soul did not want to accept this. Yet he just knew, that all he was being told was true.

'So where are my mum and dad now?'

'Your real mum and dad are being held prisoner by the magicians who have trapped you in the Box. They are there with Elia, Linda, Nina, Brian, Tony, Casper, Lorian, Crystal and Catherine.'

'Who are all these people? I don't know them.'

'These are your fellow lightworkers, David, your good friends. Fortunately, you have many friends throughout the universe who prayed for you, hence, why we could penetrate the Box to reach you. We were able to use the prayer energy to create a rainbow path into this place.'

Lady Nada and Archangel Michael placed their hands around David's third eye and, like the long lost forgotten memories, the images of his real mum and dad, Elia and all that he'd experienced, came back from his subconscious. As it did so, the pictures of angels, that David had in his bedroom, suddenly re-appeared back upon his walls. 'It was pictures of us, the angels, hanging on your walls in your real bedroom back at home, David.'

'Why did I not have them up in this false reality?'

'Because the magicians and Illusion knew that if you were to see pictures of our kind, it would remind you of your connection with us. They couldn't allow that.'

Letting David regain his composure for a time, to allow all this to sink in, it was now time to let this go.

'David, are you ready to come out of the Box? It's now or never,' asserted Archangel Michael.

'Yes, I am ready, but there's still so much that feels hazy.'

'You still have spiritual amnesia. Once you are out of the Box, your memory will return.' 'Davie, Davie, dinner's ready,' called Suzanne, 'I've made your favourite Lasagne.'

David knew this was going to be hard but he didn't know just how hard.

'Can't I say goodbye to them? I can't just leave them.'

'David, once you know that all this is illusion, and that it can no longer deceive you, the digital downloads of mum and dad will cease to exist. They appear only within your memory and, dear one, that is where they shall return, where they will stay, always in your heart, my love.'

Nada kissed him tenderly.

'What must I do to get out of here?'

'It is the biggest and hardest thing of all to ask of you, but you need to tell them that they do not exist.'

'Davie, David, son, come on, your dinner's getting cold. What are you doing up there?'

David attempted to go to the landing. It was the hardest, cruellest thing he could imagine doing.

'I can't do it. Please don't make me, please, I can't!'

'David, it's the only way to affirm in your mind that all this is fake. It's okay, we are with you, dear one. You won't be hurting them or destroying them, as these images will go back within your mind, to sleep.'

David slowly, and reluctantly, made his way to the landing, to the foot of the stairs where the images were looking up, both smiling at him.

'Come on Davie, it's time you had your dinner. Listen to your mother, David, son.'

'I'm sorry, but you're not real. I can't go downstairs because none of this is real. Come back into my mind, I love you both and I'll treasure this memory forever.'

'Davie, I said come down for your dinner right now,' shouted a now angry Suzanne.

'No, you both come back into my mind now. None of this is real, do you hear me? None of this is REAL!'

The digital downloads of Jonathan and Suzanne suddenly disappeared, with David assured that they were now back within his mind. A loud thunderous sound broke David's revue. Running back into his bedroom, David looked out of the window, as the once peerless sky, had given way to dark looming clouds, which now seemed to swallow up the entire surroundings outside his house. His whole house shook with violent tremors, as thunder attacked the exterior, like entities possessed.

'Michael, Nada what's happening now? I thought you said that was all I had to do.'

'It was, dear one, it's because you have denounced the reality of the Box, it is now destroying itself. It was designed to self-destruct, giving way to the storm, the moment the prisoner knew they were a prisoner, denying its existence. We are sorry. That must have been so hard to do.'

'Yes, it was damn hard. Please don't make me do anything like that again.'

'We won't, they are now back where they belong in your memories. Come, we've got to leave before the storm gets worse.'

'Quickly, Nada, the silver cord, hurry.' said Michael, urgently.

'Nada, what is this silver cord?' asked David, fascinated. 'It looks like it was spun from the moon.'

'It's the lifeline. All we have that connects us to our normal reality, that includes yours also. It connects your spiritual self to your physical being. You need to hold on to this, David. If you don't, you'll be swept into the storm, lost forever within the Box's vortex.'

A horrendous sound of giant quakes could be heard outside, as David looked in horror. The ground of the garden collapsed, everything was being obliterated, revealing nothing but endless vortex, swirling around like some raging torrent. Everything was gone, the garden, neighbouring houses, completely disintegrated. Davids house was the only thing left standing.

'Hang on, David, hang on,' said the angels. A terrible noise was heard before the whole house was ripped away, collapsing, just like the gardens and other buildings, into the great vortex, completely devoured.

14

THE LIGHTHOUSE

'David, whatever you do, hang on and don't let go,' shouted Archangel Michael, through the howling winds of the storm. David's body dangled about like a fragile leaf upon a tree that could have blown away at any moment. As he clung on to the silver cord with both hands, he felt the freezing winds lash across his face, as lightening zig-zagged insanely around them. The hellish noise was almost deafening. Looking beneath him, David could see the last remains of his illusionary home disappear forever into the heaving vortex. Archangel Michael had his arm placed around David's waist as he lifted him up, so that the Blue Robin now sat on the silver cord. 'Now David, listen to me. Pull yourself across with your hands. It's alright, I'm right behind you.'

'Archangel Michael, Nada, I'm scared.'

'Do not fear, dear one. We are always with you,' said Lady Nada.

'Just keep going, this is the only way. Have courage, lad,' added the masculine voice of Michael. 'Speak my mantra within your mind and know the words to be true.

Look, David, straight ahead, the lighthouse. That's where we are heading.'

David looked up. Shining like some rare grain of hope amidst the overbearing gloom, stood a lighthouse, its golden light beckoning them all towards safety. It was quite a distance away, but within reach. Nothing was impossible, nothing at all. Psyching himself up and repeating the mantra, 'Archangel Michael, above me, Archangel Michael, below me,' David continued onwards, relieved at the sight of the lighthouse, a gift from the One, to be sure. He tried not to be distracted by the rampaging lightening, it was so near to them and David felt that, at any second, they would have been struck by it. But the hand of Archangel Michael held him tightly. The Blue Robin felt the warm breath of both Lady Nada and Michael around his neck.

'Can't be distracted, I've just got to withstand the threats of this virtual reality and concentrate on what is real. My friends are here with me.' The lighthouse started to get a little nearer. 'Just got to keep this steady pace up. I must focus.'

Inside Erratus Manor, the control room seemed to have calmed down since all the tension earlier. The Magicians had regained their usual cold and calculating demeanour, and now seemed frustratingly undeterred by what they had experienced for, in their minds, they had won, just like always. Everything had been taken care of. The Genesis Crystal had been found and suppressed. The Blue Robin was out of their way trapped for all eternity in the Box, living a lie, and the woman Lotus and her friends were now their prisoners. As for the Blue Robin's parents, they were expendable and posed no threat, but they could never be released due to what they had seen. Apart from them, the rest of humanity was still in the dark. All the other earth angels and lightworkers were a cause for concern, but what could they do now without Elia, David and the crystal? Soon, they would be once again gloating about how well they had all done, congratulating themselves on still being the rulers of our world. How heart-warming, toasting their success on another expensive bottle of champagne, compliments of the taxpayer. Elia hung in the air along with her friends, still under the grip of the Black Candle. She had been looking at Lord Asphodel, her eyes a mixture of dislike and sadness, but also compassion. She longed to reach out to him, spend hours treating him with Reiki, if that's what it took, anything to melt the ice that had frozen around his heart.

'You're too late, he won't let you in, lightworker,' taunted the Wounds above them. 'He's far too lost in hate. He will never trust again. Our Wounds are too great, ha, ha, ha!'

Elia ignored them and the Illusion's menacing eyes, for she was not scared of them. Her faith in the love and light was too strong. Suzanne had noticed Elia's expression. She could tell that Elia still had feelings for this Lord Asphodel, vile though he was. Suzanne could not forgive what he had done to her son. Suzanne noticed the strange robotic drone, Orwell, that hovered close to Lord Asphodel, like some sort of pet. It then rested upon Asphodel's lap. He stroked it, as one would a cat or dog.

'Elia, what is that thing, that robot?'

'That is what happens when you encourage a big brother society,' Elia replied. 'It's an artificial intelligence designed by the magicians, to spy on the populace, just like their satellites in space. It may also be the reason why we find ourselves in such a predicament. I am sorry, Suzanne, both to you and Jonathan, for all that has happened.'

Suzanne could not quell her curiosity much longer.

'You and him,' pointing to Lord Asphodel, 'You don't have to tell me, Elia, but I take it you were together at one point?'

After a long pause, and with a sorry sigh, Elia nodded.

'Yes, we were together at one time, for that matter, a great many lifetimes ago.' Drawing a deep breath, due to the pain still being raw, Elia continued. 'Jack and I were first born over a hundred lifetimes ago. We were the king and queen of Atlantis in the time just before the Illusion's darkness began to take hold. I loved him and he loved me, but then darkness began to brew within him, due to the great advances in Atlantean technology, we were thousands of years ahead of even today's technology, but that wasn't enough for him. He began to seek power, rather than honour what we already had, preferring to control, rather than to share our knowledge. He started to look outside himself as opposed to within. He created things, such as the Box, as a means of creating other realities, rather than listening to the wisdom of the Creator. Thus, as his desire for power grew, the blackness around his heart continued to grow like some invisible fungus, that blocked his conscience from all things humane. Our high priests tried to stop him, but already he had found a loyal following. This, for the first time ever in our bright history, created duality between our people as many sided with our king and those who wished to stay true to the golden energy sided with me. They experimented with our power, with our crystal technology, trying to enslave us. The duality brought about the rise of the dark arts, and the Magicians were born.' Tears fell from the wise woman's eyes, as Suzanne looked at her with empathy. 'I tried to help him. I tried, truly I did, but the Illusion was now rampant within him. The Magicians created crystal technology, based on the darkness instead of the light. As you can see before you,' she said, pointing to the dark crystal computers within the control room.

'What happened next?'

'Eventually, he was placed on trial by the high council of Zeus. Zeus and the other high priests decided to exile him, but the duality had created so much darkness that the Creator deemed that this could no longer go on. Thus, Atlantis' fate was sealed, as the cleansing power of water washed away our once beautiful, civilisation. It was such a sad time. Many of us who had maintained the pure energies, such as David and myself, escaped, using our Mer abilities.'

'Wow, I'd love to see that one day,' said Suzanne, trying to be positive.

'Well I'm not sure you'll ever have that chance, dear one, but who knows?' said the healer. 'The pain I felt, losing my once loving husband, has never been healed. Lifetime after lifetime, Ive tried to help him only always to fail.'

'But surely, Elia, you have the ability to heal yourself with Reiki?'

'Yes, but healing through bereavement has to come about with both souls' desire to heal. I have tried to heal myself and, for the most part, I have, but Jack has not. He remained unhealed from his life long past. This is what keeps him trapped by Illusion. Every lifetime I visited him in dream state trying to find what was left of his heart. I try to help him, I try to heal him, I still love him but…'

She was cut off by Lord Asphodel, who had been listening to the whole conversation.

'And then, if I remember rightly, Elia in every dream you leave me, whenever I offer you to join me you reject me, you betray me Just like you did in Atlantis.'

'I never betrayed you. You were like all children. You were born to light and yet YOU yearned for the darkness. You left me long before I left you, Jack.' Just before Atlantis was engulfed by the waves I pleaded with you to come with me Elia, I begged you but no you wished to stay loyal to the purity. You could have been my lady, lived here at Erratus and ruled the earth from the dark realms with me.

'You could have stayed with me, Elia, and had a life of wealth and power.'

'Yes, deprived of the one thing you know I value above everything else, truth.'

'Bah, you and your truth,' mocked Lord Asphodel. 'I found the only truth in the guidance of my master. He taught me to be strong and how to survive. A bit like a father, but better. My master is the only one that's ever cared for me.'

'Quite right, Asphodel, I have always cared,' hissed the Illusion.

'No!' Persisted Elia. 'The Illusion doesn't care about you. He allows you to kill, thinking of it as a means to an end, and any civilisation, that condones the killing of another is dooming itself to destruction. Peace is the way of the future and love is stronger than anything.'

'Will you stop the babblings of this woman, Asphodel, before I do. For your information, woman of Lotus, I am not an Illusion.'

'Then what are you? If everything love is not. I am not scared of you, Illusion. None of us are, as you do not control us. It is time for every soul on earth to be free. We will accomplish this somehow, no matter how much you think you have won, for you have heard the words of Akash.'

The enraged Illusion was about to order Lord Asphodel to kill her, when a siren-like alarm filled the control room, a terrible noise. The Wounds held their jagged ears, as if to block the terrible sound.

'It's the alarm,' exclaimed Lord Asphodel. 'The alarm of the Box, its defence systems have been activated. You know what that means.'

'Oh no, david must have realised what he was experiencing was fake and activated the storm,' said Elia, fraught with worry.

'Davie, no, not our baby,'

Jonathan reached out and anxiously grabbed Suzanne's hand, clasping it in moral support, knowing full well that their son could not possibly have survived this.

'It can't be. He couldn't possibly have found out the truth of his existence,' Lord Asphodel said in shock, grabbing his miniature Box, which revealed a view into the magicians' matrix. 'Orwell, project this image onto widescreen,' ordered the lost soul.

The robot drone obeyed, as a huge image of the sweeping vortex storm filled the control room. Elia and the others gasped in alarm, as they saw the horrendous hurricane-like energy, lit by lightening. Then the lightworkers' eyes widened with hope for, within the midst of it all, they spotted the tiny figures of David, Michael and Nada, pulling themselves along the shining silver cord.

'Davie, it's Davie!' Suzanne could scarcely contain herself. Told you he was stubborn Asphodel, said a delighted Jonathan.

'And there's Archangel Michael and Nada,' responded Elia, 'But, how?'

The view of the lighthouse came into view, as David and his friends were much closer now, a good Thirty feet away. Its light shone into the control room, lighting up the darkness and forcing the magicians to shield their faces. Lord Asphodel was seething with rage.

'No, this cannot be happening. He has breached the matrix defence systems. He was supposed to have had spiritual amnesia. How could he have been able to let them in?'

'They must have found a way in, something you must have overlooked Asphodel,' hissed the Illusion, angrily.

'No, master, the Box was fool-proof, I tell you, fool-proof. There's no way the angels could have reached him, unless, unless..'

'That's it, our prayers were answered cried Elia. Dear ones, our prayers must have reached Heaven.'

Lord Asphodel glared at Elia.

'Your prayers would not have been enough to have reached him by themselves.'

'No, Jack, but what about the prayers of every single lightworker in existence, not just on earth, but throughout the entire universe. Have you forgotten just how many there are within the cosmos?' Suddenly, Lord Asphodel felt deflated. 'Their prayers merged with ours, enabling Heaven to create a pathway into even that dark domain,' Elia beamed with joy. 'There must have been so much hope all over the cosmos, so much compassion for David, that it enabled Michael and Lady Nada to get through with the silver cord. That is why David is surviving the storm.'

'Then David is safe, Elia? Oh, Jonathan, what a relief!'

Suzanne's grip tightened around Jonathan, as his heart pumped with gladness.

'I just hope he can make it,' said Jonathan, anxiously.

'They can't make it to the lighthouse, Asphodel. If they do, he will be free, it is his way out.' The Illusion now started to panic.

Lord Asphodel gestured, frantically, to his minions.

'Quickly, Astrally project into the matrix. You must try to get them off the cord.'

'Yes, Lord Asphodel, right away.'

'No!' screamed David's mum and dad, in tandem.

'Some people are just never pleased,' ranted Asphodel. 'I give him a perfect world to live in, his house, a family, possessions and security, and this is what he does. He destroys it. He'd rather brave the storm than live in a world where ignorance is bliss. Well now he shall pay for it with his life.' Pointing coldly towards David's parents, Lord Asphodel continued, 'Be prepared, for soon your son will be no more. I'd start saying your goodbyes, if I were you.'

'Keep going, David, keep going,' archangel Michael's voice had kept David going the entire way, as the Blue Robin kept repeating the mantra. They were all nearly at the lighthouse, its flashing beacon an absolute pleasure to see. 'Lady Nada, how are you, dear one?'

'All is well with me, Michael. Just focus on helping David, for we are virtually there.'

A sinister voice was heard around them.

'Ah yes, so near, yet so far! What a pity all your efforts have been wasted.'

Three figures emerged from the dense darkness, the mere sight of them, far worse than they could have imagined. David held back for a moment unable to move as fear began to crawl up inside him.

'David listen to me. Don't look at them, just keep going, my friend, keep going. Remember I've got you. It's the Magicians. They must have discovered your escape sooner than we thought. They're Astrally-projected into the matrix. Keep going, quickly.'

The menacing figures flew, with ease, through the storm. Each one wielded an energy weapon, as they floated in between the angels and the lighthouse.

'Hand over the Blue Robin, archangel. He needs to remain out in the storm. You were very foolish, earth angel, destroying that lovely home, not to mention your poor parents. Now you have nowhere to go except to be lost in the storm.'

David had had enough of these magicians with their cruel taunts.

'Well, I'm afraid I've just never been able to fit into a box. It's time for you all to start losing,' he replied, defiantly.

'Then take the consequences, boy,' cried the magicians, before firing a blood red laser beam at the Blue Robin.

Nada shielded the Blue Robin with her gossamer wings, whilst Archangel Michael unleashed the Sword of Truth, blocking the deadly weapons fire with its diamond stone, that was encrusted upon the handle.

'Lady Nada, get David to safety. I'll ward these creatures off with my sword. Go, Blue Robin, go with Nada, now.'

With a mighty thrust of his beautiful tool, Michael swept the astral magicians aside so that they were no longer in the way, allowing David and Nada to pass. The magicians hurtled through the vortex, but being masters of this horrid reality, quickly overcame this. Their dead faces grimaced at the vigour of the archangel.

'So, you want to play the hard way, do you?' said the leader of the three, as they raised their spear like weapons, the colour of electricity towards the Archangel. 'We're very surprised that a being of the light, such as yourself, carries a mighty sword to protect himself,' the Magicians said mockingly.

Michael looked down at them assertively.

'You're not flesh and blood, you have simply been downloaded into this odious reality. My Sword of Truth only cuts away dark energy, as that is what you are, figments of the dark mind. If you want him, you have to get past me first.'

The three vengeful magicians hurtled towards the great being, lashing out with their flashing spears. Archangel Michael met the challenge, defending himself with his sword, whilst skilfully balancing upon the silver cord.

'Hurry, Nada, get the child to safety.'

The great archangel bio-located his body, so that there were now three archangel Michaels defending his friends. The Magicians were surprised at first, but they were tenacious to say the least, but then so was Michael. In the control room, everyone watched with baited breath, as the events enfolded within the Box.

'Come on, you fools, more power. Already, you are letting the boy elude you,' Lord Asphodel yelled, anxiously, directing his words at the three magicians, who sat in a semi-circle, guiding their astral projections within their minds.

'Do what you must, Asphodel. They cannot be allowed to leave the Box,' hissed the Illusion, in a whispering fashion.

Suzanne and Jonathan's hearts were racing. They were so hopeful for their son's freedom, yet so scared that he would not make it, at the last moment.

'I want to help him, I feel so powerless said Jonathan.' All the lightworkers felt the same.

'But we are not,' said Elia, 'We must try not to worry, as we can pray.' Elia looked at Jonathan, saying, 'Perhaps now is the time you should pray again, just like you used to. Tell me, Jack, why is it so important that David went into the Box? Why wasn't he brought here, like the rest of us? Why did you try to separate him from us?' Lord Asphodel did not answer. 'Never mind then, I think I know.'

'Why, Elia? David is harmless,' said Suzanne.

'Yes, exactly darling, that's why the Illusion didn't want him here, because of his great innocence. You see, David is pure and it's his purity that repels the Illusion.'

'But we are pure, Elia, for we also come from our souls,' said Linda, the incarnated Angel.

'Yes, but remember that we have lived. We are older and, at times, have been tainted or challenged by life's rollercoaster. We have remembered our true selves, following these things. David has lived his life the other way around. He knew and trusted the light, before experiencing the challenges. He being a Rainbow Child of Shambhala that is why he has never lost touch with his soul. Not even the Black Candle could hold him, the way it did us. Eventually its power would have weakened against Davids own. The mere sight of him is enough to repulse Illusion, The Illusion knows this and fears it. Even amongst the lightworkers, the Blue Robin is unique and knows the language of the Creator. That is why they exiled him. But his ultimate challenge will come, once he is free.'

Meanwhile David and Nada had finally reached the rocks leading to the lighthouse. Nada hoisted the young man up onto the first rock. Pulling himself up onto the jagged surface, David looked back, concerned for Archangel Michael, who had fought off their attackers. But now the tables were being turned, as the magicians increased their mental powers. There were now even more astral entities to contend with. One of them grabbed the archangel, coming from behind, holding him firmly, another had done the same to another of archangel Michael's bodies. There were now less "Michaels" to defend David and his beautiful guardian, climbing up beside him on the barren rocks. One of the magicians caught sight of them and, whilst Michael was being detained, flew menacingly towards David and Nada.

'Michael!' shouted David. 'Nada, they've got him.'

Nada had spotted the magician, looming towards them,

'David, look out!' A blast of red hot energy had blown up the rocks they were crawling on, as David fell downwards, grabbed just in time by Nada. She held him by the hand as he dangled helplessly above the great abyss, a horrifying vortex, whose secrets were known by no one and was as profound as death. David clung on desperately to the edge of the rock. He was absolutely exhausted, as he tried to pull himself up with weak fingertips. 'It's alright, beloved one,' said Nada, holding his other hand firmly, 'We can do this, we can.'

'Ha, ha, what a shame that such a powerful soul must meet his end,' mocked the magician, who had fired at them and still loomed above them. 'Come and see this, friends. The Blue Robin is on his last legs and about to meet his end. Why don't you just accept your defeat, Rainbow Child. You're going to be lost for good in the storm, you and your pretty guardian angel. I'll just fire at the piece of rock you are on and you will be lost forever, within the oblivion. Oh, to think you could have had a life in a blissfully ignorant world. Oh well, so much for courage.'

It raised its weapon to fire. But as it did so, a ball of golden orange light shot from the beacon of the lighthouse.

'AAHHH!' screamed the magician, as the light shot into its face, pushing it out into the storm and away from David.

This gave Nada the chance she needed to pull the Blue Robin from danger and get him to safety. Looking up, they saw more glowing balls of golden orange firing out from the beacon, going out to aid archangel Michael, who was still struggling with these astral pests.

'Nada, it's the angels.'

'Yes, David, The One has sent out reinforcements to help us and our higher champion.'

They watched, as each of the orbs cast their light out into the darkness, breaking up the fight and pushing the astral projections out into the storm. The magicians fought hard to resist the angelic orbs, but their efforts were in vain, as each of them were bunched together in a large cluster by the angelic soldiers, banding around them, in a tight circle. The beautiful sound of OM could be heard, coming from within the angels. This was the language of love, the sound of the One. 'Of course, only the highest of our kind can retain their power within darkness like this and be so strong,' said Nada.

'You mean they are the seraph?' exclaimed David, in wonder.

'Yes, dear one, the highest of the high.'

Archangel Michael regained his balance upon the silver cord. Two of the seraph orbs lifted Michael over to the circle, where he towered over the projected magicians. They uttered all the curses under the sun, but it was no use, they had been defeated. With archangel Michael's great sword held high above them, they cowered in fear.

'Now, astral entities, be gone from this realm. Your darkness is no match for the light, in the name of Father Mother, my sword will dissolve you all.'

Thrusting his great sword down upon the group, they all let out a piercing scream, before dissolving within the light, melting into nothingness.

'NO!' screamed the Illusion.

Its voice could be heard throughout the Box, sending shockwaves throughout Erratas Manor, as the magicians' bodies contorted in agony, within the semi-circle, before passing out in utter exhaustion, fearing that their minds would be lost if they did not. Archangel Michael was carried over to the remaining rocks to re-join David and Nada. The worst of the storm seemed to be over, as the seraphs' song emanated with peace, drowning out the winds of the vortex. David hugged the great archangel within his arms, as did Nada. The seraphs waited a moment for the souls to regain their breath, before carrying David, Michael and Nada up to the beautiful beacon of the lighthouse, up into the great light which, at first, seemed blinding after the storm, but they soon adjusted to it.

Inside the beacon's light, David felt his strength return. He felt all his memory returning and his chakras began to open, once again, one by one, returning to their natural brightness. The clothes he had been wearing in the Box, had disappeared and been replaced, once again, by his beautiful blue/purple tunic and cloak. He now saw all his other angels, who were flocking around him, now that they could finally reach him. They tended to him, checking that he was alright. He noticed the light of Michael and Nada getting brighter, regaining their true power. They, who had never felt that feeling of powerlessness before, had survived and rescued David, against all odds.

'I would never have got out of that place but for you, Archangel Michael, and you dear Nada. Thank you both so much, bless you all.'

'See what happens when countless souls come together to pray,' beamed Nada. 'Miracles can happen, indeed they can.'

'It is thanks to the Lightworkers across the universe, that the magicians' Box is no more.' said Michael, as they turned to see the storm outside rip itself apart, the vortex completely dissolved.

The reality of the Box had been destroyed. The faces of all the ascended masters appeared within the light around them, and a voice was heard.

'Welcome back to reality, Blue Robin.'

The voice, though tender and kind, was strong and powerful. It was not the voice of Akash, though Akash could be seen, like all the masters. The voice sounded like a man's, but also a woman's, an androgynous balance of both feminine and masculine energy.

'Who are you?' asked David.

'I am the light of all that is. Do not be afraid, for the time is not yet ripe for you to see me.' The voice continued. 'The final chapters in your universe's great history are now coming to an end and the new era is about to be written. To accomplish this, you must go within the place where the Wounds still dwell and where the light of my gift to you is being suppressed.'

'Erratus Manor,' thought David.

'Yes, dear one,' replied the beautiful voice, 'for going within, is the only way you will be able to heal the Wounds, thereby breaking their cycle, which has caused history to repeat itself, time after time.'

'But don't you see? I am still afraid.'

'You're afraid of what you might find once you go inside this place. You feel unworthy, not good enough. But believe me, dear one, you are worthy, you are good enough. Your light is so bright, far brighter than the darkness within Erratus Manor. This is the last part of your journey. You will feel challenged, you will feel scared, but remember what all my children have told you. You have the power within to break the chains that are holding you all back from knowing me. You must be strong. Once you have gone within, you will give my children the permission to go inside also. You must confront that which no longer serves you and your world, for then the old shall pass away and the new reality will be birthed, as the seeds are planted, you have my word that your world will once again flourish in peace and harmony. This is my will and it must be done. You have the light and you have the wings. Just fly, dear earth angel, just trust and fly.' You are good enough, great enough, and beautiful enough just for being you, now give them Heaven. The words of the voice touched the very core of David. He did not want this wonderful experience to end. The great lighthouse faded. Just as it did so, he heard the voice of this sweet being say, 'Come, my children of light, to help David. We must prepare, for the moment has come. It's time for the Ascension.'

That was the last thing David heard as he watched the scene fade, leaving just Nada and his other angels around him. They stood outside, surrounded by the mist of the veil, within a plethora of the angels who were blocked by it, outside Erratus Manor. It was time for David to go inside.

15

DAY OF ASCENSION

David looked about him at all the angels, who stood enshrouded by the veil. They seemed to be consulting with Nada and his other angels. The shattered remains of the Box lay splintered upon the ground. David looked at the fragments of his destroyed prison, remembering how he had nearly conformed to this false reality and how he had nearly lost his life in trying to escape, but, escaped he had. He could never have done it without the help of Michael and Nada. He owed them so much, for they could have been lost, also. They had risked their lives for him, there was no way he would turn back now.

'David, dear Blue Robin, thank The One. You made it out of the Box,' said the voices of the angels, who were trapped in the veil.

'We were all so concerned when we heard what Jack had done. The lengths he will go to, to keep out the light are frightful to contemplate. He will go to such depths to achieve this,' said one of the angels, who glowed in beautiful golden light. 'My name is Tala,' said the golden angel. 'You have no idea how long we have all prayed for this moment.'

'Tala, it's wonderful to meet you all, but why are you all here? You aren't accompanying any mortals or animals. Why is that?'

The beautiful angel let out a sigh, as did they all, in tandem.

'We are blocked by the veil which you see around us. It prevents us from getting through to reach those we love. We want, so much, to be asked in but we have been kept out by their Illusion.' Tala pointed in the direction of Erratus Manor, which stood ahead of them, clothed in shadow.

'Then you mean you are the magicians' guardians?'

'Yes, that is true, beloved one. Like all souls across the galaxies, we were assigned to each one at the birth of their physical life, but ever since the last days of Atlantis, we have been kept out by their darkness,' said Tala. 'We long to touch them, hug them, embrace them, but we can only do this if we are allowed in.'

'Who is Jack to you, Tala?'

'You would know him better as Lord Asphodel. I am his guardian angel. He and his minions have kept us out here for far too long, but you have weakened the veil to such an extent, that we can now get through.'

'But, even if I am a lightworker, even a rainbow child, how can I help you to do this?'

'You have the great power of innocence. You understand the meaning of peace and your light holds the energy of Shambahla. That is something the Illusion is terrified of because your light is powerful enough to melt the darkness from all hearts. That is why you are here.'

'No wonder the Illusion wanted me imprisoned. It feels threatened by me.'

'It fears all who are of the light, but your purity would eventually overpower all their dark magic and now you are free to dissolve the veil and let us in.'

David looked sadly at Tala.

'All your love, all your beauty, and yet Lord Asphodel chooses to shun you. I don't know how these souls could ever reject you like this,' he said angrily.

'Some people in life can reject us and forget about their true selves when they succumb to the Wounds. It all depends on how deeply they allow the Wounds to penetrate. When you are as lost as the magicians are, you cut yourself off from love and your fellow creatures. The Illusion knows when this has happened, influencing those who are lost from any walk of life, to kill, to prove a point. Yet the truth, from the very beginning, was to love others and to see the light within all. When you are in that same place with The One and The One in that place with you, then you realise you are all divine Namaste.'

David smiled broadly at the angels.

'It's time, David. It's time for you to go inside and heal,' said Nada quietly, as if listening to someone who David was not privy to. 'The time for ascension is now. Go now, Blue Robin, go.'

David began to walk towards the ominous house of the Magicians. His peaceful energy shone, like a candle, amidst the darkness. He realised he would have to do the hardest thing any of us will ever have to do he was going to have to face his fear.

Inside, Lord Asphodel frowned, his lip shaking violently. The Illusion glared menacingly, hissing away to itself, but really it was afraid at the sight of David on Orwell's projected scanner, coming through the veil and walking straight towards Erratus Manor like some peaceful warrior. It seemed as though none of the magicians in the control room knew what to do at that moment. Each one had a look of fear and bewilderment at their inability to defeat the Blue Robin. Elia, Suzanne, Jonathan and all the lightworkers, looked relieved and hopeful at the sight of their son and friend. They daren't say anything, for if they did at this point, Lord Asphodel would have sentenced them to death.

'The Blue Robin, still he comes,' cursed Asphodel.

'He comes to seek the crystal, to defeat all of us. He must be insane. You must not let him inside, Asphodel,' came the Illusion's distraught voice. 'He will destroy me. He'll destroy everything we have worked for.'

'Do not fear, my master. I will ensure that he will never get in.'

'I don't understand, Lord Asphodel. He seemed so weak when we saw him,' said 19.

'Yes, so easily defeated when we put him in the Box,' agreed 84. 'I judged him so easy to take care of.'

'Then you judged too early,' answered Lord Asphodel, enraged.

'Yes, you judged his vessel without looking deeper and that will always be your downfall,' replied Elia. 'The

Blue Robin is hope. His light and faith are what helped him survive. See how he comes, as gentle as a lamb.'

'Yes, my dear, like a lamb to the slaughter,' retorted Asphodel, coldly. 'Quick, 19 and 84, go outside, take recruits, use what you must. I want him destroyed, do you understand? Total annihlation. Whatever it takes, just do it, its time to unleash the Wolves.'

'Yes, my Lord.'

'No, you cannot do this. Please, you must spare him!' cried his terrified parents. 'Elia, you must try and stop them,' they pleaded.

'Why Jack? Why, after all this, must you resort to such violence? Why not surrender to the light and let love in?' said Elia.

'Because of power,' answered Asphodel. 'We will not have power if we let the light in and my master will be gone, should that happen. My master ensures that I have control.'

'Yes, but you are also under its control,' argued Elia. No one ever knows true power if they are controlled.

'It is worth it for, in return, I have control behind the scenes of your world.'

The Blue Robin had now reached the dead tree and was nearly at the door of Erratus.

'David, look out!' warned his angels, as dozens of magicians, led by 19 and 84, flew out from secret entrances.

They emerged from the manor, pointing their weapons at the Blue Robin , burning hot spears. They looked as if they had come out of a nightmare, whilst even the branches of the dead tree, blowing in the wind, seemed to be trying to ensnare him. David clutched onto his cape and then, upon feeling a strange sensation on his back, discovered that he too now had wings. They were beautiful, magnificent to behold, almost as big as an angel's. He rose high into the air, just before 19's scorching spear came down, leaving a large smoking hole where David had just been standing. 19 snorted in disgust as he looked at the Blue Robin now flying so effortlessly through the air.

'Quickly, fellow minions, after him. He must be destroyed.'

'Yes, we'll soon clip his wings,' mocked 84.

Hurtling through the air above and around Erratus Manor, David looked at Nada, who flew beside him and his other angels, trying desperately to avoid the swishing spears and deadly red rays that shot from the magician's weapons. The angels within the misty veil looked on with hope. The way ahead of David was suddenly blocked as 19 & 84 cornered him, along with the other magicians. They moved towards him menacingly, their burning weapons matched only by their heated tempers. This boy had been an annoyance for far too long. How dare he try to stop the era of control. Now he was going to pay.

'What part of you do you want us to cut off first?' said Lord Asphodel, who had come to join his subjects.

'Lord Jack Asphodel, I presume?' enquired David, trying to remain strong.

'You've caused me and my fellow magicians much grief, dear boy.' Again, that tongue was dipped in poison. 'You will now feel the wrath of my master, channelled through me.'

'You mean the Illusion don't you, lost one,' said the Blue Robin, bravely.

'Hmmph! Is that all you've got left to help you, calling my great master an Illusion? It's going to take more than name calling and faith to help you now.'

'What have you done to my parents and Elia and the others?'

'Oh, they are safe, far more than you will ever be,' chided Asphodel. Raising a glowing spear into the air, Asphodel and his magicians smirked. 'Why do your angels desert you now? Have they now seen sense and realised they are not equal to my master's dark? They will now watch you perish and soon you will join them in Heaven.'

Lord Asphodel was about to thrust his burning weapon into David, when a great light shone down from the black void above, beaming down upon the Blue Robin and the magicians.

'Lord Asphodel, what is it, that light? it is hurting me.' asked 19 and 84. 'It's too bright.'   Lord Asphodel shielded his face as Michael emerged from this light using his great Sword of Truth. He completely destroyed the glowing spears, reducing them to dust.

'No, it can't be, it can't beeee,' Lord Asphodel screamed, as the faces of every archangel, angel and ascended master from Christ to Buddah, peered down from the great light above. 'Retreat, Asphodel, retreat.'

The Illusion was calling them back inside. Before David knew it, each of the magicians had rushed straight back into Erratus Manor, as if they were unable to take the light any longer. David didn't understand why, as he absolutely loved it. Looking up at the smiling masters and archangels, the Blue Robin graciously smiled and spoke an internal prayer of thanks, once again to his great saviours.

'It is also you that we thank, dear one, for without your trust in us we would not be able to get through like this,' they all said.

'What's happening? How can you penetrate the Illusion's veil?' asked David. Because it weakens came Michaels reply, because of your courage dear one.

'We still need you to go inside, beloved one, but beware. Within that place there are many defences which will try to stop you.'

A rocket-like sound was heard coming from below, as lasers were fired from Erratus Manor, aimed directly at David.

'Quick David, we will avoid them as much as we can,' said Nada.

'We will prepare for the coming,' said Michael, as he flew back into the great light to join his friends. Meanwhile, David dodged the relentless lasers that continued to fire at him and his angels.

The Magicians inside the control room were now desperate, each one operating the Black Crystals, which powered the lasers, in a bid to vaporise the Blue Robin, who was skilfully weaving in and out, dodging the vicious rays that sought to destroy him, along with his angels. Suzanne, Jonathan, Elia and the others watched in both fascination and horror. All they could do was hope and, of course, pray.

'How comes our son can now fly and has wings?' asked Jonathan.

'Because he now believes in himself.' said Suzanne, almost to herself.

In beautiful Shambhala in the Temple of Truth, every master, saint, galactic being, archangel and angel, sat cross legged within the lotus position. They were praying and chanting in deep meditation. The magnificent Akash floated in one position, as he was also meditating.

'SACRED LIGHT, SACRED HEART, SACRED FATHER, SACRED MOTHER,' they all chanted together. With each breath, the mantra became louder, yet still soft. Stronger and stronger, as they all repeated this.

'Concentrate, my children,' said the kind, beautiful voice that David had heard speak to him in the lighthouse. 'Remember you are all part of me and I am part of you. We are all one.'

Mother Mary, who had been holding beloved Mother Earth throughout this whole time, felt the beautiful planet lift from her hands. Slowly but surely, it rose higher and higher within the air, making its way upwards towards the great light at the top of the temple. 'It's happening, brothers and sisters, it is happening,' said the beautiful master. 'Mother Earth is ascending.'

Each of them raised their heads, before opening their eyes.

'It's time, dear ones. The Earth Mother is integrating the fifth dimension. Everybody into the mothership,' said Akash. Sananda looked lovingly at his brothers and sisters. He held his hands out to his brothers next to him.

'Mohammed, dear brother and sweet Buddah, please take my hands,' said the master. Mohammed and Buddah both smiled lovingly, accepting the invitation. They took the hands of Sananda, holding them tight. Every master then held hands with the master next to them. Archangel Michael held hands with Archangel Raphael, Raphael with Gabriel next to him, Gabriel with Raziel, Raziel with Uriel, Uriel with Jophiel, Metatron with Sandalphon etc.

'Ready to shower the Earth Mother in healing light?' said Michael to his brother Raphael.

'There is never any time like the present,' responded the emerald Archangel.

Throughout this time, each of the masters had been joined in their chanting by all of Heaven. Every soul had wished to do their bit for the betterment of the earth. In the luscious gardens of eternity, every soul joined in the prayers. David's relations, Past and Present along with all his pets, had been aware of the situation and prayed strongest of all for their Blue Robin, and for the release and safety of their children. Every being, unicorn, Mermaid, dolphin, whale, dragon, elf, fairy, sprite, griffin, phoenix and fawn, centaur, and dinosaur, along with all the animals who had lived on earth, but had now crossed over, had joined the chanting energy, as well as each of these soul's guardian angels. Many had gone to the Cathedral of Sacred Heights to amplify this joyous power. Whilst the Atlanteans all prayed and Chanted within their sacred city sending their love throughout the Sea of Compassion.

'Come, dear ones, this day marks the end of the old and the beginning of the new. 'FOR THE GLORY OF NEW EARTH,' 'AND FOR THE FREEDOM OF THE PEOPLE; cried Archangel Michael.

'FOR THE GLORY OF NEW EARTH,' 'AND FOR THE FREEDOM OF THE PEOPLE; repeated every being within the Temple of Truth.

In a great circle they elevated towards Mother Earth, their purpose to heal. The power of the chanting was already creating a vast ripple effect that was reverberating throughout the cosmos. Its golden energy was affecting everyone and everything on earth. At Erratus Manor, the wave of energy was causing the entire domain to shake, halting the laser attack and giving David a little more time. The magicians inside looked around them at their quivering domain.

'What's happening? Why is everything shaking around us? It isn't possible. Our lasers have affected the planet's geology and is causing a quake.'

'It's the earth,' came the Illusion's voice, alarmingly. 'She is trying to ascend. The closer the Blue Robin gets, the more danger there is of this coming to fruition. You mussst destroy him Assphodel, you must!'

Lord Asphodel hurriedly rushed to the magicians 19 and 84 who were operating the Black Crystal consoles.

'Hurry, you idiots. What is keeping you?' he said impatiently.

'It's the lasers. Sir, the ascension seems to have drained us of power. We are doing our best but our efforts are futile against the Blue Robin.'

'This is an abomination to all of us,' hissed the Illusion. 'Quickly, Wounds, spin faster. We must not let the relentless fool enter.'

The foul entities spun around as fast as they could, but even now they were beginning to feel exhausted, as they felt their negativity start to drain.

'Any normal person would have been vaporised immediately, yet still this one persists. Why can't he go away?' Lord Asphodel said, almost to himself. 'Please, go away. Why must you interfere with my control?'

'Lord Asphodel, why don't we kill them?' Weaver said, pointing to David's mum and dad. 'Why not cause their extinction and let the Blue Robin know that his efforts have been in vain?'

'No, we shall let them live, for now. After all, we've too much to make out of them. Besides what can they do? They can't help him, whilst under the influence of the Black Candle. If only this accursed shaking would stop.'

'Do not fear, our Lord, we will use what little we have left, lasers or no lasers, we still have more spears,' said 84.

David was nearly upon the entrance to this dark place. His spiritual heart was pumping, its glow pulsating erratically. He was exhausted now but was spurred on by the great light. Suddenly the entrance opened, revealing the menacing figures of 19 and 84, holding their dreadful weapons in their hands.

'We told you, Blue Robin, not to interfere.'

David peered in alarm at the razor sharp points of the ugly spears their tips glowing molten red hot.

'Wait,' came a cruel voice. 'Let me do the honours.'

Lord Asphodel came to the front, standing between David and the entrance. His hands were glowing with red fire whilst the embers dripped from his fingers.

'I'm in spirit form, Asphodel, and you can't trap me, your Box is now destroyed,' retorted the boy, defiantly.

'Yes, I know. Destructive little urchin, aren't you? Quite the anachist. Since you failed to conform to the Box, we shall have to find another one to put you in, preferably one that can be buried. KILL HIM!' shouted the repulsive lost soul.

'Quickly, use Reiki,' David heard his angels say, just as the magicians' spears were fired.

Rays of colours resembling rainbow showers flashed from Davids hands, as the energy rained down from above. The beautiful rainbow rays of Reiki, pushed the vile lasers back into the magicians' weapons. The magicians were pushed back into Erratus by the powerful force of love. Lord Asphodel was not affected so easily. But, even though he struggled desperately, he could not withstand the love for long as it tried to melt the ice that had long since buried his heart.

'No, stop doing that. We cannot be reached, we cannot......be ...STOP THIS!' The magician eventually broke free from the contact with Reiki. 'Now, feel my power Blue Robin, the energy of darkness.' Lord Asphodel held his hands up toward the boy as dart-like bolts of red energy shot out, engulfing David. Each one felt like hot needles stabbing at David's core. The pain was excruciating. The Blue Robin fell to the ground, screaming in agony at the onslaught. 'Yes, Blue Robin you are indeed in spirit, invulnerable to any bullet or laser, but not to my dark arts. These can still penetrate your soul. Remember how I used these against you in Atlantis?' when you tried to stop me. Now feel the wrath from the leader of the pack.

'Excellent, Asphodel, it is working,' came the Illusion's wicked voice. 'Now, Blue Robin, you have a choice.

Submit to our darkness or walk away and never return to Erratus ever again. You can't heal the Wounds, boy. Their cycle will always be in movement. I knew it was wise of me to accelerate the Wounds, I thought they were slacking as of late, Asphodel.'

'Indeed, my master. Well, Blue Robin, what do you say to our ultimatum? Leave or die?'

David's agonised face looked up. There were tears streaming from his eyes. Nada and his other angels longed to help him, but due to the acceleration of the Wounds, the veil blocking them had increased in strength, stopping them from intervening.

'Don't give up David, don't give up,' he heard them say.

'Never, I'll never give up. Not to a bully like you.'

'Master, he has refused the chance of life we offered him. What should we do?'

'The young fool has made his choice. Kill him, Asphodel.'

'Yes, Great One. Farewell lightworker.'

Another plethora of red needles shot from Asphodel's palms. Again, David let out a piercing scream as the burning needles performed their voodoo function, stabbing mercilessly at the boy's heart. David rolled on the ground, twisting in agony. Time was running out. If he could not enter within to heal, the cycle would be allowed to continue and the angels would be unable to dissolve the Wounds.

'Please God, help me, help me! I can't stop this! I cant' This was just what the Illusion wanted to hear, but then a voice spoke strongly within David, It was the voice of his

Dad, Jonathan had started to pray again after all these years, praying for his son. It was profound, yet simple.

'YOU CAN. DAVID, BLUE ROBIN, YOU CAN. I BELIEVE IN YOU, WE ALL DO YOU CAN DO THIS, YOU ARE THE BEST OF ME, THE STRONGEST OF ME. I LOVE YOU. IM SO PROUD OF YOU.'

The words echoed and resonated within David and the stabbing sensation seemed to stop, just for a moment. That moment was enough for David. He then remembered the Creator's voice, but also the sound. He had heard the sound of hope, the essence of all love, and that sound was "OM". Hearing it within him, he emulated it the best he could. The sound of "OM" shone through David, igniting within him like a ball of fire. The sound was so powerful that it lifted David up from the ground and into the air. He was a glowing angel, lighting the way for the others, as the burning red needles fell to the ground becoming just as they truly were - nothing. They vanished from sight and Lord Asphodel was shot, like a torpedo, straight back into Erratus Manor.

For a moment, David hung in the air, burning like a Sapphire Star, his wings unfolded in all their glory. He heard the voice of The One speaking within him. David closed his eyes, savouring the words.

'Through darkest night, through unkind pain, look into your heart. There you shall find me, again and again.'

David nodded, as if in thanks to what The One had told him. Looking up to the skies, he saw the beautiful mothership that he had seen when he had first entered the Temple of Truth, emerging from the light. The great pyramid craft resembled a giant Star, as it stayed high up, suspended in the air, spinning round and round before descending into the dark realm.

'Go inside, David.' It was the voice of Michael. 'We can only come in when you have entered.'

'I understand,' the Blue Robin said, humbly.

He suddenly became conscious of Nada and his other angels, who had all got through, thanks to the sound of "OM" being sung by every angel and lightworker throughout the galaxy. Each one unique and beautiful, the prayer of the universe. Gradually, the chanting hymn of the ascended masters, Akash and the angels was heard. It filled David with hope and joy, as well as the strength he needed, as he approached the entrance of Erratus. As he went inside, he sent his light into that place he knew as darkness.

A dazed Lord Asphodel staggered into the control room, his hand upon his head as he'd taken quite a knock, after being propelled through the air, at speed. Grunting in pain, he half slumped over one of the Atlantean computers, as two of his magicians assisted him back to his throne.

'Shut the door. Quick, shut the door. It's our last chance to keep him out,' he said, frantically.

The door to the control room was shut immediately, just as David's glowing figure was seen coming towards it in the gloom.

'David, we're in here,' shouted Suzanne.

'He's done it, he's done it!' shouted Jonathan, excitedly. 'He's made it inside.'

'Let me in,' David shouted from outside the control room. 'Let me and my angels in.'

Inside the beautiful mothership, whose consoles were made of shimmering crystals, glowing in radiance, each and every one of the heavenly beings sat upon the cushions of air in their lotus positions, looking down upon the sad monstrosity that was Erratus Manor. Commander Ashtar and his star squadron sat operating the ingenious crystal technology, not by pushing with their hands, but by using their minds telekinetically, causing the amazing crystals to move all by themselves.

'The Blue Robin is within, he is about to go into the control room,' came the soothing voice of Akash.

'Indeed, we can then knock to be let in,' came the equally calm voice of Sananda. 'Come, we shall be strong, yet as gentle as the lamb. Commander Ashtar, activate the violet flame.'

'Indeed, my brothers and sisters,' came Ashtar's kind voice, reaching out with universal mind. A large crystal, the colour of violet, levitated across the dazzling crystalline columns before inserting itself into a translucent tube device. A gentle humming was heard, before the magnificent sight of the violet flame burst out from the bottom of the mothership. The giant, violet flame flickered in the air before moving down towards the veil, without causing any harm or damage, the veil seemed to evaporate, its misty substance overwhelmed by the flame of violet. Cheers were heard from below as the angels, who had once been blocked, were now free to go on their way. They headed right in the direction of Erratus Manor. Commander Ashtar looked proudly upon all his beautiful brothers and sisters. 'I shall never forget this day, never. The One be praised and all hearts of those who are genuinely good.'

'Aye, sweet Ashtar, we shall not forget,' smiled Melcheizedeck, who stood close to the floating Akash. 'We shall not forget, nor what is to come.'

David had continued to hammer at the door but it was no use. It was sealed shut and the code that was used to open it had been put into lockdown by the desperate magicians, who clung inside their controlling world, as if it was their last refuge which, at that point, it may well have been. David looked at Nada.

'There's no way we can get in, Nada.'

'Yes there is, use Reiki. It will dissolve the barriers that have been put up.'

'Reiki,' thought David. Yes, of course. Reiki's love vibrational frequency can melt anything that is closed. Looking behind them, they saw the entrance to Erratus, firmly shut.

'Good, that should keep anything else out,' said Lord Asphodel, his head being tended to by one of his lackeys.

'Lord Asphodel, they have released the violet flame. It is coming straight towards us and we are powerless to stop it,' said the concerned voices of 19 and 84.

'It can only get in if we allow the angels in, and the Blue Robin is trapped outside. He may have got into our domain, but we have shut him out from the place of our control. He cannot hope to reach the Wounds.'

'Look,' exclaimed one of the magicians. 'See what descends from the craft of light.'

He pointed to the scanner and the magicians gasped in horror as each ascended master, archangel and a vast amount of angels, left the mothership. They held hands and each of the masters carried glowing torches to light their way through the darkness. Some flew like the Archangels, led by Michael upon the wings of the wind, whilst others, like Quan Yin, who rode upon her beloved dragon, Fire-Cho, sat upon the winged unicorns of the rainbow, led by Pegasus their energy blazing across the earth, leaving a rainbow trail that was spectacular to behold, a truly amazing sight for the eye.

'That's one of the most amazing things I've ever seen in my life,' said Suzanne.

'Just look at that flying horse and then theres the dragon; said an excited Jonathan.

At that moment the entrance to the control room began to shake, flashing with primary colours before starting to crack, as two fissures appeared around the door.

'No, the Blue Robin is using Reiki to penetrate us. Stop him, Asphodel,' screamed the Illusion. 'My Wounds are exhausted, they cannot spin their cycle for much longer. This is the best they can do.'

'I'm aware of that, master.'

Lord Asphodel looked on aghast, as the ascended masters came closer to Erratus Manor. They would soon be knocking, wanting to come in. Lord Asphodel felt something hit him on the head. Looking up, he saw fissures that had started to appear above. Chunks of debris began to fall from the ceiling. This accelerated very quickly.

'Elia, what's happening?' asked Suzanne, frightened.

'It's the ascension process, dear one. Our world, and everything within the known universe, is moving into the fifth dimension. Everything is being affected. Those who have stayed centred, and led good decent lives, will find the transition process quite easy, but those who have stayed in lower energy, not moving with the times, shall find their dark ways crumble around them as our ascending world can no longer tolerate their negativity. This place is where darkness can be found, those who hide in the dark are now being found by the light. 'No, I refuse to accept that,' interceded Lord Asphodel. 'This world, my empire, is far too powerful. Its foundations are too strong to ever crumble, Elia.'

'You built your so-called empire on greed, Jack. Greed and cruelty, hardly a strong foundation,' retorted Elia, fiercely. 'Why not let it go, Jack. The Illusion has had its time. Let it go, in exchange for peace.'

Before Lord Asphodel could give an answer, a tapping sound was heard coming from outside Erratus. It was Jesus Sananda, standing at the door, gently knocking. Sananda carried a lantern in his hand and stood close to the apples that had fallen, along with all the masters and angels who were each knocking at the walls of the dark place, gently saying 'let us in, let us in babies, let us in.' Each of the magicians looked both perplexed and afraid, none more so than Lord Asphodel. For the first time in his life, he didn't know what to do. For the first time in his life, he felt out of control. A large cracking sound was heard. The Blue Robin, through his Reiki, had broken through the door of the control room, along with Nada and his other angels. David looked around him in astonishment, as debris continued to fall and large fissures tore through the walls. The Illusion's hold was weakening, it surely would only be a matter of time now. David's heart leapt as he saw his mum and dad, with Elia and all their friends, who were so relieved to see him again. David glared angrily at the magicians and at the Illusion, who'd put his family and friends through all this.

'Let my parents and our friends go, Asphodel. They're nothing to you.'

'You brave fool, you dare break into the control room. It is because of your meddling that my master is sick and we are in the state we are in,' said an enraged Lord Asphodel.

'Then perhaps you should let your master go. Playing the blame card isn't going to help matters. The fact you are all in this position is because you turned your backs upon the light, but now they will be able to get through.'

'You may well feel empowered at this point, Lightworker, but I still hold the cards and the one I play now is called revenge.'

Asphodel raised his hand towards David's parents, Elia and the lightworkers, lifting them higher and higher into the air until they were at least seventy feet up. The frightened parents held hands, whilst Elia did her utmost to reassure everyone. At that moment she did not know what would happen. Jack was so unhealed, so scared and scarred, and now the only world he had known for centuries was breaking apart, falling around him. She did not know what he would do. He was drunk with insanity.

'Mum, Dad! No, please, you wouldn't dare,' said the Blue Robin, desperately. 'I appeal to the man you once were to spare them.'

'I wonder if they can fly like you, your friends wings are too weak, numbed by the Black Candle's power.'

'They will recover in seconds,' retorted David.

'Ah yes but by then it will be too late, their souls will be in pieces upon the ground,' said Lord Asphodel.

'You diabolical maniac,' said David in disgust.

'You've asked me to let your parents and friends go and that's what I shall do.'

Lord Asphodel used a cutting motion with his hand and the flame of the Black Candle was extinguished, so that it could no longer hold its captives. David screamed in horror as his parents and friends plummeted downwards. Acting instinctively, he flew up, in the hope of catching his mum and dad. But what about Elia and the others? There were too many for him to catch, he'd never do it. Just then Nada, along with each of the lightworkers' guardian angels, who could now get through to them, flew before him. They effortlessly caught every falling soul. As Nada caught Elia, David caught his mum and dad and held them close to his heart as he took them to safety. Jonathan and Suzanne, despite the danger of the magicians, were now protected by their angels, who resembled the shimmering butterflies Suzanne had seen earlier. They were nestled safely within the angels' wings.

'Thank you so much, please take care of them.'

'We will, dear one. They are now enfolded by us,' the guardian angels replied lovingly.

The look on Lord Asphodel's face said it all. He was, for sure, in meltdown.

'Please just get them to safety,' said the Blue Robin, as Elia ran up to him, flinging her arms around him.

'David, we're so glad you are alright,' before whispering, 'I'm so proud of you.'

They were joined by all the other lightworkers, who welcomed him back warmly.

'Are you alright Elia? And the rest of you?'

'Yes, dear one, we're all okay,' smiled the wise woman.

The lightworkers turned to face the magicians. Lord Asphodel held his hand to his brow as if trying to see them through the collapsing debris. A slithering dark mist was seen coming towards them on the floor.

'Leave these to me Asphodel,' hissed the Illusion, 'Go and give the ascended masters your own special welcome.' For a moment there was great hesitation. 'Well, what are you idiots waiting for? Use your weapons on them, that's an order.'

The Illusion rose up from the ground to face David and his friends.

'David, be careful, be very careful,' warned Elia, as they now stood face to face with the Illusion, which had solidified into a form they could now see.

It was a horrendous apparition, one that could have crawled out of the darkest recesses of the mind. It looked partly like the gorgon Medusa from ancient legend and part like the Minotaur, also from ancient times. Its head was similar to that of a snakes' but out of its head grew bull-like horns. Its torso had a chest with a belly and it had no arms. Beneath the waist, it sported the tail of a serpent. Elia winced in horror at the sight of it, its energy would have been enough to make you sick and its breath was the aroma of decaying meat. David was terrified at this moment, but he knew he must face his fear.

'You have dared this day to stop me, but I shall destroy you,' said the Illusion, its seething yellow green eyes flashing in anger.

'We want the Genesis Crystal, Illusion. Where is it?' demanded the Blue Robin.

'Your friends will tell you it is now lost and suppressed. You cannot hope to find it now.'

The Illusion threw back its head toward the ceiling.

'Get down, quickly,' screamed Elia.

The lightworkers darted out of the way, as burning acid spewed from the Illusion's mouth like a giant spitting cobra, missing the lightworkers by a whisker and burning everything in its path.

'Good. Our master may be able to destroy them and then our cycle is safe to go on forever,' smirked the Wound, Hate, as they watched all that was enfolding.

The magicians who had gone outside to face the ascended masters, stood at the entrance. Each of the ascended masters and archangels led by Michael, and Sananda, stood in a long line around Erratus Manor, as if waiting patiently for them to finally come out, whilst several angels were standing around the dead tree trying to pull it up. The violet flame flickered powerfully behind them.

Without uttering a single word, the scared magicians opened fire with their laser spears. Every one of the lasers hurt, or was it the hatred the masters could sense within the magicians? A teardrop fell from Sananda's eye yet he, like all of them, stood completely physically unharmed. Each of the masters and angels there, held out their hands. The laser weapons were pulled telekinetically from the magicians' hands and into the hands of the masters and archangels. All the magicians could do was stand there in shock, as what was handed back to them were not weapons, but roses. The magicians fell upon their knees to the "love" none of them had felt since infancy. They had tried to hurt these wise souls, and yet they had turned the other cheek and shown them only love. The violet flame passed through them. What became of those magicians, I cannot say, but let it be known on that day they finally realised what forgiveness truly was. Within the control room, the other magicians looked on, as the Illusion did its utmost to destroy the lightworkers, especially the Blue Robin, whom it feared most of all. Again, the Illusion spat burning acid, but the angels, led by Nada, were able to shield them with their wings.

'David, we can h-hold the Illusion back. We c-can contain it whilst you retrieve the crystal,' gasped Elia, nearly choking on the Illusion's sulphurous breath. 'I-it's underneath here.' She pointed to the floor, which concealed the hole. 'You open i-it w-with that mechanism over there.'

David leapt through the air, narrowly missing the Illusion's acid. The Illusion attempted to give chase but, at that moment, was stopped by the rainbow energy of Reiki, from each of the lightworkers who had surrounded it. Healing energy was the Illusion's greatest enemy. The Illusion seemed to hunch over in pain as the Reiki sought to find any vestige of good within the Soulless entity.

'Aahh, Love, can't stand this, I can't.'

Lord Asphodel lunged at the boy trying, in vain, to stop him from operating the control.

'Never, boy, do you hear me? Never. Give up while you still have the chance.'

He was joined in his efforts by his minions who succeeded in pinning the Blue Robin to the ground. The whole room shook, surrounded in a storm of pelting debris and ectoplasmic lightening. This truly was the battle between the light and the dark. Nada swooped down around them, managing to pick six of the brutal magicians up before throwing them aside. Lord Asphodel was the only person left struggling with David. His hands were placed around David's throat in one last desperate attempt to silence him. But David was determined, and his empowerment had made him stronger. He managed to flip Asphodel off him before struggling to his feet and finally activating the console to open the door to the Well of Suppression. Looking down into the abyss, David could see the Genesis Crystal. It was being pulled by the black hole's magic, deeper and deeper into the bottomless depths.

'David, hurry. The Illusion is doing what it can to resist our love,' shouted Elia. 'The Genesis Crystal is imperative in the dissolution of all this.'

There were no two ways about this. David dived headfirst into the hole, lighting the darkness as he went. He was now virtually upon it. He grabbed the Genesis Crystal with both hands and felt its love flowing into him. But the black energy, that had ensnared it, held it tight within its grip, as David sought to free the crystal.

'David,' came a voice. It was Akash, whose consciousness spoke to him through it. 'Michael's sword. Look up , David. Michael has sent you the Sword of Truth. Use it to cut the suppression from the crystal. Do this now, or you will be pulled down with it.' Looking up David saw the great Sword that Michael had sent the boy which had broken through the Control room, passing through the Magicians, and was now spinning down the well towards him.

David caught the Sword , and with all the strength he could muster, swiped the mist-like binding that had fettered the crystal. The black strands were cut away, its remains which went down into the black hole, wavered like reeds in the wind, as if reeling in pain, before they collapsed back into the never-ending abyss. The Blue Robin held the Genesis Crystal tenderly within his hands and then he heard the sound of "OM" coming from it. Holding it close to his heart, he kissed it tenderly before flying up towards the top, thrilled that he would be returning it into the light. Asphodel looked down at the ascending Blue Robin.

'Quickly, shut him in. I'll show him what it feels like to be suppressed.'

The door of the hole quickly slammed shut, trapping David and the crystal, but David used Michael's mighty sword to smash through it.

'No, that sound, the song of "OM" is too powerful!'

The magicians held their ears, as the Blue Robin flew high above them all. The sound filled the control room like a choir within a church. However at that moment The Illusion had finally freed itself from Reiki, causing the lightworkers to be hurled to the ground.

'You held me, but not even Reiki can stop me forever.' Looking down upon the lightworkers on the floor, The Illusion let out a menacing chuckle. 'Now I kill all of you. So much for the power of love, ha!' It was about to cover them in acid, when David appeared from behind, thrusting Archangel Michael's sword into the Illusion. 'Arghh!' With a huge cry of pain, it fell to the ground, electrical surges coursing through its vile form. It felt its power and its hold drain away, like blood. 'You cant defeat me. My control, my power, it's g-going.'

The Illusion, that which had kept the world in duality and revelled in the killing of others, now lay wounded by the Sword of Truth.

'May I help you, my lady?' smiled David, looking down at Elia.

'You may,' answered the wise woman.

Lord Asphodel nervously fumbled in his pockets.

'I can't stand this much longer. I need a light,' he said, just as a huge light filled the destructed control room. 'Not that sort of light,' he said.

The walls of Erratus Manor shook like jelly before blooming outwards, resembling giant boils. As it burst, it revealed the Heavenly beings who had asked to be let in, and now they could do so. The procession was led by Michael, with Sananda closely behind him. Every master, archangel and angel entered, making their way towards the magicians, who stood hypnotised by the beings of light. Their guardian angels, led by Tala, approached Lord Asphodel, enfolding him and everybody in wings of love and light.

'No, fools,' croaked the Illusion, 'Don't let them make you weak. Don't.'

It was too late. David, Elia and the others watched as the robes of deceit, that had long since clothed the magicians, began to melt away, literally evaporating into large, black puddles on the floor. The robotic droid Orwell spun round and out of control, before blowing up, as did every dark Atlantean computer, until they were nothing but smoking ash. As Erratus Manor was now consumed by the violet flame, the old tree was pulled up completely. Most extraordinary though, was that the magicians now had eyes, for they now saw the truth. The brightness was overwhelming for them, It was as if they were children who had never seen the light. They were now fully naked, like a first born baby, freed from the captivity that they had endured. They had all been puppets for the Illusion, dancing about whenever it had pulled their strings. Now the dance was over.

'David, Elia, dear ones. Are you alright?' asked the great archangel Michael.

'Yes, Michael, we are all fine. David has found the crystal.'

'Indeed, dear one. Blue Robin, you have paved the way for the new world and now all that no longer serves humanity shall be healed.'

As the angels continued to tend to the magicians, as did the angels of all the mortals present, the Wounds that had once spun their cycle so fast, appeared to slow down radically to the point that they stopped moving altogether. Archangel Raphael floated up to the Wounds. They tried to resist him, but his healing light was far too bright. Gazing lovingly at the Wounds, Archangel Raphael spoke these words that sent tingling up everyone's backs.

'Through this darkness we have found a never-ending light that shines around. Now we, who stand here in preparation with the divine, transmute negativity transcending all space and time. With humanity, which has until now, remained asleep, watched over by The One, whose love for us is so bright and ever so deep. And From this nightmare humanity shall awake, when all is healed the Illusion's cycle shall break.'

As Raphael spoke these words, the Wounds were engulfed by the violet flame and within a blaze of light, were indeed transmuted into butterflies of gold. Where monsters once lurked, creatures of beauty now dwelled. The transmuted Wounds bathed in their new-found ecstasy. They seemed serenely joyous, even relieved. The once Wound of Hate now, like the others, a shining butterfly, looked down at David and Elia.

'Let it be brighter, let us go,' it said.

Each of the healed entities now flew away towards the great golden light that shone above. David and all his friends watched as they disappeared into the bright sunlight, accompanied by healing angels.

'Elia,' said a quiet voice. It was Lord Asphodel. 'I'm sorry for all that I've done. But now I am free, we are all free.'

Elia smiled sweetly at this man she had once loved.

'I'm sorry too, Jack, that it has taken you this long to find peace within your heart.'

The wise woman bent down and kissed him tenderly upon the lips.

'You seem as eager to kiss me now as you once did in the bedroom,' Jack said.

It was lovely for Elia to hear Jack Asphodel speak in this way. It had been a long time since he'd ever spoken to her like this. I didn't wait lifetimes just to ignore you now came the wise womans reply. Memories flooded through both the adults' minds. Memories of all that had been, and for what might have been.

The Archangels and Masters walked towards the Illusion, who lay sprawled out upon the ground. It looked a pathetic sight as its snake tail tried to move. Its eyes, tried not to look up at Michael, who towered above it.

'You have defeated me, why?'

'Because the Creator decreed your darkness could no longer go on.'

The Illusion looked in hatred at the angels and masters and then gazed upon the Blue Robin, scornfully.

'I caused the downfall of Atlantis. What makes you think I can't do the same to the next utopia you create?'

'Because now we have moved within the fifth dimension, and the Wounds that you fed off, have all been completely healed. The multitude of lightworkers that now live on earth will never allow this,' said the great archangel.

'Then why don't you kill me?' gasped the Illusion. 'Wouldn't you like that?' Then, looking at David's mum and dad, 'Wouldn't you, after all I did to you and what I put your son through?'

It was trying to goad them into being angry and hateful, thus giving it more power to feel that bit stronger.

'You're not pulling that one on me. Not after all I've seen and felt,' said Suzanne. 'I've seen through all that has happened and learned that there is hope.'

'I'm no longer afraid,' said Jonathan. 'I now trust, and have faith.' For I have seen, I have heard and I have felt.

'We have only one thing to say to you,' said Archangel Michael. 'WE FORGIVE YOU.'

With this, the Illusion let out one final last breath before exploding in a ball of violet fire, vanishing completely, its evil lifted, gone from the earth. An exploding flash of great White light surrounded every soul present at that moment, engulfing all that was left of Erratus Manor and all of the dark realm as Mother Earth turned bright gold. Then there was complete silence before everything went dark.

16

A NEW BEGINNING

David looked about him in the darkness, lit only by the light of the Genesis Crystal trying to make out where he was the now quiet sound of OM could still be heard coming from it.. He became aware of his mum and dad standing beside him.

'Mum, Dad, are you both alright?'

Suzanne and Jonathan hugged him, holding him tight for they were both as puzzled as he was.

'David, Suzanne, Jonathan, Oh, thank goodness you're all fine,' came a familiar voice.

It was Elia. The Blue Robin looked relieved as he saw the familiar forms of his Reiki Master and the other lightworkers running towards them. Nada and everyone's angels were hovering close by. Each and every ascended master floated high above them, once again, having formed a great circle. Along with Pegasus and each of the Unicorns, Fire- Cho and every spiritual Creature. Archangel Michael seemed to be at the centre of the great circle, his hands raised upwards in victory. He was looking proudly down upon the mortals and that could only mean one thing that the light had triumphed.

'Where are we?' asked Suzanne.

'Where's Erratus Manor and where are the magicians?' added Jonathan.

'You now stand in the "between",' replied the hopeful voice of Michael. 'The Pause, The In breath before the outbreath. This is where the seeds must be planted, for it is the moment we have all been waiting for.'

'All? You mean all of humanity?' asked David.

'Look behind you, beloved ones.'

Standing behind them were, not thousands, but millions of souls. Men, women and children from every culture, religion and creed, not to mention every creature that existed on present day earth, from land, air and sea. Some of the many mortals were asleep, but a great many more were awake, for they had all heard the song of peace within their hearts. David noticed other members of his family within this vast menagerie. There was his aunt and uncle and his cousins, his oldest cousin, with her young daughter, Amelia, lying within her mother's arms, fully awake and gazing around her in wonder. He also saw his grandma, who was one of the sleeping ones. They were all present, not to mention his neighbour Rob and all his family and all his cousins who lived in Australia, friends whom he had known throughout his life, not to mention every past life. Everyone now stood together. They had all been given new hope. Every other animal was awake, their eyes wide open, alert to all around them.

'Michael, why are some people's eyes open while others are closed?'

'There are those in your world who have raised their vibration to love, and those who have not. Those that have are now, as the Buddah likes to call it, awake, whilst others, who have let ego rule their lives, are still within a sleep state. Nevertheless, they have the opportunity to awaken, now more than ever. Each and every soul is loved equally. Each one is allowed into the fifth dimension. David, Elia, dear sweet lightworkers, come forward and place the Genesis Crystal before us.' The time has come to birth the New Reality.

David, who held the glorious crystal in his hands and had not dared let it go, led the procession of lightworkers, followed by Elia and the others before the great masters and archangels.

'You have done so well, dear ones. David, we are proud of you,' said Sananda. 'You have conquered that which you were afraid of, and fulfilled all that you needed to do. You have needed the love and guidance of dear Elia, but ultimately you braved the storm, denouncing that which was untrue, taking your light into the darkness to heal that which needed healing.'

'Now, from the ashes of the old, a new world shall be born,' said Nada, joyfully.

Archangel Michael gestured with his hand, as David placed the great Genesis Crystal before the divine beings. They began to say in unison, along with all the lightworkers,

'Peaceful seeds of new earth, come out from the crystal and give us rebirth. Transcend all darkness gone before, heal all hearts that are still so sore. For any heart that has known only night, remove all dark, so that we now see only the holy light.'

At this, the beautiful sound of the crystal began to magnify, becoming louder and louder. Then a burst of emerald energy veered upwards, before solidifying into a trunk. David, Elia and the others watched in awe as this emerald energy skilfully splayed outwards, venturing in different directions and forming into branches. The lightworkers stood in wonder at what was before them. The seeds of the crystal had grown, as if time had been speeded up, into a huge beautiful Oak tree. Its emerald coloured leaves were ripe with the promise of spring, for the tree symbolised hope to all who saw it.

'Behold, dear ones, the new tree of life has now been born for all of you,' said the optimistic voice of Michael.

Then, without warning, a light resembling the majesty of morning dawn opened up within the middle of the tree.

'It's so beautiful,' said David in amazement. 'Nada, the light, what is it?'

'Do you really need to ask us, dear one? It is harmony. Harmony's Doorway is opening up to you all,'

Harmony's Doorway continued to open within the great tree, getting bigger and bigger until finally it stopped. They were met by the great whale Akash, who proceeded to swim out of it.

'Akash!' David and Elia exclaimed, in delight. They might as well have been excited children as they embraced the great whale. 'Mum, dad, please come and meet Akash.'

Suzanne and Jonathan gingerly approached the wise creature.

'He's a whale. By all that's mighty, he's a whale!' said Jonathan. 'Davie son, you must be in your element.'

'Greetings, beloved ones. The Creator's vision has now come to fruition, as my consciousness has been allowed to manifest.'

'So, this is what your consciousness is, Akash. It's the new Tree of Life,' said David.

'Yes, It is the symbol of new life and hope for your world, beloved ones. How I have dreamt of this moment for centuries.' And this time the Tree shall never die it will grow in health for all eternity.

'Wait,' said Linda. 'Elia, David, look. Who's that?'

The others looked towards Harmony's Doorway. Someone stood inside the light. Everyone watched as the mysterious figure walked towards them, coming nearer and nearer. David strived to identify this person, as the light of the doorway was so bright. Then he remembered. It was the strange figure who he had seen watching him that morning outside Elia's house, then in the fields on the way home and, once more, outside David's house by the lamp post on that fateful evening. He felt his heart beating faster. A magician coming out of Harmony's Doorway.

'Everyone, look out. It's one of the magicians, it's a trap!'

The great beings simply smiled and laughed.

'No, David, look deeper, dear one. We promise you, this one is nothing like the magicians at all.'

'This one,' thought David to himself.

A kind, familiar voice came from within the veil that shrouded it.

'Help me get through the last bit of Illusion, so all my children can awaken David.'

It held out its hands to David, just as it had done the night it watched him from the lamppost.

'Go on, David, don't be afraid. Help The One to reach us all. Lift the veil,' said Elia, encouragingly.

The Blue Robin walked slowly, but confidently, towards the mercurial figure. Reaching out, he touched the hands of the figure. As he did so, the shroud of the figure began to open up, bit by bit. As each part of the garment fell down, it revealed the petals of a huge, pink coloured rose, which opened in full bloom. Standing upon this beautiful flower, in full glory and surrounded by blazing white golden light, was the Creator, The One. There really are no words to describe the true beauty of the Creator. Light, the colour of sunshine, covered its entire form, and The One seemed to grow higher and higher, as each petal fell before it. Two beautiful, giant eyes of liquid Sapphire looked kindly upon its children, as every master, angel and archangel, even the great Michael and the marvellous Akash, bowed before the Creator. As for David, Elia, Jonathan and Suzanne, they were overcome in humble humility, as were the rest of humanity. Cupped within the Ones hands tenderly was the Universal Heart beating away for all to hear.

'So, it was you, who I was afraid of. You are the Creator,' said David in fascinated awe.

'I am indeed. I am sorry that I frightened you that day, dear one. I could not, at that point, reach you, though I tried. The Illusion's veil was keeping me out, hence in physical reality, I was shrouded so that nobody could see me.'

Once again, the beautiful voice sounded androgynous, a balance of masculine and feminine.

'What do we call you? Do you have an actual name?' asked Suzanne, astonished.

'I am known by many names through all walks of life. I am generally referred to as The One by all my children in Heaven, but to make it more personal, I should like you to know me as AznaOM. Azna is the feminine aspect of me and OM my masculine, for I am the balance of Mother and Father.' As David already knows.

'AznaOM, what happened to the magicians and the Illusion? Where did they go?' asked David, curiously.

'They shall trouble you no more. Their darkness could no longer be tolerated upon the earth, nor any such souls who spread and energised such pain. Jack Asphodel and all the magicians were removed by their guardian angels.'

Upon hearing this, Jonathan could not help but ask,

'When you say "removed", do you mean they've been sent to Hell to be punished?'

Azna/OM's voice was assertive, but loving upon hearing this. Dear one

'I have no desire to condemn any of my children to fire. For even in the darkest of hearts, I see hope. No matter how dark a soul has become, my light still burns within them, constantly. For remember, dear ones, all hearts are one heart and one heart is all hearts. To hurt another means that you are also hurting yourselves. We are all interconnected within Creation. If I was to hurt any of you, I would be harming myself. No, dear ones, the magicians have been taken back to eternity where within the Halls of Healing they shall undergo Soul retrieval. They may return to new earth in many years as babies, but not until their souls have been cleaned of lifetimes of darkness, by which time they will be healed.'

Every soul listened intently to these words, especially Elia, as she felt a strong sense of relief course through her mind when she thought of Jack. Closing her eyes, she saw the Halls of Healing. It was a chamber of Silver bright light and the vessels of the magicians laid upon couches of healing. She then saw Jack Asphodel, his once frozen heart now beginning to thaw, trickling away into large droplets of water, which were carried away by healing angels, who assisted this process. Elia smiled as Jack Asphodel's Soul, that he'd long since lost, was returned to him, glowing in pink light, having been washed and cleaned by his angel. It was beating with eagerness, ready to be returned to his vessel.

'Hello, sweetheart, I'm so glad you've found me after so many years and lifetimes. Can I come back inside? Will you have me?'

Jack nodded.

'Yes please, come back inside dear Soul, I've missed you, I truly have.'

Tala, the guardian angel of Jack, who held his Soul, placed it back into his chest. Elia chose to look no further. She opened her eyes, her own heart now rejoicing, as the weight of the old had been lifted from her. Elia's angels enfolded her within their wings, as a final tear fell from her eye. She was now content, as her old karma with Jack Asphodel had been severed forever. The wise woman smiled to herself, knowing that, at last, they had reached the end.

'As for the Illusion,' continued AznaOM, 'It was just a build-up of negative energy that feasted upon the Wounds within humanity. By going inside, you were able to heal the Wounds by breaking its cycle. You then did what the Illusion could not withstand.'

'What was that, AznaOM?'

'You forgave it, dear one. When you forgave it, despite all its horrors, it had no choice but to leave. Your compassion and love are the antidotes for darkness. Within that antidote, the Illusions only poison.'

'Didn't David thrust Michael's Sword of Truth into it? Isn't that what finished it?' said Jonathan.

'Dear one, the Sword of Truth never kills, it simply weakened the Illusion's power. When that occurred, my children of light were able to get through to heal the Wounds, but ultimately it was forgiveness that vanquished the Illusion, and that alone, otherwise it would have remained alive forever.'

'You're saying it was my destiny all along, to go inside that place?'

'Yes, Blue Robin. I oversaw everything, ultimately. You all had no choice but to go within. Sooner or later, everyone has to. My higher Will guides everything. Even when you were captured by the magicians and you thought everything was lost. It wasn't, for the higher good will always triumph over all, always remember that. It was all meant to be. Never lose your hope, or sensitivity, for that is your true strength.'

David smiled, as he looked at the vast plethora of ascended masters who enfolded AznaOM and the great new tree. He found himself smiling even more when he noticed that Sananda's little lamb, who'd always tried to be friends with ascended master Afra's power animal, the lion, had decided to give it one last try. Floating closer, the little lamb feeling quite brazen licked the great lion's face. To its pleasant surprise, the lion, Sampson, did not try to frighten it away. Instead, Sampson rolled over on his back before returning the licks, then placing its huge paw upon the lamb's head, gently stroking it. They lay together in harmony. It was such a moving sight. Already the fifth dimension was working its special magic.

'And now, everyone,' called AznaOM. 'Come, my children, I welcome you into the fifth dimension through Harmony's Doorway. There you will be in new earth, where you shall all know Peace. It is a world free from Illusion, unhampered from trickery.' A world purified by flame, where each and every soul shall be free and no longer controlled.

'What about my physical body, AznaOM?' asked David. 'And Elia's, also.'

'Your physical body is still in your house on the earth of the fifth dimension, dear one. You'll be able to get back into your physical bodies as soon as you've passed into Harmony's Doorway, for it is the earth where your homes still are. The energy has been raised to much higher levels than you have ever known before. As the years go on and the dimensions rise higher and higher, you will no longer need your heavy vessels. You will always be able to fly, Blue Robin. You will not feel the need to possess anything, for you shall have all that you need within.'

'Great. Do you suppose things might go back to normal now?' said Jonathan.

'I sincerely doubt it,' responded Suzanne.

'I hope not,' added David.

'This is the new era, my friends,' said Elia. 'Expect there to be many more miracles in future. Now, let us all go forward in peace and love, for that is all there is.'

David took his parents hands either side, and everyone walked towards the great light within the tree. They each felt such joy, such elation and hope, as they passed through it, slowly but surely.

'To think, thought David. All this started with a dream and it became a reality.'

'I love you,' whispered Jonathan in his son's ear.

'I love you too, Dad.'

Suzanne put her other arm around David and squeezed him tight. Elia smiled, they were all in such bliss. Suddenly, the past did not matter anymore. What mattered was now and the future. They had a whole world of peace before them, as did everyone. It was up to them all to make the best of it and they were determined to do so. Thus, upon that day, it all came to be, as a new chapter was written in the long history of Gaia. The masters, archangels and angels smiled lovingly at one another, along with Akash, who playfully swam or floated around the edge of the new tree. Michael winked and nodded encouragingly at all his friends.

'Well, my children, thanks to you all,' said AznaOM.

They drifted higher, back into the sparkling mothership.

'This is a day I shall always be thankful for,' said Sananda to Michael.

'Indeed, my friend. None of us must never forget that the love of The One will shine for all, until the end of time.'

They were all returning back to the kingdom of Shambhala, but now they would always be able to reach humanity as there was no veil between worlds to stop them. All souls would now find it easier than ever to talk to their angelic friends and, as the dimensions would rise upon the earth, humans would live in harmony with all creatures and would enjoy long periods with the ascended masters and star people, who would visit the people of earth often.

As for the Blue Robin, he would indeed continue to fly higher than he could ever have thought and would go on to teach many others to do the same. His parents lived happily for the rest of their lives. Both accepted what they couldn't change, but they now had the courage to change what they could. They now had the wisdom to know the difference. Elia's light continued to naturally shine. She became a close friend of David's family and all those who would come to her. She was never again treated with any hostility from those who initially feared their light. People were now starting to look within, as they never had before. There was even talk of a romance that had blossomed between her and a man she had met whilst giving healing to him. This time she truly had met her soulmate. This one loved her truly and, funnily enough, his name was David.

Each year, fireworks were lit in remembrance of the day of the new dawn, when people would gather around from every culture, their arms around another, brother with brother and sister with sister. They would sing and laugh together, remembering the day when they found the light within. The days of war and fighting were long gone, for people were now so much wiser and kinder, seeing themselves in another, and another within themselves. They were never ever told what to do by a government, or anyone outside themselves, as people realised all they had to do was to look within, to find the answers. Then they could ask the angels, who would help them find the solutions to all that was needed. Mother Earth, who now had a golden aura around her, was supported completely by the rainbow hands of God. The entire planet was now restored to its true glory, shining like a jewel within the depths of outer space.

One day, people will all realise and see the light within themselves and in others. Yes, it may take time and there will be those who are awake and those who are still asleep, but, eventually, we will all awaken to the truth, to that which is love, as we each take our first steps and walk through Harmony's Doorway. Just wait and see!

THE END [OR THE BEGINNING]

Printed in Great Britain
by Amazon